STOKER'S SERENITY

THE VIRTUES BOOK IV

A.J. DOWNEY

COPYRIGHT

❀

ISBN: 978-1-950222-21-6
Editing by Barbara J. Bailey
Book design by Maggie Kern
Cover art by Dar Albert at Wicked Smart Designs

DEDICATION

To my dear readers who wanted more. Here it is. Also, to all my Metal friends. Your nobility is duly noted and inspiring. Like MC folk, you guys are a cut above. It was time that was recognized.

1

$\mathcal{S}$erenity…

The din of the concert venue was out of this world. I guess I hadn't expected it to be so loud as Linny drew me through the crowd by my hand, laughing.

I'd had to borrow her clothes. I didn't have anything she'd deemed worthy for a night out on the town and by 'worthy', I mean 'revealing'. I wore a pair of tight-fitting jeans and knee-high black velvet boots. Those were at least mine... the boots. The jeans were a new purchase, and the top was Linny's.

Shiny and metallic, it was held up by strings around the neck and around the back like a bathing suit.

The shiny silver material fell like water, pooling between my breasts, which were quite a bit bigger than Linny's and by sheer force of will, seemed to defy gravity enough to make the top bearable.

Still, I felt all kinds of exposed, and the only thing that helped keep me from feeling like I was running around naked was the black velvet choker that was around my neck.

No ornament, just simple and black, to match the boots and dark jeans.

"Come on!" Linny cried. "Closer to the mosh pit!"

I rolled my eyes but acquiesced to her enthusiasm as the metal guitarist on stage shredded his solo into oblivion. The crowd, whipped into enthusiasm, rolled and roiled like the sea on a stormy night and my link to my best friend was severed.

"Serenity!" she cried out, but she was swallowed by the crowd and I was swept in the opposite direction, buffeted by a tide of muscle, sweat, leather, and chains.

I yelped in surprise as I was thrust up hard against a guy with a red Mohawk, practically shirtless, his tee in shreds around his waist, the guyliner dripping from his eyes like ruined tears from how hard he was sweating.

"Hey, baby, what you doing out here?" He grinned and I tried not to cringe at his discolored teeth. Meth mouth was something prevalent out here.

I was grabbed and pulled another direction, hands reaching, groping, and helping themselves to my body, a handful of my ass, a breast, even so bold as to grab me by the front of my jeans over my crotch.

I cried out and found myself fetched up against another man who crowed like a rooster, his head thrown back, and clearly drunk. He snatched a fistful of the front of Linny's silver shirt and jerked.

I screamed, my arms going up and covering myself as the strings holding the material to my body gave way, popping loose from their moorings and leaving me exposed for real. The cloth was dragged from my body, fluttering to the floor to be trampled under a mix of black combat and steel-toed work boots.

"Hey!" someone shouted, and a wall of leather moved in between me and my assailant. A scuffle ensued and I forced my way away from it, rounding my shoulders, hunching forward, moving my smaller frame between the crush of bodies whenever a gap or opportunity presented itself, working my way doggedly toward the edge of the undulating crowd, most of them oblivious to my distress.

"Hey, hey, hey! It's okay!" I heard just as thick leather, warm with body heat, enveloped my shoulders, and cut me off from view of any would-be prying eyes.

Tears slicked down my cheeks as an arm went heavy across my back, guiding me out of the mash of people. My white knight tucked me into the front of his much larger frame and bodily shoved people when necessary, moving us both out of the concert crowd and toward the front of the building where the bathrooms and the merch tables were.

"Hang on, hold up; wait!" The voice was warm, velvet with a core of steel and I froze, letting my long dark hair hide my face. I stopped in my tracks, my chest heaving.

The voice shouted over the top of my head, hands kneading my shoulders through the thick leather of his coat reassuringly.

"Rory! Gimme a band tee!"

"What size?"

"I don't care!" the voice barked. "Just give me one!"

Whoever Rory was, he flung a tee, and the person at my side caught it one-handed and thrust the warm cotton over the top of my right shoulder and into my hands. I struggled to grab the offer of more substantial cover without letting the coat that was my only shield for my modesty gape, rendering it ineffective.

"Come on, this way," he urged and took me to the line of waiting ladies for the bathroom. He marched me past all of them and thrust me toward the door, telling a couple to leave me alone when they got upset.

"Quit'cher bitchin'! She's not going in there to pee, your spot in line is safe!"

He stopped me with a shouted, "Hey!" and I paused, turning half-way, but still not looking at him. I kept my eyes fixed studiously to the wall, instead. "Bring me back my jacket and cut as soon as you get that on," he called to me. I gave a curt nod and darted into the bathroom and away from the din, confusion, and dirty looks from the girls out there in line.

The atmosphere inside the beat-up bathroom was vastly different from outside of it.

The ladies in that bathroom were everything, helping me into the tee as I sobbed, listening to my story as I shook, and thrusting the man's jacket into my hands as they fussed over me and fixed my makeup so I didn't look so dreadful going back out there.

I stared at the colorful embroidery on the back of the patch, a giant orange octopus dragging a ship under the waves. I'd seen it before, but on very rare occasions, out on the highway.

"There you go, hon. Good as new," a blonde woman proclaimed, as she took a final swipe of a damp paper towel under my eye.

I thanked her, my voice shaking, and, unsteady on my feet, I stumbled back out into the noise. The cacophony of wailing guitars and screamed-out lyrics was overwhelming; the dim light, broken by strobes, confusing; the hot, oppressive atmosphere too much.

Thank God he came up to me and took his coat back from my trembling hands. I hadn't thought to look at him before, through my anxiety and humiliation. I didn't know who he was, but as he swung his coat around and put his arms through the heavy sleeves, I nearly swallowed my own tongue.

He was gorgeous.

Muscles lean, body cut, long black hair, and a face that belonged on a classic statue or painting of the devil himself, freshly fallen to earth.

Most people don't realize that the devil isn't as horrific as he is typically portrayed. No, he wasn't all horns and cloven hoof. The fallen angel who reigned in Hell was quite the opposite, said to be so beautiful that it hurt to look upon him.

This man was like that, too. So beautiful to me it took my breath away, a sort of fractured ache taking up residence in the center of my chest, where my heart still quailed from my humiliation and recent trauma.

"The name's Stoker," he shouted over the noise, folding himself at the waist to put his lovely lips closer to my ear. "What's yours?"

"Serenity," I answered, swallowing hard. "My friends just call me Ren."

"Sorry, I can't hear you," he half-shouted and I tried again, raising my voice.

"Serenity!" I called out.

"Nice to meet you, Serenity," he shouted for my benefit. "Are you okay?"

I shook my head and blurted out, "I just want to go home!"

He frowned in empathy and put his hand on my shoulder giving it a quick squeeze, turning me towards the open doors and the deep Florida night just outside. "Come on, let's get out of here. I'll take you home myself if I have to."

2

*S*toker…

"I don't know where she is, her boyfriend drove us here. We got separated in the crowd and, well, you know the rest…"

Her cheeks flamed under the supernova-harsh blue-white light of the floodlight at the front corner of the venue. The captain was in hard-core conversation with some of the bouncers, no doubt giving them a rip for not being more attentive. He had a talent for tearing your ass a new one without doing it in such a way that you got all butt-hurt over it. No doubt, knowing him, knowing our history with coming up against traffickers and sexual predators, he was talking them into looking the other way while the rest of the crew beat some fucking ass out in the parking lot. The little shoving match close to the pit was just a preview of coming attractions; those assholes inside just didn't know it yet.

I turned back to little Serenity. She was a petite thing, almost doll-sized, practically drowning in the band tee Rory'd tossed my way. He was the guitarist for the band I was in. We'd been one of the opening acts earlier in the night.

Her skin was pale for Florida living, her eyes large and dark under long and equally dark hair that fell to her waist, just above the perfect curve of her ass, which was hidden by the dumpy black band tee, and yeah – I know – it was my band's tee, but she was suited to something like a size small, something that would hug the swell of her breasts and caress the inward curve of her body before the flare of her hips.

She was beautiful, a perfect hourglass figure under the extra-large shirt.

I knew, because I'd been planning to talk to her before she'd been swept away by the surge and roll of bodies at the edge of the mosh pit.

Her voice was light and lyrical as it broke through the feminine spell she had unintentionally cast on me. *Fool, you cast it on yourself,* I chastised myself, but didn't spare it another thought, tuning in to what she had to say.

"I need my keys and my purse… I can't get into my apartment and all I have is my ID in these damn jeans." She slid her hand into her back pocket and extracted the little laminated rectangle of cardboard, then put it back.

"Wouldn't be a problem if they gave us some actual pockets," she complained and scrabbled her fingertips against where, it appeared, front pockets existed in her jeans. But they were sewn shut, no pockets to be had. I never got that. Still, she was being hella cute and I cracked a smile and had to chuckle.

"I don't get why they do that to girls," I said, for lack of something smooth or clever to say instead.

She frowned. "Same reason they do anything. Money and greed," she said simply. "No pockets means we have to buy their accessories, like wallets and purses. Fashion trends dictate we have to buy a purse and shoes for every outfit. It's a racket." She pressed her lips together and averted her gaze, her cheeks coloring bright pink all over again as she muttered, "Don't get me started."

I laughed a little and said, "I'm sure your friend is looking for you; she'll find you out here soon enough. I can wait with you."

"Thanks." She hugged herself like she was cold, which was a joke in and of itself. It was like standing in somebody's sauna out here. Mid-eighties and humid despite the deepening night. Summers in Florida were nothing to fuck with, especially this far inland. I was seriously missing the inner coastal region where Ft. Royal lay, practically on the bubble of the curve of the penn.

It wasn't cooler by much, but any breeze off the ocean was better than the stagnancy out here.

"Where do you live, anyway? I can maybe take you home."

She opened her mouth to reply, the rush of her inhaled breath sharp, but she closed it so sharply before speaking I could swear her teeth clacked.

"I mean, I have a ride, I just have to wait for them to come out. I don't want to put you out any further than you already have been."

"Hey, I told you." I spoke gently. "It's no trouble, and before you even suggest it, I'm not leaving you out here to wait all alone."

She smiled and it was edged in a sadness, but she murmured a thank you. A long pause ensued and she let out a shuddering nervous breath before asking, "So what do you do when you aren't saving hapless females from concert ruffians?"

I had opened my mouth to reply when the fast-paced clacking of approaching boot heels interrupted me, followed shortly thereafter by, "Ren! What are you doing out here!? I've been looking all over for you!"

"Oh, God, Linny!" Serenity intercepted her friend, brushing past me, and her perfume, a light, airy, floral scent tickled my nose slightly. I liked it. I figured I would like her, given a chance to get to know her. I turned and her much taller and much blonder friend embraced her smaller, darker, counterpart.

"What happened?" Linny demanded. "And where's my shirt?"

Serenity went about filling her friend in, and she couldn't help it, she got tearful again. I got the impression that she didn't get out much, which was a shame. She was a beautiful girl.

Her friend hugged her when Serenity started getting apologetic about losing her friend's shirt, of all the dumb things, and shushed her. "It's fine, it's just a stupid shirt!" she exclaimed.

"I know, but you trusted me to wear it and –"

"You didn't even want to wear it, you goof, and I'm not the least bit worried about it. I'm worried about *you*." Her friend looked up at me, and said with a sigh, "Thank you for looking out for her. I hate to ask, but do you think you could wait with her for just a little while longer while I go find my boyfriend?"

I nodded and said, "It's no trouble at all, you do what you gotta do. She's cool." I winked at Serenity, who was looking back at me over her shoulder, and her friend stepped back and let her go.

"Two minutes, I swear, and then I'm getting you the fuck out of here. I've never seen a crowd do that before. Usually metal guys are like him." She thrust her chin at me. "Some of the nicest guys out there. I'm so sorry, Ren."

"It's okay," Serenity said, taking a step back from the taller blonde. "I just want to go home, though."

"Absolutely, two minutes, I promise!" her friend called, walking backwards back to the door. My captain and his woman were looking this way and I gave them a nod. They went back to talking softly, over by the bikes, and I turned back to Serenity who was wincing as she looked at me.

"You must think I'm a total headcase," she said.

I shook my head. "No. I have to figure you don't get out much. Makes me feel bad for you that when you finally let yourself be talked into going out this is the kind of shit you have happen."

She let out an explosive breath. "You're right," she said, gazing out toward the street with its occasional passing set of headlights. "I haven't been getting out much aside from work. Partially because money, but mostly because I'm just a homebody. Linny really wanted me to come, although I prefer low-key to all of –"She waved her hand back at the building and the drone of muffled bass pounding out from the walls. "This."

I smiled and nodded, burying my hands in the pockets of my frayed jeans. "I'm headed that way myself," I said honestly, sucking in a breath between my teeth. "The older I get, the more I'm liking spending time on the beach by the bonfire versus the constant grind of gigs that cost me more money than they pay out, only to get absolutely nowhere. It's frustrating, you know?"

She nodded and said, "I can only imagine."

I gave her a crooked smile and was about to say something else when I was interrupted by her friend, keeping to her 'two-minute' promise. Here she came, a dude striding alongside her. He was clearly irritated.

"She wants to go home, Tyler, and I know it's not fair, but making her stay isn't fair either," she was saying to him, and I knew Serenity had caught it, because she visibly wilted, her shoulders dropping, her chin dropping too, her entire body radiating defeat.

"Yeah, well, I'm not ready to go," Tyler practically snarled.

Serenity piped up.

"It's okay, I can just wait out here. I would just feel better if I had my purse and keys. I'm really sor –"

"Hey, no. Don't apologize," I said at the same time Linny cried, "Honey, no!"

Tyler pulled his keys out of his pocket and the lights flashed on a nearby Prius, which figured. The guy looked like a poser and he'd already proven beyond a shadow of a doubt he was a fucking douchenozzle. Serenity made a break for it like she expected the dude to hit the locks and keep her from her things. I half expected him to.

He and Linny were getting into it and I had to say – I liked Linny a lot for standing up to her boyfriend.

The way she was looking at him with murder in her light brown eyes said he wasn't going to be her boyfriend after tonight, though.

Hell, I hoped not, but as pretty as Linny was, in that tall, blonde, willowy modelesque way, my gaze was drawn back to Serenity, who was pulling her small purse out from underneath the passenger seat of the Prius. Her heart-shaped ass was displayed nicely where she bent over through the open back door of the cage and I'd be lying if I said she hadn't piqued my interest in the slightest.

"Look," I said, stopping Linny and Tyler's low-key quarreling. "My set is long done, and I'm about ready to head outta here myself. I would be happy to take Serenity home if you guys are all cool with it. I mean, it's really up to her."

All eyes turned to Serenity as she stood frozen in the open doorway of the car, just far enough inside the reach of the pool of floodlight we were standing in for us to make out the surprised expression on her face. She looked at me, and I stared kind of calmly back at her, silently willing her to take me up on my offer. I wanted to get a shot at getting her number.

I figured that I could give her the ride home, score her digits, and be on my way home to Ft. Royal. Nice and tidy. Plus, I didn't think she would want a front-row seat to the ugly fight brewing between her friend and her fuckboi. Clearly there wasn't anything else there, the more I watched the two of them. I mean, I don't know what the fuck else any female would see in this guy other than the looks, and possibly his taste in music.

"Sounds good to me," Tyler said and Linny backhanded him against his shoulder, the slap of her fingers against his studded leather jacket snappy. I bit the inside of my cheek to keep from laughing and waited for Serenity to make up her mind. She was looking at Tyler and Linny and her eyes abruptly flicked to mine, where she grabbed hold of the offer like I was throwing her a lifeline.

"You're sure you wouldn't mind?" she asked.

"Not at all. I wouldn't have offered if I did," I said, smiling.

"You guys, I feel like I've already ruined your evening, you go on back inside. I'll catch a ride from Stoker and I'll text you as soon as I get home," she told Linny. "I promise," she added hastily when her friend looked like she was going to protest.

The look on Linny's face said that Tyler was a dead man. I didn't even feel sorry for him.

"Look, it's like a half-hour from here to your place." Linny held up her phone and the flash went off in my face. I blinked and she said to me, "I'm giving you forty-five minutes. If she doesn't text me the minute she gets to her door, I'm taking this picture straight to the cops."

"Easy." I waved her down. "Nothing's going to happen to your friend. I mean, if it does, it will literally be over my dead body. Don't forget who was there for her inside," I said and tried to be nice about the stinging remark.

"Fine," Linny grated and Serenity came up and hugged her.

"Got my keys, got my wallet, and got my phone. I promise, I'll text you as soon as I get there."

"God, this feels so stupid," Linny whispered, and I pretended like I didn't hear it.

"It'll be fine," Serenity whispered back. "I have a good feeling about it."

I tried not to smile and give myself away that I'd heard anything.

"Cool, thanks, man, I'm going back inside," Tyler said and Linny scowled but went with him. Dude was about to have a shitty rest of his concert experience.

"So, uh, where's your car?" Serenity asked me when they'd gone.

I laughed and said, "Bike's over here."

3

*S*erenity…

I eyed him with a bit of trepidation that was quickly giving way to excitement. I'd never been on a motorcycle but I'd always wanted to go for a ride. I never thought I'd ever get the chance.

"You're not joking, are you?" I asked.

"No. My bass can go in the van with the rest of the equipment, I can get it from the captain's place tomorrow. Just got to let him know about it."

"Alright." I gave a nod and slung my purse across my chest where it was secure.

"Come on, that's him over there with his Ol' Lady, Hope." He jerked his head to a small knot of people in the same jackets and vests with the big octopus patches on the back. I followed along to the side and just behind him as he went up to the people and said, "Hey, Cap. You mind grabbing my bass from the van and keeping it at your place tonight? I'm going to break off from you here and run Serenity home, if that's cool?"

The man he spoke to eyed me with a sparkle of mischief in his brown eyes and an easy grin on his face. A tall, lithe woman with hair as dark a brunette as my own and eyes an even darker shade of brown let her gaze rove over me tranquilly from where she leaned into his side.

"You okay?" she asked.

I shifted slightly on my feet and replied honestly, "Not really. I just really want to go home."

She gave a nod and said, "Stoker's good to take you. We'll take care of everything here."

I didn't know precisely what that meant, but I did know she wasn't just talking about making sure his guitar made it to the house of the man she was leaning against.

"Thanks, Captain."

"No sweat," the man replied and gave me a wink.

I gave a bit of a weak smile back and followed Stoker to his bike. He sat down on it after plucking the full helmet with its deeply tinted facemask off the seat. He parked it in his lap and asked me plainly, "You ever ride before?"

I shook my head and he raked his bottom lip between his teeth and gave a judicious nod before saying, "Okay. Safety rundown first." Then he launched into some basic rules of being a good passenger. To lean with him and the bike, never against it. To try not to shift too much in my seat, to hold on, and even how to hop off the bike and be sure not to burn myself on the pipes, which would be hot when we stopped.

He went to help me into the helmet and I asked, "What about you?" before he could put it on me.

"I have the requisite health insurance, I don't have to wear it. I just do because I like my face and if I ever bite it I kind of want to keep it."

I gave a bit of a laugh and he grinned. "I'll be fine. I don't always wear it, just on long rides on the highway. Besides, you're more important."

I felt a certain little thrill at his words, a blush of a strange sort of unexpected pleasure that he would think so, let alone that he would say so... I mean, we'd only just met. *Was he flirting with me?* I was always so bad at picking up things like that.

"So, where are we headed?" he asked. I filled him in, gave him directions and he said, "You'll have to show me. Just point and yell at stoplights."

"Okay."

He stood up and took off his jacket, peeling the leather vest off of it. He laid the thick leather coat across the seat while he shrugged back into the vest over the fine, sleeveless black mesh shirt he wore beneath it. The mesh was crisscrossed by shiny pleather straps and equally shiny silver buckles. I was a little taken aback by the physique peeking through the mesh of that shirt. The arms were something admirable, too.

It seemed like a body lean and muscled from hard work and possibly more than a few skipped meals more than one honed in a gym somewhere. He held out his jacket once his vest was back on him and I obediently and silently slipped my arms into the sleeves which were way too long. He rucked them back to free my hands and I took over, pushing the sleeves up to my elbows.

He got on the beastly motorcycle and turned to eye me. I swallowed hard and got on behind him. He let me get settled before he turned it on, but I still couldn't help but jump. I had never been a fan of loud and sudden noises. It was silly, but it was the music and the buildup and the loud sound whenever something jumped out that did me in completely for horror movies. I couldn't stand the sharp sounds and the fright, so I didn't tend to watch them.

It was somehow always worse when I knew it was coming, and this was no different. I mean, it was a motorcycle, I knew it was going to be loud. I knew it, I dreaded it just a little, and so, of course, I jumped, and jumped hard when it finally roared to life.

Stoker gave a bit of a laugh in front of me, something I barely heard over the chug of the motor, but I did hear it when he called over the even thrum of the engine, "Hold on to me!"

I put my arms around him and held on, and I wasn't the least bit surprised to feel he was just as hard, just as solid, as he looked.

Riding was just as fun and exciting as I always imagined it would be and I loved the sensation of butterflies in my stomach, the light sensation of fear sweeping over me. The kind of fear when you knew you were safe but were irrationally scared anyway, like when you faced going on a ride at an amusement park. You knew it was safe, that the rides are regularly inspected, maintained, and had been researched and had safety features installed to the point there wasn't any reason to be afraid at all… but it was still there. That little thrill of excitement, anxiety, and all-around feel-good energy.

It was the same on the back of that motorcycle, except with it was a heavier sensation of being afraid which was inextricably linked with the absolute mortal danger of the pavement whipping by below us at sixty-miles-per-hour when we hit the highway.

I'd told him what exit was mine and tapped him twice on the shoulder when it was the next one up. He gave a clear nod and steered us onto the off-ramp, and when we reached the stoplight at the bottom, I called out to him, "Right!"

It went like that, calling out 'right', 'left', or 'forward' until we got further away from the highway and surrounding strip malls and businesses and further into neighborhoods, first past apartments, and then into little subdivisions of houses on their little plots of land.

He slowed and came to a stop at a stop sign and I called out, "Left, and like six houses down on the left, that's me."

He turned us left, and my tummy did that funny bottoming-out feeling every time we leaned on the bike, the irrational fear of falling off bubbling through my system. I tapped him twice on the shoulder and pointed, and he glided the bike smoothly up to the curb in front of the small house owned by my little old landlady and stopped.

"Nice place," he said, then the silence was interrupted only by the soft ticking of his cooling engine, almost louder than the ride had been. I got off of the motorcycle and turned, and he twisted on his seat to face me, his long fingers going to the sides of the helmet, gently lifting it off my head. He planted it in his lap, between his legs, and I tried not to let my gaze follow and linger.

"Thanks, um, I'll tell my landlady so. I live in the little mother-in-law apartment above the garage."

"Oh." He smiled, his eyes glittering in the dim porch light from the detached garage as something like relief swept over his face. I smiled back, and he reached out and plucked at his jacket sleeve.

"Oh, right!" I blushed furiously with embarrassment and slipped out of it, handing it over, where he flopped it over his helmet and cocked his head, raising his eyebrows.

"Waiting right here until you're safe inside," he said, and I felt myself develop a soft spot for him right then and there.

"Why are you being so nice to me?" I asked gently.

He searched my face and sighed. "Starting to get the feeling you don't get many people who are nice to you."

"Not really, no." I swallowed convulsively at having given myself away on that front.

He smiled and bowed his head, nodding.

"I'd like to change that, I think," he murmured. "Give me your number?"

He was asking. There was definitely a question mark at the end of 'number' and I wanted to so badly, but it was almost too good to be true. I bit my bottom lip and made the decision.

"Seven-five-four…"

He pulled out his phone swiftly and entered it in, and I jumped when my phone buzzed in my purse, which rested against my hip.

"There. Now you have mine," he said calmly. "I hope to hear from you, and don't forget to text your friend."

He reached out and moved some of my mussed hair behind my ear, his fingertip lightly tracing the edge of my ear and I tried not to shiver. It had nothing to do with the ambient temperature out here and everything to do with a very different kind of heat.

"Thank you for the reminder," I murmured, digging both my phone and my keys from my little bag. I entered his name into my phone alongside his number and then fired off a text to Linny telling her I was home.

"Okay, you good?" he asked, when my friend texted back almost immediately.

"I'm good, but, out of curiosity – where do you live?"

That dashing crooked smile of his came out and he said, "Ft. Royal."

I blinked and blurted out, astonished, "That's almost two hours away!"

"And?"

"And I live clear in the opposite direction you were going!"

"And?"

I blinked at him stupefied. "And why would you do that for someone you don't even know?"

"Maybe I just figured it would give me a better shot at getting your number."

I laughed. I couldn't help it. Like I was going to deny a man this kind and this gorgeous anything. Especially after he was nice to me.

"Are you going to be okay? I mean, it's late, and that's going to be one very long ride…"

"I'll be fine," he said. "I'll stop for an energy drink or a cup of coffee at a gas station and it'll be all good."

"I mean, it's not the finest gas station coffee or anything, but I have some upstairs, can I make you a cup?" I offered, desperately wanting to show him even a tenth of the kindness he'd shown me tonight.

He smiled big, his teeth very white in the dark and asked, so flirtatiously it was obvious even to me, "Are you inviting me up to your place?"

"For coffee," I established clearly, laughing nervously, "and to talk some more… sure."

He got off his bike and took his keys, helmet, and jacket. I led him past the detached garage, the place between my shoulders tingling slightly as he followed me. I went up the switchback back stair with its climbing clematis vines. They turned the railings into a living thing, cascading with deep green foliage and white blossoms with frilled purple centers.

I unlocked the door and opened it right into the little studio I called home. The kitchen to the far right, the little dining table between the door and it. Straight ahead, my queen bed facing the wall-mounted television. Beside the black dresser below the television was the door to the bathroom, which also contained a small stacking washer and dryer.

I loved my little home. It was so me, cozy and a curious mix of light and dark. I hung my keys on the little wrought iron key hook plaque by the door and my purse on the heavy, free-standing, matching coat rack set on the hardwood floor beside it.

I hadn't wanted the feet to gouge the floor, and I'd needed the thing to slide easily, so I'd found this round black placemat that'd fit perfectly beneath it with enough cushion to preserve the wood floor.

I was forever cleverly repurposing things like that, and the style was reflected here and there among the skulls and gothic artwork on my shelves and walls.

"Metal," he said with a smile, approval coloring his voice.

I blushed slightly and said, "Funny enough, it's really more like gothic; metal is Linny's scene. The music actually kind of gives me anxiety. I can't listen to it when I'm driving or anything."

"Oh, really? So what were you doing at the show then?" he asked, hanging his coat and helmet on free arms of the coat rack.

"Concerts are different," I said shrugging. "Like, um, the difference between watching a live sporting event and the same event on TV. One is an experience the other is just… meh."

He smiled and nodded. "I completely get that, actually."

I pulled out a chair at the table for him and went into my little kitchen, crossing the open floor plan threshold marked out by a transition from hardwood floor to ceramic-like tile in a soft, neutral, light tan.

"How do you take your coffee?" I asked, switching on the pot, which was set up for tomorrow morning, to brew.

"Ah, I can do black, it's no trouble," he said.

I laughed slightly and said, "I use creamer because I like myself."

He smiled, "Okay, what 'cha got?"

"Amaretto, Irish Cream, and French Vanilla – and no I'm not an alcoholic, I promise. I don't really even drink."

"Amaretto sounds good."

I nodded and slipped into a seat across from him. He leaned

back, somewhat twisted in his seat so he could throw an arm casually behind it as he leaned. He let his deep brown eyes sweep my face.

"So what do you like to listen to, then?" he asked.

"Okay, this is totally going to sound weird, but I like things like Florence + the Machine and Loreena McKennitt. Um, out of the two, though, I would probably only want to see Loreena live, though, because I listen to their music to hear their music, not to listen to a bunch of people scream over them, and I know that out of the two, Loreena would be the only one where people would be quiet during the songs."

He laughed and said, "You're very peculiar, I'll give you that, but you also know what you like, know what you want, and I can respect that."

I colored faintly and didn't quite know what to say so I just kept quiet.

"Did I embarrass you? Because if I did, I apologize. Wasn't my intent."

I shook my head. "No, not at all, I just... I guess I don't take compliments well." I twitched in my seat.

"Not used to getting them?" he asked.

"No, not really," I said, and my cheeks did flame with humiliation, then.

"That's a shame," he said, and the way his gaze lingered turned up the heat in my face for a very different reason. I got up abruptly to bring down two coffee cups and add creamer to the bottoms of both, just needing the busywork, unable to sit still.

"You probably think I'm some kind of pathetic," I said, laughing nervously.

He shook his head.

"No."

I scrubbed my face with my hands and said from behind them, "Oh, God. I'm sorry, I'm so terribly awkward."

"I'd say, out of practice," he said charitably.

"Never had much practice to begin with," I said bleakly.

"I find that hard to believe." He cocked his head and swept me with his gaze.

I asked him, "Why do you say that?"

He smiled like the cat that'd eaten the canary and murmured, "You're a beautiful woman. I find it hard to believe you don't have to practically beat guys off with a stick."

I rolled my eyes at the ridiculousness of it and sighed, "I think we know what type of guys I attract." I winced, thinking back on being trapped in that press of bodies with their groping hands.

"Shit, I was hoping not to go back to that," he said, and sighed unhappily.

"It's okay, I'll be fine after a long hot shower."

He nodded slowly, "You should go take one, get comfortable; I can pour the coffee when it's done."

"Oh, I don't know," I laughed. "Seems a bit rude to shower with a new guest in the apartment."

"Even when the guest insists?" he asked, arching a brow.

"Um, I should give you your shirt back at the very least," I murmured.

He shook his head. "It's yours. Use it as a nightshirt or something. No selling it now."

"Oh, this is your band?" I asked, pulling it out from my body and staring down at the logo on the front.

"It is."

I peered at it and tried to recollect when they'd gone on. I mean, I could picture the logo on the front of the drum set, but I couldn't for the life of me recall seeing him on stage. I confessed as much and his lips split into a wide grin.

"It's okay, it was a battle of the bands, and a lot were up there tonight leading up to the main act. We were the third on stage."

"Oh, we got there late, like arrived in the middle of your set."

"See, that explains it. Mystery solved."

"I forgot all about the 'battle of the bands' lead up, you didn't even get to stay to find out if you won?"

"Don't worry about that," he said. "I'm just happy to play my music and have people listen. I don't care about bragging rights or ego rushes."

"Yeah, but…"

"But, nothing, the guys'll let me know."

I fell silent, guilt nibbling at the edges of my soul, and I hated that I'd pulled him away.

"Hey."

I chewed my bottom lip and let my eyes flick from their fixed position on my table to his dark eyes.

"I don't go anywhere I don't want to go and I don't do anything I don't want to do."

I smiled a bit at that and asked lightly, "Like, ever?"

He shrugged his shoulders and answered, "For the most part."

"Must be nice," I conceded.

"Sometimes. Sometimes, like with anything else, it's a struggle to be free and stay free."

"I can relate to that for sure."

The coffee maker gurgling and dribbling into its carafe filled the deep silence between us. It was dimly lit in my little apartment, the salt lamp by the bed and the single light over the sink in my kitchen casting a muted golden glow to beat back the deep night outside. The air conditioning hummed quietly, but it was still warm in here as the gulf between us slowly filled with unspoken attraction. It was palpable, like you could reach out and touch it like a living thing, just there, shimmering invisible between us.

"I really hope you'll call me," he said suddenly, but it didn't break the spell.

"You have my number, you could always call me, too."

He smiled and raised an eyebrow, and I laughed.

"I'm really bad at this flirting part and the rules of engagement are absolutely mystifying to me," I confessed.

"Oh, yeah? How's that?" he asked, laughing.

"Like, if I called you tomorrow it would make me look desperate, right? But if I wait until the day after tomorrow, is that enough time or do I still look overeager? Then if I wait two days, is that too long? I don't want to give you the impression I'm not interested..."

He laughed and said, "You're overthinking this."

"I'm good at that. Like, really good at that. People are just so confusing!"

"Nah, people just like to make things way more complicated than they need to be," he said and I pursed my lips and nodded slowly.

"I'm good at that, too," I murmured.

"Nah," he shook his head, "I don't think so."

"How do you know? You've barely met me."

He grinned. "I have a good feeling about things."

I turned to fix our coffees, the maker finally through, and also so he wouldn't see me blush. I couldn't believe this was happening! To *me* of all people...

I stirred the creamer up from the bottom in each black cup with their delicate red and white glazed blossoms and brought them over to the table. He took the one I offered him, and an electric thrill traveled from where his fingertips brushed mine.

"Thanks," he murmured.

"Welcome."

We talked a bit more. He brought up Tyler and laughed when I made a face.

"I love her to death, but it's a good thing Linny goes through men like dirty socks. Tyler is a passing fancy, and I guarantee he'll be gone by tomorrow."

"Good, that's good. Maybe it will knock some sense into him."

"Doubtful," I said, after swallowing a sip from my cup.

"Truth. Most guys like that never figure it the fuck out."

"No," I agreed. "They don't."

He sighed, and it was the kind of sigh that said all good things must come to an end, and it was the end of my night. I was a mix of disappointed and grateful. He roved over me with his gaze and asked softly, one more time, "You sure you're alright?"

I nodded slowly.

"I'm sure, thanks to you."

He nodded.

"Okay, I'll call you sometime this week."

I smirked. "No pressure."

He laughed.

"Never," he said and I caught the double meaning behind the word and it made me relax just that much more around him.

"Thank you, Stoker… for everything."

"You're welcome, Serenity."

He stood and I watched as he shrugged out of his vest, pulled on his jacket and put the vest back on over it. He fetched down his helmet from the coat rack and opened the door to the outside world.

"Goodnight," he said and I smiled, hugging myself a little, sad to see him go.

"Goodnight."

4

*S*toker…

I wanted to call her the minute I got home but it was pretty much just before the asscrack of dawn. I knew she would likely be showered and asleep by the time I rolled in to my place, two streets off the boulevard in Ft. Royal. Still, it didn't stop the desire.

I split the difference and shot a text to her phone saying: ***Made it home. Call you in the next few days. Promise.***

There wasn't a reply. I didn't expect there to be.

I crashed and crashed hard. When I finally came to, it was pretty late in the afternoon. I checked my phone first thing to a few text alerts.

Rory: Third Place.

Captain: Hope whooped some ass, you missed out. It was beautiful.

Serenity: Thank you for letting me know. I'm sorry I was asleep but glad to know you made it. I look forward to hearing from you. I hope you got good sleep. She'd even included a smiley emoji.

I didn't text back right away, instead answering the first two texts with a 'that sucks' and an 'I bet. Just got up. Be at the house, soon.'

I dragged my ass into the shower and sighed as the hot water

25

rushed over my skin, easing some residual soreness from my muscles and washing the road down the drain. I didn't much feel like doing shit today except catching up on laundry and taking my ass to work the next morning.

I got my jeans on just as a heavy knock fell at my front door. I went for it and opened it up to Atlas on the other side. He held up my bass and bounced his eyebrows asking, "Hear you may have hooked your-self a hottie last night."

I laughed and opened the door wider, taking the soft case from my crewmate and letting him into my house. It was small, a cozy place that'd belonged to my grandparents and had fallen into some disrepair. I was fixing it up, slow but sure, since they'd left it to me. That's how I'd come to Ft. Royal in the first place. My folks, they lived in Louisiana over by Shreveport. Well, my dad did. My mom died when I was seven from breast cancer, and the grandparents who'd left me this place were her parents.

Atlas let out a gusty sigh and dropped into my recliner. I leaned my bass up against the wall and swung the door to my place shut.

"She's different, that's for sure," I said.

"Aw, yeah? How's that?"

I went over and dropped onto my couch and looked at him.

"She's timid, dunno why. Shy, but at the same time brutally honest and unafraid to just say it."

"Say what?" he asked, laughing.

"Whatever it is that's on her mind."

"You got her number?"

"Yeah."

"You gonna call her?"

"Definitely," I nodded.

"What else you know about her?"

"Her first name and sort of where she lives, that's it."

"Gonna have Radar look her up?"

"Naw, man. I don't want any spoilers, not with her. She's chill."

"Good deal." He nodded along and finally sighed and put his feet up and asked, "Got any weed?"

I huffed a laugh and said, "Yeah, hang on."

I GOT MY SHIT DONE, ready for the work week, hung out with a few of the guys and watched some television, and sent 'em all packing when I needed to crash so I could get up for work the next morning.

I lay in bed that night and stared at the lit screen of my phone and smiled to myself. Serenity had been on my mind all fuckin' day and I couldn't wait a minute longer. I dialed her up.

"Hello?"

"So, does this make me desperate or overeager or what?" I asked and she laughed lightly on the other end of the line.

"Neither, I think… it would only be those things if I did it."

"What kind of logic is that?" I asked, smiling like a fool.

"A crazy person's," she said simply. "You've officially been warned."

"Good to know."

There was a pregnant pause, heavy with promise and a little bit awkward. Finally I spared us both and broke the silence.

"I wanted to check and see how you were doing, you know, after last night."

"I'm okay," she replied softly. "Thanks to you."

"How about your friend? She good?" I asked.

"Much better, she lost around a hundred and sixty-seven pounds last night and has never looked better."

I laughed at her totally serious, totally deadpan delivery.

"I think we both had to guess that was going to happen."

"Right?" She gave a gusty sigh as she asked, "So, what are you doing?"

"Chillin' in bed, about to go to sleep. I gotta get up for work tomorrow morning."

"Ah, me too… the whole work thing. What do you do?"

"Construction, actually. I frame houses and buildings, put up the skeleton, the plywood and the like."

"Oh, that sounds… really tedious and boring."

I laughed out loud. She was an interesting girl. Timid, yes, but also completely fuckin' fearless. I wanted to know more, so bad.

"What about you?"

"Um, boring and tedious, thy name is retail," she said, sucking a breath between her teeth. I laughed again and she cried, "No, seriously! Don't judge. I graduated high school and I knew there was no way I could go to college and be able to pay my student loans on the other side, so I just have a high school diploma and it sucks, but I don't really know what else I'm supposed to do… you know?"

"Hey, I only have a high school diploma," I told her. "Who am I to judge?"

She made an exasperated noise and said, "Yeah, but you work in a trade, which is at least noble work. Not like me, twenty-seven bouncing from job to job with no prospects whatsoever, but unwilling to incur a massive load of debt only to still have no prospects… Ugh… I feel so trapped and it sucks, and I don't even know why I'm telling you any of this. Oh, my god you must think I'm crazy. I am so making a terrible first impression, aren't I?"

"No, actually, I like how frank and honest you are. It's like what you see is what you get – no bullshit."

She sighed and it held a tiredness, a sort of sadness which was echoed in her voice when she murmured, "Yeah, well, I feel like the world would be a much better place if people were more honest with each other."

"No doubt," I agreed, and got the suspicion that maybe people hadn't always been honest with her.

There was a long silence as we each got sort of lost in our own thoughts, but it was a comfortable silence. At least, it was for me.

"Should I let you go?" she asked and I glanced at the clock on my phone.

"Shit, yeah, as much as I hate to say it – it's getting late for me."

"What time do you have to be up?"

I cleared my throat. "For this job? Four in the morning. Takes me that long to get where I'm going."

"Bad commute?"

"Yeah, not much traffic at that hour but it's a ways, that's for sure."

"Alright, well, be careful."

"Call me tomorrow?"

Another long pause full of promise before she said, voice shaded with surprise, "Uh, yeah. What time is good?"

"Uh, either before two or after four-thirty," I said.

"Okay. I'll call you tomorrow."

"I'm looking forward to it," I told her honestly.

"Me too," she murmured.

"Night, Serenity, sleep well."

"You do the same," she said, and I loved the sound of her voice, soft and gentle, velvet over the line. I could fall asleep just listening to her talk. It was probably one of the most soothing sounds I'd ever heard. Somebody had named this girl right, that was for sure.

I disconnected the call before I was tempted to keep it going, to keep her talking. God, it was tempting though. I felt like a goddamned teenager with a hardcore crush.

I sighed and set my phone aside on the end table and closed my eyes. I swore if I breathed deeply and slowly enough, I could just catch the faintest whiff of her delicate perfume.

5

 erenity…

"Shit." I sighed and put my phone back in my purse. It was after two, I couldn't try to call until after four-thirty, and as soon as my lunch was over I was working until six, so… yeah. I chewed my bottom lip as I sat in the mall's food court and wondered how late was too late to call when he had to get up so early.

I was a world-class worrier, no doubt about it.

"Uh-oh, what's that look for?" Linny asked, dropping into the seat across from mine with a hearty sigh.

I shook my head and said, "It's nothing."

"Oh, you suck at lying. Please tell me you hooked up with that hot guy from the MC."

"No," I said, but I couldn't hold out. I let out an explosive breath and told her the truth. "We've been talking, though."

"Oh? What's that, now?" She perked up entirely too quick and I cringed inwardly.

"We traded numbers and we've chatted on the phone a few times."

"Oh, ho, ho! See, I told you it was a great idea you came out with me on Saturday night."

I frowned. "I was groped six ways to Sunday – almost literally might I add, at that show."

"And you were picked up by a seriously hot member of one of those bands," she said, sticking a bite of her salad into her mouth, staring at me with her inquisitive brown eyes, and chewing slowly, waiting for me to concede defeat on the point.

"Fine, yes… you're right," I said, and she smiled brightly.

"Thank you," she sang out, and I rolled my eyes so hard I nearly checked out my own ass.

"I wanted to call him but it's after two."

"What happens after two?"

"I think he has to commute home. Kind of hard to answer the phone while driving… or riding or whatever."

"True, so just call him when you get home."

"Yeah," I said and tried to keep the glum feeling that the wait was killing me out of my voice.

"You like him?" she asked.

"Yeah, Linny… I do. I'm not sure what it is about him, but I really do."

"Well, if he's a douche, never fear. I got your back and will totally kick his ass for you."

I laughed and shook my head. God, I loved my friend…

THE DRIVE HOME was such a drag. I'd lucked out. My land lady's eyesight had gotten so bad, she couldn't drive anymore, so she'd sold me her car – a little 1990 Honda Accord with barely any miles on it – for dirt cheap. In exchange, I took her shopping and to her doctor's appointments pretty faithfully.

She was sitting on her front porch when I pulled into the garage and perked up and waved at me when I walked out to go around to the stairs.

"Hello there, Serenity!" she called.

"Hi, Mrs. Sedgwick!" I called back.

"Come have a glass of tea!"

"Oh, I wish I could, but I have a phone call to make. Rain check?"

"Absolutely, my dear! My door is always open."

"Thank you, Mrs. Sedgwick!"

"I told you already, call me Nellie!"

I smiled and shook my head and disappeared around the corner and dashed up the steps to my apartment. Once inside I performed my coming-home ritual. Shoes off, sigh of relief at the cool hardwood beneath my feet, soothing the burning, throbbing ache from being on them all day, and then divest of the rest. Keys on hook, purse on rack, shoes on the shoe rack by the door behind the coat rack, grab phone, and a running leap onto the made bed.

I bounced twice and let myself just melt into the softness, letting out a gusty sigh. I lit up my phone and called Stoker.

"Ahhh, I was starting to wonder if I was going to hear from you today," he said without preamble.

"Yeah, sorry. By the time I got my lunch it was after two and I worked until six. I just got home. Is it too late?"

"Nope, not at all. You sound tired."

"I am tired," I said.

"Come see me," he said.

"What? Now?"

"No, not now," he said laughing. "This weekend."

"I wish I could, but retail… My schedule isn't always set. I don't have this weekend off. I get them every now and then but my next one off isn't until next weekend."

"Aw, that's balls."

I hesitated and finally suggested, "You could always come see me… you know, for dinner. I mean, I could cook."

"When's your next day off?" he asked gently.

"Um, I have split days this week, so Thursday, and then Monday, but then I have the weekend after that off, both Saturday and Sunday."

"How about I come by after work on Thursday, we can grab a bite to eat somewhere?"

"I'm actually a really good cook. I mean, I like to cook, I just never have anyone to cook for."

"Okay," he agreed. "Dinner, Thursday night."

"It won't be too far out of your way?" I asked meekly. Like I said, I was a world-class worrier.

"Nah, I'm actually working out that way for now."

"Oh," I said, a bit taken aback. "God that must be awfully far for you."

"It's no picnic but I've done worse." He sounded dismissive of the commute, which baffled me.

"I couldn't do it," I said.

He chuckled. "You do what you gotta do if you want to keep a place of your own and food in your face," he said and I sighed.

"I'll concede your point, there."

"Oh, goodie! I like to win," he said and I could hear the smile in his voice. I laughed, probably harder than I should have.

"Well, it won't be hard with me. I very rarely, if ever, come out on top."

"Mm, maybe we'll have to change that luck of yours."

I lost my breath at the low, sultry tone of his voice, and it took me a couple of tries to find my own.

"I-I think I'd like that, someday."

"I like that you're open to the idea," he said, and his voice glowed with a pleasure to match.

I smiled, blushing furiously, and suddenly couldn't wait for Thursday. We chatted a little more, cooling it with the double entendres, and just talked about our respective days. It was nice, and I was sad when we had to hang up, him to go to bed and me to fix myself something to eat.

I DIDN'T GET to talk with Stoker at all on Tuesday, but I woke up to a good morning text telling me that I was on his mind and to have a good day. On Wednesday, we exchanged texts and managed a short evening talk about how excited we were for the next night and getting to know one another some more.

I spent my day off getting my apartment into shape. I mean, it was always clean, neat and orderly. I couldn't stand clutter or mess. It made me feel all kinds of anxious, so really it was cleaning what was already clean, going down the usual checklist of day-off chores like getting laundry started, with a few extras like making sure fresh towels were on the towel rack in the bathroom and that my makeup was put away.

I made sure with a quick text that there weren't any food allergies or anything he couldn't stand, and when I got the all-clear, I sat down at my table to go through my cookbooks to figure out what I wanted to do. I spent a half hour or so choosing what I wanted to make and making a shopping list for what I didn't have and would need. I ran to the grocery store and picked up my missing items and, worrying my bottom lip at how much my checking account balance had dropped, made my way home.

I set everything to marinating in my fridge, giving the flavors time to marry. Realizing it was still pretty early in the day, I let myself out to play – as in, went down to indulge in one of my favorite pastimes.

It wasn't just Mrs. Sedgwick I loved about living here. There was also what had been a little plot of grass growing out behind the garage in the side yard of her house. A little plot of grass that was just begging for a greenhouse.

With her permission, I'd built one for myself, out of cheap pavers, cinder blocks, and reclaimed windows. It was sturdy, and cozy, and more than a bit ramshackle, but I loved it out there. It allowed me to tend to my orchids, a thing I'd grown to love with a high school horti-culture class.

The greenhouses behind my high school had given me a place to essentially hide during lunches and even some assemblies. I'd been horribly bullied for being different... poor, for one, but my penchant for depressing music, literature, and comics, as well as wearing all black all the time, and even some of my more unique religious explorations, had made me a prime target for the popular crowd. I'd been marked out as something 'other' since junior high, and God it had been awful.

It made it hard for me as an adult to trust anybody. I was always expecting the very worst that humanity had to offer and I found I was very rarely, if ever, disappointed on that front, which was just sad.

It was one of the reasons that Stoker had my interest. He was so… different. No one except for Linny had ever stood up for me or looked out for me like he had and I was so very curious about him, about what made him so different from other guys.

I misted some of my plants, checking for mites or any other signs of distress. I was excited to see that a few of my babies were getting ready to bloom.

I talked to them, told them how happy I was to see them. How excited I was for the evening, and how I would see them soon, but that I needed to go get a shower and get dressed. I didn't know how long it would take Stoker to get here from his job site and I didn't want to leave any margin for error in looking a hot mess when he got here.

I carefully chose one of my casual dresses – at least, casual for me – and laid it out on my neatly-made bed.

I showered, made sure everything was shaved, and brushed through my wet hair and braided it over my shoulder. I didn't always dry it, preferring not to heat damage it if I could avoid it. I didn't exactly have a lot of money to go around, so expensive salon visits were out of the question. I could barely afford to get it trimmed every three months; usually I went six or more between haircuts.

I stared into the mirror and huffed out a breath, my shoulders dropping as I took in my plain appearance. There wasn't enough makeup in the world to fix it. Linny insisted I was a pretty girl, but all I'd ever gotten from most anyone else was a passable 'cute.'

Long ash brown hair, I would say a medium brown in color, that was pretty unremarkable save for its thickness and length. Skin too pale for the Florida sun, which I did try to avoid. I mean, I only really had two colors – glacier and lobster. Even my eyes weren't much to write home about. Just plain brown, an almost even match for my hair.

No bronze or amber highlights, nothing unique at all about me really. Just any old girl from anywhere in the world lost in the crowd on the street.

I put on a black bra and a black pair of matching panties before slipping the black bohemian mini-dress over my head. It was a simple tank top that fit me well at the top and flared perfectly into a flirty skirt at my hips, showing off my figure. It was one of my favorites, and so, it was faded with wear and washing, the embroidery standing out darker against the light cotton and rayon mixed fabric that almost appeared stonewashed now.

I was in my own house, and didn't feel the need to put on any sandals or shoes so I just kept barefoot, checking my deep burgundy toe polish for any chips. Finding none, I found myself with nothing to really do except wait, so I tucked myself into the little reading nook I'd made for myself in the corner of the wall that led to my front door and the wall that ran behind the head of my bed. It had windows on both sides, allowing plenty of natural light in over my shoulders.

The wing-back chair that I'd parked there was a garage-sale find that I'd reupholstered myself.

It wasn't the best job of lining up all of the upholstery tacks, but was passable from a distance. I'd found a nice black-on-black damask-patterned upholstery fabric. There had been just enough to cover the front and the back of the chair and its seat in the bargain bin at the fabric store. I'd pieced it together with a plain, inexpensive black velvet on the arms and the back of the chair, and it'd turned out nicely.

I'd found a closely matching ottoman at another garage sale and I had recovered it in some of the same black velvet and, with the little round high table perched beside the chair to hold my drink and my book or phone, it made quite the cozy little reading space.

When it got cold, which it rarely did in the Sunshine State, I just used an amethyst chenille throw – again, found in the bargain bin – and I couldn't be bothered to come out of my snug little world for hours.

It was where Stoker found me when I finally came up for air. I was reading along and got this strange feeling like I wasn't alone and when I looked up, I'd yelped and then put a hand over my mouth as if I could somehow take the sound back. He was standing just on the other side of the screen door.

It wasn't too bad out today and I tended to turn off the A/C unit in the apartment and throw open doors and windows if the heat was something I could tolerate. It saved money.

"Sorry," he said, and pushed open the screen, stepping across the threshold. "I didn't mean to scare you, I just couldn't help myself."

"What do you mean?" I asked, setting my book aside and uncurling myself from the chair, standing so I could come around the little ottoman and greet him.

I stepped over to him and looked up at him. He was tall. Easily six foot or more to my whole five foot three.

"You were just, I don't know..." He laughed and it sounded a bit nervous, which was funny to me – him, nervous, around me? Ha. "You looked like you were really into it and you were just so beautiful, I had to stop and just look for a minute."

I stared at him and blinked stupidly. *Me? Beautiful?*

"I'm glad you're here," I murmured and he smiled.

"Yeah?"

"Yeah… can I get you something cold to drink?"

"Uh, yeah." He lifted a gym bag, "I kind of came prepared. It was kind of brutal out there today, you mind if I get a quick shower? I'd hate to stand around stinking up your place."

"No, not at all, bathroom is through there, take your time. Are you hungry now?"

He nodded. "Food sounds fabulous, actually."

"I'll get it started."

He moved past me with a smile and a nod and we'd been standing just near enough that the air was just a touch cooler for him moving away. He didn't stink, not one bit, at least not to me but I could understand not wanting to feel grimy after a hard day's work.

I moved into the kitchen and filled two glasses with ice and poured from the pitcher of lightly sweetened ginger-and-pear white tea I kept in the fridge. I liked the exotic taste and, though like any southern girl I liked a good sweet tea, this was just healthier than the copious amounts of sugar found in most traditional sweet teas. Besides, honestly, the tea bags weren't that much more than your regular ol' Lipton or whatever.

Bonus, white tea contained less caffeine than green or black teas, and as much as I worshipped caffeine in the early mornings or as a pick-me-up throughout the day, I didn't need it before bed or in the evenings. My nerves and anxiety were more than enough to keep me awake staring at the ceiling long after I should have been asleep.

I set the table and took our food out of the fridge, dropping the liner to my Instant Pot into the housing. It was the best Christmas gift I'd ever bought myself; I'd gotten a major deal on it for Black Friday. It had been marked down to seventy-five percent off the original price, plus more with bonus rewards coupons and an employee discount on top of that. In fact, I'd gotten such a great deal on it, I'd been able to afford the accessories set that went with it. I barely, if ever, used my oven for anything anymore, and that included making breads or cakes, since I'd gotten it.

Sealing the lid, I set it to cook, and added rice to my little five-cup rice cooker along with the requisite amount of water. Everything was so efficient that I was essentially done before he'd even had time to turn on the shower.

Feeling quite pleased with myself, I set his glass of iced tea near his plate and went back over to my little reading nook with mine, setting it on the little side table and taking up my book once more to wait for him.

The food would only take around twenty minutes to cook once the pot came to pressure. Ten minutes to cook, an additional ten minutes to rest, and *voilà*, dinner was served.

I tried very hard to immerse myself back into my book, but it was hard, and it was mostly due to the fact I couldn't stop picturing his hard body all naked, steamy, and wet in my shower just behind my bathroom door. I stared at the door and blushed, jumping slightly when the tap shut off and quickly returning my gaze to the lines of text that blurred together on the page.

God, the last thing I wanted him to do was come out here to me staring at the door like some... pervert or something. Desperation, thy name is Ren, I thought to myself.

The last thing I wanted to do was give any kind of hint about how hard up I was for friends. I had Linny, sure, but she was pretty much my only friend and that was by way of some fucking miracle, I'll tell you what.

I was lonely, but I knew she couldn't be my end all of be all's when it came to friendship, so, as lonely as I was, I usually pretended I was just dandy with my solitude. I knew Linny would feel some kind of guilty if she knew otherwise and I didn't want that on my conscience. Besides, it wasn't her fault people didn't want to have fuck-all to do with me. It wasn't really mine, either... it just was what it was, I guess.

The door to the bathroom opened up a moment later and Stoker stepped out. A plume of steam and the scent of clean man wafted over to me and I tried not to press my thighs together. He smiled at me and gave me a wink, his long hair pulled back into a ponytail so tight it gave the illusion it was short. His light gray tee hugged his chest and shoulders nicely and was darkened in places by some errant water droplets.

He set his duffel bag by the open bathroom door and came over, his booted footfalls across the hardwood deep and resonant. He dropped onto the ottoman with a satisfied and gusty sigh and he rested his hands on the calf of one leg where I was curled in my seat. I sucked in a tremulous breath at just how good his calloused fingertips felt against my bare skin.

"Now I feel like I can greet you properly," he said with a crooked grin. "C'mere."

I set my book aside and put my feet to the floor, standing up straight; his hands went lightly to my hips and he stood too, hugging me to him gently. He immediately leaned back with a wink and asked, "So how was your day?"

"Pretty low-key," I murmured. "Dinner should be up in about fifteen minutes or so."

"That fast? Wow."

"You said you were hungry now."

He nodded. "I'm ravenous, actually." His gaze lingered on me a bit long after he said it and I laughed a little, blushing. We broke apart and retook our seats.

"What you reading?" he asked.

"Oh, um…" I grabbed my book back up and handed it to him.

"Nice," he said and turned it over. "*The Woman in Black*, by Susan Hill. Horror fan, then?"

"Not really," I said. "I have an eclectic taste in books and movies. I just decided to read this one because I saw the movie with Daniel Radcliffe and I liked it, so I thought I might like the book better."

"You a movie-before-the-book kind of a girl, then?" he asked.

"Absolutely. If you read the book before the movie, you'll almost always be disappointed in the film adaptation, but if you see the film before reading the book... When you liked the movie... well, if you liked it enough give the book a try, it's almost a guarantee that the book will be a thousand times better, so win/win."

"You never find it tough to get into the book when you know what's going to happen?"

"Sometimes, but not always," I said.

The Instant Pot beeped and he straightened slightly, "Need to get that?" he asked.

I shook my head. "Ten more minutes."

"Cool."

He handed me back my book and I put it back in its place, taking up my tea.

"Your glass is on the table," I said and he smiled, standing up and giving me space to do likewise.

We wandered over to the table and he picked up his glass taking a sip.

"Let me know if you don't like it or if it needs more sugar or something," I said.

"No, this is nice, actually. What is it?"

"Ginger and pear white tea."

"Nice! It's good, really good."

"Thanks…"

6

*S*toker…

She was beautiful, like, holy shit, unimaginably lovely. I don't know what I was thinking but the memory of her from last Saturday night didn't do her justice. She was simply gorgeous in the light of day, all woman with lush curves, the dress she wore hugging every line of her body ending in a flirty hemline at mid-thigh. I couldn't get over it, but I really couldn't get over how nervous she was, her posture unsure, her gaze fixed anywhere but on me as a light blush painted her cheeks.

She moved stiffly around her place and treated me like I was way out of her league even though I was pretty sure it was the exact opposite. I didn't get it, like at all, but I wanted to figure her out so bad.

"So," I asked, taking another sip of the spicy, fruity iced tea, "aside from letting your friends drag you to concerts with music you don't necessarily like, what do you do for fun?"

She laughed a little and it transformed her into something other-worldly.

"I, um, I listen to music I do like, and I read, obviously… I like to make things, and fix things that are broken or unloved up into something useful again."

41

"Oh yeah? Like what?"

"I redid that chair and ottoman," she said, gesturing to where she'd been sitting before.

"No shit?" I asked. "I never would have guessed. You did a good job, I thought it was store-bought."

"Mm-mm." She shook her head. "Two different yard sales and the fabric store. Same with my book cases and dresser. Old things refurbished, just like new."

I looked around her place, and I mean *really* looked this time, and I had to say it was eclectic as hell, but it still all went together at the same time.

"Your place is nice," I said. "Way nicer than mine. I should have you take a look at it and make some suggestions on interior decorating. Looks like a bachelor's pad, for real."

"I mean, that's fair, isn't it?" she asked. "You are a bachelor."

"True, I guess."

"I even built my own greenhouse out of reclaimed windows," she said casually as she went to the fridge to bring out her pitcher of tea. I ambled on over for a refill and blinked in surprise at her words.

"That greenhouse out back by the stairs? You built that yourself?"

"Yeah, I really like cultivating orchids. I, um, I'm trying to —"She let out a shuddering breath and tried again, "If I trust you with something, I mean, show you something, would you promise not to tell on me?"

I set my glass aside on the counter and cocked my head. "Yeah, why would I narc you out?"

"I don't know." She crossed her arms, pitcher abandoned on the counter beside her. "It's just something people do."

"Not me." I shook my head. "Snitches get stitches where I'm from."

She swallowed hard and nodded.

"I'm trusting you," she murmured, and checked her cooker thing. "It'll keep a few minutes, come on."

She refilled our glasses and led me out the door and down the steps. We went into her little greenhouse and she took me to a back corner. It was humid as fuck in here and hotter than it was outside. Oppressive, but beautiful, green and dotted with color and even some white blossoms. She stopped beside some delicate lacy blooms and I knew immediately what they were. Was hard to live in south Florida and not know what they were – and it was illegal to have them.

"Ghost orchids?" I asked in a bit of awe.

"Started with one that I kiped from the swamp, but I've managed to keep it alive, and…"

"I thought these were impossible to cultivate in captivity."

"They are, um, but I figured it out."

"That's nuts. You're hella talented, Serenity."

She blushed with pleasure this time and I liked the look on her. I was struck by how much I wanted that look underneath me, those lovely brown eyes of hers heavy-lidded with passion, a halo of her dark tresses scattered over the pillow.

Fuck, I was getting chub just thinking about it, so I shut it down quick and tried to hide it by swallowing some of my tea.

"Call me Ren," she murmured, and took me on a little tour of her collection. While the Ghost orchid was obviously her crown jewel, she had quite a few other equally beautiful blooms, even if they weren't nearly as rare.

"You're something else, Ren."

"Thanks," she whispered, and with a smile that held the gentle light of the moon even though it was still full sun, she turned and led me back out into the yard. I caught her scanning the street.

"I didn't think I heard the bike," she said, closing up her little greenhouse, which was pretty fucking sturdy, all things considered.

"Oh, no, that's my truck," I said pointing out the old 80s Ford pickup. "I gotta bring my tools with me most of the time, so I don't typically ride into work."

"Ah, that would explain how you managed to sneak up on me."

I smiled and we paced slowly back toward the stairs up to her place. A little old lady waved at us from a rocker on her front porch. Serenity lit up and waved back at her.

"That's Mrs. Sedgwick, my landlady," she said.

"She cool with me being here?" I asked.

Serenity laughed. "Probably overjoyed that I have someone over other than Linny. Come on, let's eat."

The food was good, the company fantastic. She turned the tables on me once we were seated, though.

"So, what's life like in a motorcycle club?" she asked lightly.

"Structured," I answered carefully. "Comfortable. At least for me. We live and die by our own rules when the majority of us don't have a hope or a prayer of fitting in anywhere else. Citizen life just isn't made for us." I gave a half-assed shrug. It wasn't much of an explanation but it was hard for me to explain at the same time.

Serenity chewed slowly and eyed me carefully. She swallowed gracefully and said, "I get that. Probably more than you might think," she said softly. "The whole 'not fitting in anywhere.'"

Now that I could believe. She was definitely, unabashedly, and uniquely her, and I liked that. Something was still nagging the fuck out of me about her timid nature, though. I'd figure it out eventually, though. Just time and trust. I was part of an outlaw MC — trust didn't come easy to my kind either, so I knew it would be slow going. That was okay, though. I wasn't in any kind of a rush and good things came to those who waited or some shit.

"How come?" I asked her and fixed her with a look.

"How come what?" she asked softly, shifting nervously.

"You're beautiful, smart, funny, kind, and obviously creative and crafty. How can you not fit in anywhere?"

"I just don't, at least, not really," she said, and misery accompanied her tone.

"Okay." I nodded slowly. "Fair enough."

I didn't like the silence that overtook us after that as we worked on clearing our plates. She'd made some Asian-inspired chicken dish with honey and garlic over rice and it was fuckin' good. Made me wish I knew how to cook better than I did. I mostly lived off of sandwiches and the occasional pot of spaghetti.

"Put some of your music on," I suggested when the silence had stretched on too long.

"What?"

"I'm pretty sure I've heard Florence + The Machine before, but the other gal you were talking about, Lorna something-or-other –"

"Loreena McKennitt?" she asked.

"Yeah! That one. Put some of her stuff on."

"I mean, are you sure? She's not exactly Saints of Corruption," she said, and I was pleasantly surprised that she knew my band name. It wasn't on the tee-shirt, just our logo: a skeleton robed in saint's sweeping garb, holding an electric guitar, a crown of thorns as its halo.

"Pretty sure the band name isn't on our tee, a mistake we were planning on fixing on the next run of 'em we made."

"Linny told me when I described the logo," she said with a sheepish grin.

"I don't really listen all that much to what I play," I told her. "I'm willing to give anything a try."

"Okay," she said, giving a nod. She rose from her seat, and I followed her movements as she padded over the tile and across the threshold between flooring material. She went over to the bedside table and picked up a little speaker, pressing a button on the bottom.

"Powering on!" a woman's electronic voice belted out of the little box, impressive with its volume. "Ready to pair!"

She set it down and picked up her phone.

"Paired!" the speaker declared. She scrolled through her music and let out a shuddering breath, hitting play.

The notes that filtered out were gentle and folksy with a definite Irish sort of flare. The woman's voice was gentle and lilting. It was calming, soothing, and I liked it. It was different, but like anything else I'd encountered where Serenity was concerned – uniquely her.

"That's nice," I murmured and she smiled and shook her head, laughing slightly as she came to collect her plate.

"You're just saying that," she said.

"Am not," I told her honestly. She giggled slightly and I had to smile.

We did the dishes together, listening to the soft strains of music, talking gently about life in Ft. Royal versus here around Ft. Lauderdale.

She was twenty-seven, went to work right out of high school and felt stuck like a lot of people our age. Blue collar, working poor, barely making ends meet. Survival a pain in her ass. Hell, if it weren't for the extra coming in under the table thanks to the MC, I'd be a hell of a lot worse off than I was, so I could feel her.

She cleaned her small space while we talked and put everything to rights and I liked that about her. She kept her place so clean it looked like it belonged in a magazine spread. What she did have out to signify it was actually lived in looked like it could very well be staged that way.

I caught her hand when she turned to go back to our seats at the table and reeled her gently toward me. She was slightly reluctant, borne of nerves, leaning back from me, but I didn't mean her any kind of harm.

I just wanted to dance with her. Hold her close, breathe her in, sway gently to the music.

I just wanted something solid and real with this woman, if only for a minute, before I had to let her go for the night. She made me want to get close, slip in between the plates of armor she wore and kindle an intimacy.

It seemed like it'd been a long time since she had it – if ever.

"What are you doing?" she asked, as I gently shifted my weight from one foot to the other with her in my arms.

"Shh, just dancing with this beautiful girl I met."

"Oh," she whispered, voice husky with surprise.

The way she looked at me, eyes wide with surprise, dark eyes, expressive and so alive, I could drown in their depths. I could deep dive into the bottom of her soul and suffocate and die, and never, not once, even consider resisting the siren's call of her lonely heart that dragged me to my death.

I brought up a hand and touched her cheek, her skin smooth and soft beneath my calloused fingertips. Her eyes fluttered shut, the lashes dark against her pale skin and she turned her face into that light touch like it was everything. She craved contact, and I knew the feeling, but not like this. I don't think I'd ever met someone so nervous to be touched yet so touch-starved in my life.

"Can I kiss you?" I asked, my voice hoarse with my restraint, but after Faith, I couldn't be sure what kind of trauma lurked in Serenity's past. All I knew was I saw all the signs and that there was trauma there. Something dark and deep, something that set her apart from the rest of the world, kept her bound with fear and pain.

Her eyes flicked open and up to mine, her lips parting seductively even if she didn't know it, and she asked, breath held, body and chest so still, "You're sure?"

I didn't understand how she could think herself so undesirable, but I damn sure wasn't going to ruin the mood. Instead, I closed the gap between us slowly, carefully, inch by excruciating inch, giving her every opportunity to step back, turn her head, pull away – anything to stop me but she didn't. She inhaled sharply, just before my lips touched her and it was like being struck by lightning.

The jolt of pleasure, amplified by anticipation, traveled straight from our softly touching lips to my dick, warming me through the chest, sensation cascading down my limbs as her hands slipped along my ribs to rest on my denim-clad hips. She stepped closer, tucking herself into the shelter of my body, and whimpered softly as I flicked my tongue against her bottom lip.

Her mouth opened to me, lush, warm, and inviting, and I took the invitation, kissing her like she should be kissed, tasting the desire, the want on her lips fused with the spicy fruity flavor of her iced tea.

Fuck, she was perfect.

7

———

*S*erenity…

His kiss was everything. As if it somehow wiped my slate clean, a new beginning just at my fingertips, if I were only brave enough to grasp it and hold on. It shook me to my core, suffused me with a warmth I hadn't known for a very long time.

It scared me, how deeply his kiss made me feel, and I tried to hold on, I did, but the fear overwhelmed me to the point I jerked back, breaking the kiss, snapping the magic, the moment falling away and shattering around us.

He let me retreat graciously, his thumb smoothing soothingly against my cheek as I tried to regain my faculties and pull myself back from the brink.

"Um, wow," I breathed, my chest rising and falling unsteady with the cascading thrum of my heartbeat, so strong I felt it in my spine and against the inside of my ribs.

"Yeah." Even he gave a little nervous laugh. "A little more intense than I was expecting."

"Mm, yeah," I murmured, pressing the back of my hand to my swollen lips, trying to keep the sense memory of his lips against mine

48

in place as long as possible, my eyes closing unbidden as I savored the lingering tingle.

"I want to see you again," he said.

"I'd like that," I whispered, lowering my hand, smoothing my other thumb against his ribs, over the butter-soft tee just above the waistband of his jeans.

"Yeah?" he asked, and he sounded uncertain.

"Very much so," I murmured, my voice thick with emotion.

"Good first date," he whispered, and I smiled in spite of myself.

"Best first date I've ever been on." I was staring pointedly at the floor and raised my eyes to his; he was staring at me so intently it put a sudden knot in my throat.

"It's late, I should have gone a while ago," he murmured, and he was right. The light had grown dim in my little apartment, the reddish glow of the setting sun through my kitchen window painting the opposite kitchen wall in fire and heart's blood.

"Stay with me." The words were out of my mouth before I could stop them and he smiled, pleased.

"I mean, it only makes sense. Your job is here, and I've kept you out way too late and I don't really do sex on the first date, but I feel so bad I've kept you and –"

I was rambling, and he shushed me with a light touch of a fingertip to my lips.

"You had me at 'stay with me', and I just want to hold you," he whispered.

My heart dropped into my toes. Just clean fainted in melodramatic southern belle style, hand raised to its forehead and all.

"I'd like that," I breathed, amazed my vocal chords worked at all with how tight my throat was.

"Go put on something to sleep in," he ordered gently and I nodded, suddenly struck mute, mouth dry as my brain caught up to what my heart had done.

Oh, my God. He was staying the night. I just invited him to a sleepover on the first fucking date. How desperate do I look?

"Shush," he said. "Stop overthinking things. Just going to hold you, just going to sleep, just going to kiss you if you'll let me. It's all on you how far things go. Always."

"Wh-why would you do that for me?" I asked.

He traced a fingertip along my hairline, starting at the part, running the gentle caress toward where my braid hung over my shoulder, tucking my errant hair behind my ear. His deep dark gaze roved my face, taking me in as if I were a work of art, and my heart wept with the beauty of it. With its desire for more.

Enjoy it while it lasts... my mind whispered. *The past will catch up with you eventually, it always does.*

I thrust the thoughts away when he began to speak.

"I get the impression you need a soft touch and a steady hand. I don't think you've been treated very fairly."

Oh, my God... does he already know?

I flicked my tongue over suddenly dry lips.

"Why do you say that?"

His eyes met mine, solemn, steady, an unspoken promise in their depths.

"Just a hunch," he said, and there was no trace of deception.

He didn't know. I was just worsening, the cracks in my veneer getting too large to hide. I needed help but I didn't have the money nor the resources to get it, and so the hurt, the sorrow, and the fear, it got out. People saw it. People like Stoker. Only he wasn't like the rest. He didn't appear to want to leverage it at all. He simply saw it and didn't pick or pry at it.

"I'll just go change," I whispered.

"Be out here waiting. Take your time."

I went to my dresser and pulled open a drawer, extracting the tee he'd given me, then went into the bathroom, shutting the door firmly, letting out a shuddering breath as emotion welled painfully in the center of my chest.

I took deep and even breaths, attempting to regain control of myself. My heart and my mind were at dreadful odds with each other.

God, I was such a basket case. The story of my life.

I took a full minute, then a minute more, before I pushed off from the back of my bathroom door and went to the sink. I set the shirt over the towel bar and braced my hands against the porcelain pedestal sink, staring at myself in the mirror above it.

What are you doing, Ren? I silently asked myself, but I had no answer for the woman in the mirror. She wasn't a girl anymore, but she might as well have been.

I turned on the tap and splashed cool water on my face. It helped. After a couple heartbeats, I dried myself and pulled the tie at the back of my dress to loosen it so I could pull it off over my head.

I put it straight into the wash and ditched my bra in there too. I threaded my arms through the sleeves of the tee and dumped the rest of it over my head, tugging it down past where the dress had fallen on me.

I didn't own pajamas, preferring to sleep in the nude, so it was fortuitous I had this to fall back on.

I switched out the light and opened the door after a fortifying breath and froze to take him in. He was already right at home in my bed, shirtless and delicious, the blankets bunched at his waist, his face illuminated by his phone as he held it above him tapping out a text or something. I pressed my lips together and padded around to what I supposed was going to be my side of the bed tonight.

"Nice," he said, with a grin when he saw the tee.

I lifted the blankets and slid between the crisp sheets that were already growing warm from his body's heat.

He lifted his arm closest to me inviting me to get close and I took the invitation, cuddling into his side, laying my head on his shoulder.

"This is going to be so nice," he murmured, bending his head at an awkward angle just so he could kiss my temple.

"Yeah?" I whispered as he put his phone on the bedside table.

"I get more than two hours of extra sleep with a beautiful woman, so, hell, yeah," he said and I had to laugh.

"Why you laugh like that?" he demanded.

"I'm not beautiful." I denied it automatically.

"Beauty is in the eye of the beholder, Ren, and I'm the one looking at you, and I say you are."

I swallowed hard. "Did I mention I'm really bad at this whole dating thing?"

"You mentioned it," he said, and smoothed a hand over my body, over the tee.

"You can't say I didn't warn you."

He chuckled. "No, I can't. Do me a favor and close your eyes." I did as he asked and closed them, and he murmured, "Good, now repeat after me: I am a beautiful woman."

"What? No. I'm not saying that," I giggled.

"Come on now! Not going to let you sleep until you humor me."

He went straight for my ticklish spot like he just knew where it was.

"Oh, ho! Leverage!" he cried, triumphant.

"Hey, no! Stop that!" I cried, laughing.

"Not until you give me what I want," he declared and rolled onto his side toward me, intent on torturing me with tickling touches to my ribs until I capitulated.

"Okay, okay! I am a beautiful woman!"

"Thank you, and you're damn right you are. Never forget it." And to make his point, he covered my mouth with his with a kiss that had me practically arching off the bed and into his arms.

"REN," he whispered in my ear and I winced, cuddling further into the warm nest of blankets on my bed.

"Ren, baby, kiss me goodbye, I gotta go to work."

I whimpered and sat up, flinging my arms around him and attempted to drag him back into bed.

"No, I don't want you to go."

He laughed and kissed me, his fingers along the side of my neck, thumb stroking along my jaw.

"I don't want to go either, but I have to. You go back to sleep and call me tonight, yeah?"

"Mm, I promise," I murmured.

"K." He pecked me on the tip of my nose and withdrew from my grasp and I felt bereft for the moment. I closed my eyes and listened to the birds chirp outside, his bootfalls as he descended the stairs and eventually, his truck firing up out at the street.

I sighed, missing him already and half afraid I was growing far too attached far too quickly.

8

*S*toker...

"Where the fuck were you last night?" Marlin asked as I dropped into my seat at the table.

"Stayed in Lauderdale," I said, and his eyebrows shot up.

"Oh?"

"Yeah, went on a date."

"Did you score?" Radar asked, grinning.

"Sort of." I shrugged one shoulder.

Cutter laughed from his throne, up on its little dais at the head of the table asking, "What's that supposed to mean?"

"Didn't fuck, but I stayed the night."

Silent glances were exchanged between my brothers.

"She the real deal?" Pyro asked.

"I don't know," I said. "I know I've definitely never felt this way about anyone before."

More looks.

"She the girl from last Saturday night?" Hope asked.

"Yeah."

"What's her name?" Galahad asked.

"Serenity."

"Pretty," Hope murmured.

"Yeah," I agreed and I wasn't talking about her name. Grins broke out around the table.

"Something about her," I said. "She reminds me of Faith when she first got to us."

New looks were exchanged, worried ones this time, but not for me. I smiled inwardly at that.

"She got a history?" Marlin asked.

"Pretty sure she does, but she hasn't opened up to me about it. We're taking things slow and I'm cool with it."

"Want me to do some digging?" Radar asked.

"No, actually, I don't. Whatever it is, I'd like to hear it from her. I don't think whatever it is it's anything we have to worry about as a club."

"Do some digging," Cutter ordered. "Whatever we turn up, we ain't gotta tell you unless it could fuck with the club. What's her last name?"

I laughed and shook my head. "You know, I never asked. Of course, she doesn't know my real name, either."

"You know where she works?"

I nodded. "Would really appreciate if you'd trust me on this Captain."

He stared at me judiciously and finally nodded slowly.

"You got a solid feeling about her?"

"I do," I said and wasn't the least bit surprised that it was the God's honest truth. "She's a loner, an outlier – but she's good people," I said.

He nodded and said, "Fine, but if something about her comes up that could fuck with the club or our vibe –"

"You'll be the first to know," I said. He nodded.

"Good enough for the rest of you?"

"Stoker's never done us wrong, Captain," Marlin said and I tossed my head in a nod of appreciation.

He threw me some chin in acknowledgment.

"Cool, let's bring this to official order, then." Cutter leaned forward and picked up his gavel, knocking it against the arm of his electric chair.

The meeting was smooth, quick, and pretty uneventful.

I couldn't wait for it to be over so I could call Serenity back. She'd called me just as I'd been about to drop my phone in the basket kept behind the bar during our church meetings. I'd answered just long enough to ask her to let me call her back.

I was stopped by a hand clapping down on my shoulder. I turned to the captain who was checking in with me.

"You need any help, you just say the word," he said.

"Appreciate that, Captain."

He smiled at me and gave me a shake before moving off to the bar himself to get a drink. I went for my phone and took myself, and the call, outside.

Fridays were tough for me. First, I had church with the captain and the rest of our crew, then I had band practice.

Still, I had a couple of minutes I could eek out to talk with my girl. I said bye to the guys and went outside where it was quieter, and I could hear Serenity talk and dialed her up, dropping onto the seat of my bike as the call rang through.

"That was quicker than I expected," she said by way of greeting. "How was it?"

"Can't say, it's the way it is."

"Ah, I see." And to her credit, she dropped it, just like that. "So how was the rest of your day?"

"Real good, actually. Probably another week on this job, maybe a week and a half," I told her and I'd be lying if I said I wasn't hopeful for another night like last night. Just with maybe clearing a few more bases. I'd kept it to kissing and a little dry humping, but goddamn, did I have a set of blue balls this morning.

"I hate that commute for you," she said. "But I'm glad you'll be closer even if I don't get to see you."

"All you gotta do is say the word and I'm there," I told her and didn't miss the smile in her voice when she said, "Okay."

"When's your next day off?" I asked.

"Sunday, I switched with one of the other girls so she could take her little girl to a doctor's appointment."

"Heeeey, mine too. Think that little Honda of yours is in good enough shape to make the drive on out this way? We're having a barbecue and later a bonfire on the beach."

"You know, I'd like that. Would you mind if I brought Linny?"

"More the merrier."

"What time?"

"As early as you can get here. I don't want to miss a minute I could be spending with you."

She laughed, and murmured, "Okay, let me call Linny…"

"Okay, great."

I went to band practice, we tore some shit up, and I figured it was going to be a new and interesting kind of hell getting through my Saturday when all I could think about was Serenity's soft skin and those lovely big brown eyes staring up at me.

I TOOK a ride with the club on Saturday. It helped clear my head some, being on the back of the bike. I couldn't help it, though. I found myself increasingly irritated that I couldn't just break off and go see her. I was like a lovesick puppy, but I couldn't bring myself to be any kind of upset about it. My masculinity just wasn't that fragile.

I just missed her.

It was a strange feeling, and I couldn't decide if I liked it or not.

I mean, I liked Serenity, no doubt about that, but I really didn't like how much I missed her when I wasn't with her. It led to some messy ruminations as we rode. Mostly, me wondering how soon was too soon to care about someone so deeply. Someone you barely even knew.

We rode through the 'Glades and I was acutely aware that we were headed in the general direction that Serenity lay. We stopped at a nice spot to picnic and Charity wandered over.

"Hey, you doing alright?"

"What? Me? Yeah, I'm alright."

She laughed at me and said, "Dude, this whole day you've had such a long face. Like you're seriously moping. What's going on?"

Faith wandered over and suddenly I had an audience as I rooted through my saddlebag for my lunch. A bunch of the guys were goofing off, throwing a Frisbee around, laughing, and I just wasn't feeling it like I usually was – because she wasn't there.

"I got it bad for this girl…" I said out loud and Charity and Faith exchanged a look.

"Awww!" Charity cried. "Where is she?"

"Work. The Galleria Mall in Lauderdale."

"She coming to the beach party tomorrow?" Faith asked.

"Yeah," I nodded. "Bringing her friend Linny."

"You going to make it?" Charity teased.

"Honestly," I laughed some, "I hope so."

"Awww! Wish Galahad missed me that much."

"What?" he called. "How can I miss you when I never let you out of my sight?" he demanded.

"Good point!" she called back happily, and I laughed.

"It's only a few more hours." Faith winked at me and I smiled.

"Yeah."

"You do have it bad," Charity said. "I can't wait to meet her."

"Just go easy on her. She gets overwhelmed real easy."

I fixed my eyes on Faith and she smiled. "I don't know anything about that." She smiled and rolled her eyes as she said it, and I chuckled.

"There's something there," I said. "Not sure if it's the same type of bad, but something bad happened."

"How do you know?" Charity cocked her head, her interest piqued.

"Just do." I leaned my butt against the seat of my bike and opened the can of soda I brought with me, taking a drink quickly as it foamed from the vibrations of the ride. I shook excess of the sticky soda off my hand and looked at both the girls.

"She does the same things I did when I first got to you guys, huh?" Faith asked. "Jumpy, always apologizing, a nervous wreck?"

"Yeah." I nodded slowly.

"Oh." Charity looked thoughtful. "Anxiety? PTSD?"

"My guess is both, but she hasn't told me why. Not yet. Things are still really super new, but she trusts me, or is starting to. I'm just afraid of fucking it up."

"You really are serious about this girl," Cutter called from over at his bike, tracing his thumb over the screen of his smart phone.

"Yeah, Cap. I am. I don't know what it is about her, but I really like her."

He looked up from his phone and over the top of his aviators and said firmly, "Then don't fuck it up."

Just like that. Like that was somehow magically going to keep me from doing whatever thing had the potential to torpedo this whole thing with Ren. I laughed to myself and shook my head.

"Aye, aye, Captain. Aye, aye."

9

*S*erenity…

"Holy shit, Ren, where did you bring me?" Linny was looking over her sunglasses in the direction of the beach and the knot of men standing around with beers in their hands, laughing. All of them were wearing the same kinds of leather vests that Stoker had with the same dirty patches, over their bare chests and board shorts.

"Close your mouth before you catch a fly in the back of your throat," I said.

"Oh, I'm going to catch *something* in the back of my throat."

"Ew! Gross!" I cried but couldn't help but burst out laughing as I turned on my signal and pulled into the lot to the Marina. Stoker waved from the curb over by the broad set of cement stairs leading down to the sand.

"That him?" Linny asked.

"You know it is," I admonished.

She rolled her eyes and pushed a hand into her hair, leaning her elbow on the car door as she sized Stoker up. It always made me nervous when she did that. I mean, she was so much prettier than I was and so carefree, I always worried someday she would swipe the guy I

60

was with from under my nose. Granted, this would only make the second or third guy I'd attempted to date since, well – since.

"You did good for yourself, babes. I like the look of him, but I think I'll go for tall, darkly tanned, and blond over there if he's not already – shit. Annnnd, he's taken." She pouted as a blonde woman with beachy waves in her long hair went up to the man Linny'd been scoping out. He lifted her up and swung her, shrieking and laughing, in a circle and I laughed.

"I can't imagine many of these guys are going to be available," I said, parking and pulling my emergency brake.

Stoker didn't waste any time. He was at my door, lifting the handle to get it for me. I smiled up at him and unlocked it so he could open it.

"Hey! You made it."

"I did!"

He leaned down to look in the open door and said, "Hey, Linny."

"Hi!" She smiled at him politely and I bit my bottom lip and eyed the rest of his club friends. I was always nervous meeting new people. You never knew who might know…

"Come on." He straightened, reaching down, holding out his hand to me.

I undid my seatbelt and slipped out of the car, taking the hand he offered. He immediately pulled me to him and kissed me, which surprised me. I mean, I wasn't used to guys doing that. Kissing me in front of their friends. Comfortable with public displays of affection. It was different for me. It was… nice.

I blushed furiously when the cheering and whistling started, lowering myself flat to my sandaled feet to thunderous applause.

"Shut up!" Stoker called out to his friends, but his deep dark eyes were fixed on me and he winked, a crooked smile on his perfect lips.

"Come on," he murmured, and steered me around the car.

"Hang on, let me grab my stuff." I opened up the back car door and picked up my black mesh macramé beach bag from the back seat. Linny grinned at me from over the roof of my car as she fetched hers on her side.

"You got sunscreen?" Stoker asked.

"Yeah."

"Cool, let's get some on you."

We walked under the shade of an easy-up canopy with camp chairs under it and a wreckage of towels, flip flops, and beach bags. Stoker picked up a can of sunscreen in a spray can and I slipped out of my beach cover up, self-conscious in my two-piece black swimsuit with its gothic, strappy harness across my chest in an inverted five-pointed star.

I wasn't religious. I didn't care. I just liked the way it looked.

I'd had a hard time swallowing any kind of religion as a believer with how awfully my God-fearing Christian parents and the 'good' Christian folk had treated me after... Well... just after. Even though I hadn't done anything wrong.

I giggled and laughed as he joked and hosed me down with sunscreen, and after I felt dry enough, shrugged back into my black velvet burn-out kimono with its black-on-black floral patterns and light flapper-type fringe.

With it and my simple black flip-flops, I felt elegant and chic, even though I'd found all of it on clearance through one avenue or another and had probably spent forty dollars on all of it combined.

He passed the canister off to me so I could do Linny's long, lean figure in her blue-and-white striped bikini even as some of the guys and their girls started to draw near out of curiosity.

"Hey, Ren, Linny. I'd like you to meet..."

The introductions were a little overwhelming with just how many people there were to remember faces and names.

I was worried when one of the youngest men, Gator, seemed to have a momentary spark of recognition in his eyes, but then he said, "Oh, yeah, yeah, yeah! You were wearing the silver shirt last week!"

I let out a breath I hadn't realized I'd been holding and nodded.

"Yeah."

"Right on," he said. "Welcome to the madhouse."

I laughed a bit nervously and said the only thing I really could, "Thanks."

It was a blessing when Stoker took my hand and led me down the beach, away from the crazy. Linny was situated and having a blast with a woman named Hossler, and flirting up a storm with a club member named Lightning. I never had to worry about her making friends wherever she went. She was beautiful, bold, brave, and absolutely fearless; everything I was not.

I sighed and let some of the nervous tension go, my fingers linked with Stoker's as we walked to where the water met the shore. He'd left his hair loose and I had too; the breeze picked up tendrils of our long hair and swept it out towards the sea.

"You know, I don't even know your real name," I murmured.

"I was thinking the same thing just the other day," he said. "I mean, I know your name is Serenity, but I don't know your last name."

"Weatherly," I said. "And you?"

"Ah." He laughed a bit nervously and said, "I'm originally from Louisiana, so it's Michel."

"Oh, I always liked that for a boy's name," I told him honestly.

"Yeah?"

"Yeah, it's unique. It fits you," I said. "What's your last name?"

"Arceneaux."

"Michel Arceneaux." I tasted his name and had to smile. "I like it a lot."

"Yeah, well, stick with Stoker if you don't mind."

"Not at all," I said with a giggle. "I'm actually pretty surprised. You don't have an accent."

"Ah, yeah. I wasn't really raised around it. I had one more, when I was a kid, but I was made fun of enough for sounding 'dumb' that I ditched it pretty quick."

I stilled a bit at that. I knew what that was like, all too well, although there was no changing the fact I'd grown up poor. Not as simple as changing the way I spoke... I envied him a bit that that was all it took.

"You cool with maybe leaving the beach for a couple of hours?" he asked out of the blue, and I cocked my head and shaded my eyes; even behind the black lenses of my sunglasses it was bright out here.

"And go where?" I asked.

"My place is only a couple of blocks from here. I figured it might be nice for you to get out of the sun for a bit and…" he hesitated and I stopped my leisurely stroll.

"And?" I prompted. He squared off in front of my, casting me in shadow, his hands on my ribs, thumb smoothing over the velvet and mesh of my cover up.

"I want to love you."

My heart stopped.

"I can't stop thinking about you," he murmured, "and I want you to myself for a little while. Don't have to go all the way. If you're not ready I totally get it, I just really want some you and me time."

"Oh, okay," I squeaked out, stunned.

Wow.

"Okay as in?" he asked, trailing off.

"I'll go with you," I said, my mouth suddenly dry.

"Yeah?"

"Yeah."

"Right on. This way, my lady."

"I should tell Linny."

"I'd planned on it. You think she'll be okay?"

I cast my gaze back in the direction of the easy-up and Linny was in a full-fledged game of Frisbee, girls versus boys.

"Looks like she's already been adopted as one of their own," I said, laughing.

"She moves fast," Stoker agreed.

"That's Linny," I agreed.

I worried about what I was going to say. I didn't want to announce to a crowd of people that Stoker and I were off to have sex, be back later, ta-ta for now! I wasn't crass like that. But Stoker was already miles ahead of me.

"Hey, Ren's getting taken in by the sun a little, we're gonna head to my place and chillax for a bit, get her out of it."

"Okay!" Linny called and winked at me behind everyone's back.

"Hope you feel better," Faith murmured and I smiled and gave a nod.

"Oh, I'm sure I will. I don't know how I managed to draw the genetic short straw being so fair in Florida." I laughed it off.

"Be back by four. Food's on then," Cutter called, unloading his super-soaker water gun at his girlfriend, who yelled out, "Hey!"

"This way, Ren," Stoker murmured and I followed him up the steps and through the marina lot to the street. We walked around two blocks up and stopped at a crosswalk on the boulevard, crossed first one lane, paused at the cement pad in the center separating the lanes, and as soon as traffic was clear crossed the next lane.

"Place is a little run-down, my grandparents owned it. When they died, they left it to me. I decided rather than sell it to move in and fix it up, but it's just me, so it's pretty slow going. Outside looks better than the inside. Put a new roof on it after that hurricane a couple of years back and painted it just last summer."

I listened to him talk and found myself surprised I wasn't the least bit nervous. Now that it was just me and him, I was feeling calmer by leaps and bounds. I kept my fingers threaded through the spaces between his and we idly swung our conjoined hands between us as we walked. We were only two houses in from the corner off the boulevard and he stopped in front of a nice little white house trimmed in an aquamarine, the roof gray, the yard yellow and dying but neatly mowed, the flowerbeds mostly weeds, which made me a little sad and I had the desire to get my hands in the dirt.

"It's adorable," I said smiling. "You've done lovely out here."

"Thanks, come on in out of the heat." He opened the front door and I blinked.

"You don't lock your door?"

"No need around here. Town knows who we are."

"Oh. But what about all the people not from town?"

"We don't worry about them, the locals would tell us if something was up. We take care of each other here."

I stepped into the dimly lit and much-cooler interior of Stoker's home and it was a definite time warp. The wood paneling on the walls, the carpet on the floors, and even the décor was straight out of the nineteen-seventies.

"Yikes," escaped my mouth before I could stop it, and I clapped my hands over my lips.

"Hey, no," he laughed. "Not offended. Not in the slightest. I told you the place could use a touch like yours."

He closed the door on the bright sunshine and the hustle and bustle of the beachgoers and the little town outside and I felt more tension melt out of me.

I put my sunglasses up on top of my head and looked up at him somewhat shyly, but I'd like to think more in anticipation.

I wanted him to kiss me so badly and he didn't disappoint, lowering his mouth to mine and kissing me like he was ravenous and I was a banquet laid out before him.

I leaned into him enthusiastically, letting my cares and worries fall away for the time being, concentrating solely on his hands on my body, his lips against mine; submerging myself into the sensations of his attentions.

"Gonna have to get you in the shower," he murmured playfully against my lips.

"Oh?" I played along. I was not exactly feigning innocence, but more I didn't understand the leap of logic.

"Mm, I want to taste every inch of you – just without the chemical tang of sunscreen."

I laughed and whispered, "Lead the way."

He did, walking me backwards, deeper into the house, his hands on my hips, leaving his flip-flops behind with a couple of strides, shrugging out of his leather vest and hanging it on a closet doorknob as we passed it. He slipped my kimono off my shoulders and hung it on the knob of the bathroom door as he walked me inside.

"Don't judge." He winked at me, going for the drawstring on his orange board shorts.

I giggled and said, "I wouldn't dare."

"I was talking about the bathroom," he said with a broadening grin and I let my jaw drop with an indignant sound.

"You going to look at it?" he asked, when my eyes hadn't wavered from his.

"Can't," I murmured, and pulled myself closer to him. "You look so good I can't take my eyes off of you."

"Pretty sure that's supposed to be something I'm supposed to say," he breathed against my mouth and we were kissing again. His shorts dropped to the ugly off-white and green linoleum.

He backed me against the bathroom counter, that faux marble-printed Formica that was chipped and even burned in a couple of places, though from cigarettes or a curling iron or whatever, I couldn't tell. It wasn't important. What was important was his hands running up my ribs, his fingertips rough with guitar callouses skimming lightly over my body until he encountered my bathing suit's top and hooked his fingers beneath the band.

I felt a certain sort of thrill that I was about to have my top off in front of him. I was concentrating very hard at not staring at his cock which was flush and resting against his body, turgid and long, the girth – at least for me – seemingly manageable, the length more than slightly intimidating, reaching nearly to his belly button.

God, he had one of those magic, long and lean torsos that went on for seemingly forever, that carved 'V' of flesh and bone drawing my eyes right to his length, which easily had to be nine inches or more.

"You alright?" He stepped between my legs, arms going around me, pressing my nude upper body against his, his cock, thick and hot, pressing against the bottoms of my swimsuit, the lycra material the only thing between us in that most intimate of places, driving me wild, my pussy giving a tortured little throbbing ache of anticipation.

"Fine," I whispered shakily.

"You need me to stop, all you gotta do is say the word," he whispered close to my ear and it was so hot.

"I don't want you to stop," I whispered back and turned my head in his hands to press my mouth tightly against his.

We made out, me sitting on the counter, for several minutes, his cock growing hotter the longer we made out. I gathered my courage and wrapped my fingers gently around him and he moaned into my mouth. I stroked him in my hand, long, sure strokes, gripping firmly but gently, the arousal from him slicking the palm of my hand as I rubbed it gently over the head.

He sucked in a breath between his teeth and shuddered, moaning, his breath rushing back out, fanning the side of my neck, the warmth of it sending a blush of tingling erotic energy out over my skin.

"God, I want you so much." My voice was barely recognizable, tight and breathy, girly and needy.

"Hold that thought," he whispered, pulling his hips back. I watched him as he leaned through the sliding glass shower doors with the swans on them and turned on the bathwater, pulling up on the thing to get the shower going. The tub came into focus, and God, it was awful, avocado green, the toilet white and clearly having been replaced, the sink set in the counter beside me rust-stained and old, original, and just as ugly a green as the bathtub.

"I am totally judging your bathroom," I said and he laughed, straightening up and holding out his hands to me. I slipped mine into his and hopped down from the counter and went to him. He bent and kissed me again and the lightheartedness slipped, falling away as passion and deep emotion welled to take its place.

His hands trailed down my body, skimming over my hips, his long fingers plunging into the waistband of my suit bottoms and skimming them down. They fell in a pool at my feet and I stepped sideways out of them.

"Come on," he whispered, and helped me step up and over the deep lip of the tub, over the metal track set on its edge. I stood with warm water beating on my back as he stepped in after me, sliding the door shut behind us.

His hands washed me, his lips ravaged mine, and I was content to just stand there forever, kissing ardently, his hands skating over my body warmed by the water.

He washed me gently with soap and his hands, teasing me between my legs with soapless fingers, backing me into the corner of the shower and kissing me, fingertips teasing against my clit with a firm touch, my head and shoulders pressed against the wall, his other arm against my lower back, pulling my hips out, tilting them back, supporting me for better access to my pussy.

He touched, licking and biting my lips, feasting at my mouth until it no longer satisfied him and he moved down my jaw, along the side of my neck, nipping at my shoulder, kissing down my body, paying attention to my breasts, moaning softly as he worked my body to a near-fever pitch with his mouth and his hands.

"No, lean back, I got you," he growled when I tried to straighten up, and I did as he told, leaning back into the wall as he went to his knees in the tub.

"Trust me," he said, looking up my body at me. "I've got you."

I yipped when he draped my leg over his shoulder, going on tiptoe and feeling totally off balance.

"I've got you," he said again and did the same to the other. "Lean back into the wall," he ordered, and I did, effectively sitting on his shoulders as he flicked his tongue out to taste my most intimate parts.

"Oh, God!" I cried and leaned my head back, my breath coming in ragged pants as he dipped the tip of his tongue inside me, running it up the seam of my pussy lips to tease that little kernel of sensitive flesh at the apex of my thighs.

I gasped, a throaty cry escaping my mouth as I buried my hands in his hair and pulled his mouth tighter against my body.

God, yes! That felt so good.

He slid his middle finger up inside me and I cried out, trying to hold still, feeling like I was awfully precarious, perched on his shoulders like I was, but he held me fast. One hand and his mouth working my body, the other arm wrapped around the outside of my thigh, his hand pressed to the top of my leg, holding me steady.

"Stoker!" I cried, breathy, on the precipice of release and he growled, encouragingly.

I jerked in his grasp, the electrical impulses coursing through me, carrying pleasure, overloading all my synapses at once. I saw stars at the edges of my vision, despite the fact my eyes were squeezed firmly shut as I trusted him to hold me up and I tried not to flop like a landed fish.

I came back to myself and looked down at him, his eyes closed as he nuzzled the inside of my thigh and placed a reverent kiss against it. He smiled when he looked up at me.

"You good?" he asked and I blinked.

"How can you even ask that?" I asked, and he laughed.

"I meant to stand up on your own," he said. "I'm not done with you, yet. Not by a long shot."

I swallowed hard and nodded carefully, after taking the time to decide if I was okay to get down.

It was a little awkward getting down off his shoulders, but not too bad and he was there to catch me, keeping me steady, pressing me back into the corner, the walls propping me up as he got back to his feet.

He shut off the shower and, holding onto me, slid the door back on its metal track. He whipped one of the towels off the towel rack and wrapped me in it. The large beach towel swallowed me and instantly absorbed the water beaded on my flushed skin.

He stepped out first, grabbing his own towel, and helped me out of the shower. I carefully stepped out onto the warm, shaggy bathroom throw rug set by the tub and scrunched my toes into it out of habit.

"I want you in my bed," he murmured, stepping into me, holding me close, and dipping his head so he could claim my mouth with his.

"Mm," I half-whimpered, half-moaned against it with want and he took a step back, fingertips trailing along my arms, beneath my fore-arms, the tip of his middle finger of each hand trailing down my inner arm along a razor's path – God knows I had thought of it enough times; I'd just never been brave enough to follow through.

I closed my eyes and immersed myself in the tickling sensation as he drew that feather-light touch along each palm, all the way out along my middle fingers before twisting his hands upright to thread his fingers in the spaces between mine.

I felt gratitude that I'd managed to hold on and be here long enough to meet a man like him and smiled as he tugged on our joined hands gently, leading me from the bathroom across the hall into his bedroom.

It was like any other bachelor pad. Pretty much precisely how you would picture a rock musician's bedroom to be – a black blanket tacked over the window, the bed unmade but inviting, black sheets, an orange and black Harley-Davidson fuzzy blanket the only other blanket to be seen.

"Condom?" I asked and he nodded.

"Got plenty," he said with a half-smile.

I rolled my eyes slightly and said, "Not surprised."

He pulled me in close and murmured, "Knew you were coming, have to keep you coming."

It was such a sinfully delicious thing to say. I giggled and he let his towel drop and pulled mine free from around my body, turning me and walking me back until the backs of my thighs hit the bed. I sat down and wrapped my fingers around his cock before he could even think about going anywhere, stroking him firmly in long, sure strokes, twisting my grip, massaging, staring up at him as he took in the sight, his eyes heavy-lidded with lust, his face going slack with peace as he got into the sensation.

When he threw his head back and let out a shuddering breath, I took him into my mouth, taking him as far as I was comfortable, using my hand lower on his shaft to make up the difference. He swept my hair back from my face so he could watch me and I tensed, always afraid in that moment, in the back of my mind, that the man I was with would force himself into my throat, that I wouldn't be able to breathe. It was an irrational fear, one that had never come to pass, but was always there none the less.

"Easy, you don't have to." His voice was low and husky, unintentionally sexy, and he was just plain sexier still for giving me the option to stop, but I didn't. I teased my tongue back and forth, side to side, along the underside of the head of his cock instead, and listened to him suck in a sharp breath.

"God, Serenity… babe, baby, you gotta stop," he whispered.

I pulled back and asked, "Are you okay?"

"God, yes, but as good as that feels I've never been able to get off that way and I fuckin' need it. I need you," he said, and reached into the cubby of the headboard and pulled out a foil-wrapped square.

I took it from him, tearing it open and letting the wrapper fall to the floor. He watched me, and my pussy tingled with anticipation as I rolled the condom down his considerable length and scooted back on the bed, turning so I was on it properly and he could join me.

I lay back and reached for him, and he came to me willingly, eagerly, and got between my thighs.

"You are so fucking sexy," he whispered, teasing his cock against the seam of my pussy lips, slapping it against my clit. I moaned, and he lowered himself on his arms, sliding up inside me as he pressed his lips to mine.

I wrapped my arms around his shoulders, arched my body into his by way of offering, and let him love me, knowing nothing this good could last forever. Not for someone like me... so I'd best enjoy his warmth for as long as I could, because nothing good would ever stay.

10

Stoker…

Her body fit mine like a glove. Warm and silken wet, she was so soft around me, her eyes tender as she gazed up at me, giving herself over so completely. She was so beautiful, her long hair spread over my pillow, her lovely brown eyes heavy-lidded and filled with passion and I could tell she felt everything just so completely, gave as good as she got, her pelvic muscles gripping me tight, pulling me in, her arms gentle, her hands smoothing over every inch of me she could reach.

She was so present, so fully here with me. I'd never been with a woman who didn't just lay there and take what I gave her with not so much as a care as to whether I was getting off. Serenity wasn't like that. This was something uniquely different. This was a true sharing, a meeting not just between our two bodies, but our two souls… and I was here for it.

I lay over the top of her, cradling her face, bracing against the bed so I didn't crush her, but rather embraced her. She climbed my body like a little spider monkey, her arms around my neck, legs around my hips, meeting me thrust for thrust, an enthusiastic partner in sex and I couldn't ask for more. She was so wonderful, so beautiful; kind, funny, smart, sexy, and cool for me – and yet she didn't think she was worthy. I could see it in her eyes, in those little nervous blushes, in the way she wouldn't make eye contact with me, and finally in her little self-deprecating comments.

I tried my damnedest to chase all of those doubts back into the black where they belonged. Tried to tell her with the way I worshipped her body that whatever was past had passed, and that the here-and-now was all that mattered.

I didn't know who had hurt her, who had damaged her, but I was damn sure going to be the one to keep it from happening again. I'd die before I did her dirty – well, depending on if she wanted it that way or not, if you know what I mean.

"Stoker!"

Her voice sounded desperate and it was the clear desperation of being so close to the fall but just that one last little bit shy of taking the plunge. I worked myself inside of her, climbing to unearthly heights just behind her. Higher and higher, our souls twining in concert, dragons dancing in the sky, beautiful, unreal, points of light flitting and flashing from their scales at the edges of my vision.

"Oh, God yes!"

Her voice was high, breathy with the wind bracketing us as we made that clear, perfect, imaginary fall from euphoric grace where everything became sensation, the touch of her body, the flicker of her pussy tightening around my cock, milking it dry as I spilled into the condom inside her.

The world ceased to exist for several moments as I drowned in the sound of our heartbeats, thundering like wings against the sky as our souls stayed high without us, riding the thermals of the passions we'd just created.

"Serenity…" I whispered her name, a prayer, a plea for her to stay with me. I was past having it bad for her. I may not have known her well, but it was clear to me I needed to learn. I needed to know everything about her and I wanted her to know everything there was to know about me.

She felt far overdue for a real taste of freedom…

"STOKER!" *Bam! Bam! Bam!*

Serenity stirred against my chest and I groaned, looking down at her. She smiled serenely, her chin atop her hand, which rested on my chest as she smiled like the Cheshire cat, her hair mussed, that freshly-fucked look radiating from her, and I felt an echoing glow of pride at having satisfied her so thoroughly.

"Yeah! What?" I yelled back, and the pounding on my door stopped.

"Hurry the fuck up! Captain wants everyone at dinner, sent me to come get you two."

"What time is it?" I growled.

"Dinner time, now move it!" Lightning called through my closed bedroom door.

Serenity burst into a fit of quiet giggles.

"My suit is out there," she said in a scandalized whisper.

"I got it," I said grinning, thinking it was adorable how she was pointedly ignoring the fact that everybody on the beach had known we'd gone off to fuck. It was okay, though. If she needed to preserve some modicum of an illusion that we'd been in here just talking and sipping iced tea, I'd go with that.

I got up and poked my head out my bedroom door and muttered, "Goddammit, Lightning."

"What is it?" Serenity asked, and she sounded alarmed.

"Nothing, baby. He's gone, he just left my front door wide open, so stay in there for now."

I bolted down the hallway and shut the door, then gave her the all clear. She peeked around the edge of my bedroom doorway, clutching my bed's top sheet around her and I put my hands on my hips, standing there naked as the day I was born. She laughed and turned her face and I etched that moment, the sheer unabashed beauty of the sight in my mind's eye forever.

"Come on, you've gotta be hungry by now," I said, grinning, and she nodded.

"Starving."

"Dinner awaits." I winked at her and she stepped into the hall. I went to her and she turned her face up for a kiss which I granted her gladly. She drifted into the bathroom, picked up my board shorts and tossed them out the door to me. They hit me in the chest and I caught them, she laughed and closed the door behind her, sealing herself from my view, but you know what? We were new and I didn't need to see her pee.

I got dressed, shrugged my feet into my flip-flops, and my arms into my cut. I had her sheer wrap with the velvet and the fringe at the ready when she stepped out in her suit.

"Oh, thank you!" She turned and I helped her into it, dropping it onto her lean shoulders, slipping my fingers under her hair and unthreading the thick mass from under her collar for her.

She turned and I smiled at her, smoothing my hands over her shoulders.

"Come on, let's get back to the beach, and get you some food."

"Okay," she murmured and stepped into her thongs on the way past them in the hall. I opened the door and she perked up in surprise.

"How late is it?" she asked.

"I think we napped for a good few hours," I commented.

"Shit, I hope Linny's not mad at me." She bit her bottom lip.

Linny was, for sure, nowhere near mad. She greeted us enthusiastically when we hit the stairs leading down to the beach.

"Ren! Hey!"

Ren went to her friend without thinking twice.

Marlin sauntered up to me and raised his eyebrows and I grinned, shaking my head. He nodded, made a look like he was impressed, but stayed silent.

I had to smile as Linny took Serenity aside and both of them spoke quietly and earnestly, their heads together. The smiles said everything was fine, everything was better than fine, and I loved this. That she was here, that she was happy, and that my brothers and sisters of the club were here to see it.

"Hey, we late to the party?" Rory, our drummer, called out. He was coming down the steps with Gideon, our lead singer, a cooler between them that looked on the heavy side.

"Fuck, yeah! Beer was running low!" Pyro called out.

"Where's Pat?" I asked and he called out, "Right here!" as he crested the steps and jogged down our way.

The easy-up was coming down, the bonfire was already going, and the sun was in that state of more than half-set, the light growing dim, but still there for the hardcore beach bums to get in that last round of Ultimate Frisbee or whatever else fuckin' game they were playing.

Linny and Serenity yipped and put their hands out as they were sprayed with sand from an errantly booted soccer ball.

"Sorry!"

A tourist type – as in a dude not from Ft. Royal – came running up to grab it. Linny picked it up and held it out to him.

"Hey." He straightened, his eyes fixed on Serenity. "I know you," he said, and she wouldn't look at him.

"No, I don't think you do," she said and everything about her had gotten stiff. Linny started this way just behind her and said tartly over her shoulder at the dude, "You got your ball, now go back to your friends."

I started walking, a bunch of my brothers straightening up.

"Yeah, it is you!" the guy called, and then looked back over his shoulder at his friend and shouted something truly bizarre. "Hey, guys! It's Murder Whore!"

"Seriously?" Linny cried. "Fuck off!"

Serenity had frozen, her shoulders collapsing under the weight of what this fucking little cockbite had called her. I went to her as some of the guys started shifting, silent thunder over the fact one of ours was clearly hurt by what the dude had said rolling through our mini-party camp.

"Serenity?" I asked, but she brushed past me and went straight for her beach bag. She sniffed and Linny started coming our way, exchanging barbs with the dude who was walking away.

"I don't want to ruin your party," Serenity said, and her voice was hollow – gutted.

"What the fuck did that guy call you?" Radar demanded.

"Nothing, it was nothing," she said, but it was definitely something. Silent tears coursed down her cheeks and she was shaking, her hands convulsing, trembling so bad she almost couldn't get them to work.

"Oh, babe. Don't listen to that asshole, don't let him ruin –"

"I just want to go home, Lin!" Serenity's voice was high and tight, and I exchanged a look with Marlin who jerked a nod and went for Faith.

"Pyro! Atlas! Go pay our new friend with the soccer ball a visit, would you?" Cutter asked – but he wasn't asking.

"Talk to me," I whispered, putting myself into Serenity's path.

"I can't," she said and she sniffed again. Linny was grabbing her shit and throwing it together.

"You can tell me anything, babe." I put my hands gently on her shoulders and she hugged herself, trying so hard not to sob and failing.

"Linny?"

"Right here, we're out of here," Linny said, and she took my girl from me.

"Call her in a couple of days, yeah?" she asked and raised her blonde eyebrows, looking at me pointedly.

"Yeah," I grunted, but to hell with that. I was going home, throwing some shit in my bag, and taking my truck. I'd be getting to the bottom of this, but give her a couple of hours, the drive home, to calm down.

I watched them rush up the stairs and into Serenity's car. She got behind the wheel and her tires screeched in protest at how fast she backed up. She stopped for a second, her shoulders rising and falling as she tried to hold it together. Linny said something to her from the passenger seat and she snapped at her friend and peeled out.

Marlin came over and handed me a wadded-up tissue.

"Shit, she gone?"

"Yeah, not for long," I said and he nodded.

"Go get her," he said. "I'll square things with the captain and let you know what Pyro and Radar find out."

"Yeah, text me," I called back over my shoulder as I jogged up the steps and in the direction of home.

11

*S*erenity…

"You want me to drive?" Linny asked, and I felt horrible almost as soon as the words were out of my mouth, but I snapped at her angrily, "I'm fine!"

I slammed my little automatic into 'Drive' and peeled out of the lot and onto the street. My heart was racing, I couldn't get the tears to stop, but I just wanted out of this town. Away from them, away from the past I could never escape.

"Serenity, slow down," Linny said in a soothing voice, and I couldn't handle her sympathy, couldn't stand the confused look on Stoker's face, couldn't deal with the idea that it was over so soon, before anything had even had a chance to get started, the seeds barely planted, not even allowed to sprout, let alone grow.

"Serenity, you're freaking me out, please slow down!" Linny cried.

I screamed, "Alright! Alright!" before jerking the wheel of my little car and pulling over onto the gravel shoulder on the side of the road. I threw it in 'Park' and promptly burst into defeated tears.

Nine years and counting… I thought to myself.

"Oh, honey, it's okay… it's going to be okay…"

I collapsed sideways into Linny's arms and let my best friend hug me and hold me as I wept in utter despair.

"Shh, it's okay." She made nonsensical soothing sounds while the bitterness poured out my eyes.

She sighed and said, "I wish they would just let it go and leave you alone."

I was with her… I honestly didn't understand why she was still my friend after it was all said and done.

You can't have nice things… you don't deserve them, I told myself resolutely. *It was stupid of you to even try.*

Stoker's face floated to the surface in my mind's eye and I lost it harder, all over again, for a completely different reason. I liked him, a lot, had given him a piece of my heart today, and even though I had known it was a bad idea – I had dared to hope.

I guess, like the popular A&E song, *Hope Dies Last…*

Stupid, Ren… You're so stupid!

My car door opened and both Linny and I screamed. I turned, and stared right into the deep, unrelenting gaze of Stoker's dark eyes.

"Come on, baby. I got you." He unbuckled my seatbelt and with a guiding hand on my knee, turned my legs out of the open door of my car so he could put his arms around me.

I collapsed against his chest, his truck running just a few feet behind my stopped car, and wept all over again, hope, just as unrelenting as his gaze, bubbling up in the center of my chest.

"Take this for me," he murmured, and unwrapped a napkin, plucking a little yellow pill off of it.

"You got any water or anything?" he asked Linny.

"Uh, yeah, here."

She passed him the half-empty water bottle I'd filled up that morning for the drive.

"You trust me?" he asked, and I nodded, surprised to find that I did and wanting whatever oblivion that tiny yellow pill had to offer at this point.

"'K, drink up."

I tossed the pill into the back of my throat and swallowed it down with three big mouthfuls of water.

"Okay, Linny, you're gonna have to drive. She's going to be no good for it in the next twenty minutes."

"Okay," Linny agreed immediately.

"You want to ride with Linny or with me in the truck?" he asked me.

"I'd better stay with Linny, in my own car," I said feebly as my mind screamed, *Choices, decisions, yes! Take them! Take them all... I don't want to do this anymore.*

The panic and the angst swirled in my breast and Linny cut in, "You don't have to stay with me, girl."

"I want to," I lied, and she bought it and nodded. She undid her seatbelt and leapt up out of the car.

"Come on, up you go." Stoker held out his hands and leveraged me up out of my seat, and walked me around to the passenger side of my own car. I got in and he buckled me in like a child. It felt nice that he still cared for me right now, so I let him do it.

"I'm right behind you," he swore, and pressed his mouth to mine in a swift kiss that was bittersweet with the salt of my tears as panic flowed through me like lava, scorching me from the inside out.

"Okay," I whispered, scared for an entirely different reason.

What if you tell him and he doesn't give up on you? What if he stays?

I'd never had that happen before.

He shut my door and I let my eyes follow him as he went around the front of my car. He stopped at Linny's window and she rolled it down.

"Drive careful. She'll probably rack out once she calms down a little more."

"What'd you give her?" Linny asked, blinking up at him through the open window of the driver's side door.

He braced his hands on the sill and said, "Ativan." He patted the window sill and with a last worried, lingering look at me, trudged back to his truck.

"He gave you the good shit," Linny mused as she adjusted my seat for her longer legs and fixed my mirrors for her taller frame.

I huddled in on myself and willed the drug to take effect. I stared into the side mirror outside my window at the beat-up old pickup behind us, Stoker indistinct through the sunset-laden sky reflected on his windshield.

"So, um, how was it?" Linny asked, turning on my headlights and hitting the signal to rejoin traffic.

I didn't answer and she huffed out a sigh.

"Well, I like this one. He's different and I like his friends. I hope they give that asshole on the beach a what-for."

"I hope not," I said.

"Why?"

"You know it won't stop, Linny. It never stops. I need to stop fooling myself that it will. You also know, the more you fight back, the worse it gets…"

"We aren't kids anymore, Ren." Her voice held a steel edge of admonishment.

"You're right. We're not," I answered, but I knew if she knew what I was thinking it wouldn't go over well, so I didn't voice it out loud. What I was thinking wasn't anything good. Mostly it was how I needed to stop letting myself be fooled by the childish idea that just because there was the way the world was supposed to work, that didn't mean that it would ever actually work that way.

I rested my head against the window glass and closed my eyes, huddled in on myself, and felt marginally calmer. An almost detached feeling coming over me.

The drugs were working.

"It'll be okay, Ren. I have a good feeling about this one," she said, and it was the last thing I remember.

12

*S*toker…

"Captain," I said by way of greeting, cradling my phone against my ear, trapping it with my shoulder as we barreled up the freeway. We didn't have much farther to go. Maybe a half an hour or so.

"Yeah, it's me." He gave a gusty sigh and asked, "So you want the spoilers or not?" he asked.

"I want to hear it from her, but I need to know what the fuck is going on to be able to do anything at the same time."

"Now you're learning," he said and grunted. "Your stray has more than a little bit of trauma in her past, I reckon."

"How's that?" I demanded.

"Well, according to the douchebag on the beach, once upon a time her boyfriend was that Kyle Ian Covington kid."

"Why does that name sound familiar?" I frowned, scouring my memory for it.

"He's the one that shot up that Lauderdale high school about nine years back."

"Oh, shit…"

"Yeah."

"And you're trying to tell me Serenity was in on it?" I asked, skeptical as all hell.

"Now, I didn't say that. You know how it is with these fuckin' citizens – hell, with anybody. Guilt by association and all that. Radar's already digging into the whole thing and says that the pigs investigated your girl, but that they let her go. Insufficient evidence to suggest she knew about her boyfriend's plot."

"Shit. Was she there?" I asked. "The day of the shooting?"

"Yeah, but that is her story to tell, we can't know what went on… I just suggest you tread carefully, my friend."

"What did that dude call her?" I asked. "I missed it."

"Murder Whore."

"Fuck."

"Yeah, these merry band of idiots sure know how to pick 'em when it comes to taunts and the like."

"Some pretty unoriginal shit," I agreed.

"Well, listen, you drive careful and we'll see you when we see you. You stay in touch."

"Aye, aye, Captain."

"Talk with you later."

He ended the call and I let out a pent-up breath full of frustration at the sheer mountain of garbage in front of me.

Humans were the worst.

I parked on the street outside Serenity's place, grabbed my duffle off the seat next to me, and locked up my truck. Linny was stretching outside Ren's car, her hands pressed to her lower back to ease the stiffness.

"She alright?" I called softly.

"Out like a light."

"Mind taking this and getting her place opened up?" I asked.

"Sure." She took my bag and raised an eyebrow. "Plan on staying a while?"

"As long as it takes," I assured her.

"Uh-huh…" She sounded skeptical.

"Shit, she knows how to pick 'em, eh?" I ventured.

"Let's just say, Ren has something like the absolute worst taste in men."

"Good thing she didn't really pick me, then, isn't it?"

She raised an eyebrow as I reached for the passenger-side door handle of Serenity's car.

"How does that work?" she asked.

I smiled and said, "I saw her first."

She shut the driver's side door and Serenity jumped slightly on the other side of the window glass. I opened up her door.

"Mm," she muttered sleepily.

"Come on, baby. I've got you," I murmured, plucking her beach bag off the passenger floorboard and slinging it over my shoulder. I leaned into the car and unbuckled her seatbelt as she frowned and looked around her surroundings in utter confusion.

Faith's meds had hit her like an eighteen-wheeler and I was glad for it. She needed to sleep it off. I reached down and she leveraged herself to her feet, unsteady as all get-out. I held her to me and kissed her hair.

"Take your time."

She pushed away from me and I let her go, swinging her car door shut when she was clear. She wrapped both of her slim arms around one of mine as we shuffled out of the detached garage she lived over and around the corner into the driveway.

"You good?" I asked quietly and got no verbal reply. Instead, she simply shook her head slowly back and forth.

Linny had the lights on and was standing at the door when we reached the top of the stairs.

"I'm going to grab my shit and make sure the garage is closed up," she murmured and I tossed her a nod.

I sat Serenity on the edge of her neatly-made bed and slipped her thongs off her feet.

"How you doing, Orchid?" I asked her.

"I just want to lay down, sleep for like a thousand days."

"Okay." I nodded carefully and said, "Let's get you tucked in. Where you keep your nightgowns?"

"I don't."

"Well, alright then. Let's get you undressed and let you lie down."

I helped her slowly out of her clothes for a second time and pulled back the blankets. She lay huddled on her side and I tucked her in, placing a kiss on her temple, even though I figured she was out and probably missed it. It was enough that I knew I'd done it.

Linny had returned up here and was eyeing me from the front door.

"You're good with her," she said, and I turned my head her direction.

"Thanks."

"Come on outside and let's talk."

I chuckled and stood up from where I sat on the edge of the bed beside Serenity, trudging in my work boots across her hardwood floor. I'd thrown them on along with jeans and a tee the second I'd gotten home. Threw some other shit in my bag and had hustled out to my truck to find out what the fuck was going on.

I had an inside line with Linny here, and I wasn't about to pass it up.

"Look, let me start off by saying that what you saw, the meltdown or whatever – that's not usually Serenity. Ren doesn't do that often, like at all. I haven't seen her have a panic attack like that in –God… a while. Years at least."

"What happened to her?" I asked, feigning innocence.

Linny leaned her butt up against the railing wrapping the little landing outside Serenity's front door and crossed her arms over her stomach.

"I met Ren our senior year of high school. She transferred in to my school after they told her she wasn't welcome back at the one she'd come from. Believe me, it was total bullshit. Ren didn't do anything wrong." She put out her hand as though she was going to need to stop me from thinking the worst about her bestie, but there wasn't any way.

For as much as I didn't know the minute details, I knew Serenity, and she was a good girl.

"What's with the dude at the beach?"

"One of our classmates, I think. He could have been a lower classman. At any rate, Serenity's first real boyfriend was Kyle Ian Covington. He shot up their old school and killed all those kids – which, if they were anything like the one you saw on the beach? I can't really say I blame him." She put up her hands to ward me off when all I did was raise an eyebrow.

"I know, I know! You shouldn't really wish death on anyone, but the absolute shit they put Ren through? I mean it was a constant barrage. 'Murderer's Whore' eventually just got shortened down to 'Murder Whore' for expediency's sake, but yeah. That was the name she came to my school with and it's literally stuck to her like nobody's business ever since."

"Jesus," I muttered, hanging my head and shaking it.

"She didn't know what Kyle had planned. She didn't even know he was the one shooting until she ran into him in the cafeteria while she was running for her own life."

"Jesus Christ."

"She was horrified, he shot himself, and she's been dealing with the fallout one way or the other ever since." She looked bleakly through the window and I followed her gaze. Trouble and worry clouded her light brown eyes as she stared at Ren's sleeping form.

"How long has this been going on?" I asked.

"Nine years," she said, letting out an explosive breath. "These little incidents have gotten fewer and further between, but they do still happen. I'm surprised it happened in your little podunk town."

"Hey," I fired off by way of a warning shot.

"Sorry," she muttered. "It's a nice town. It is, it just happens to have an asshole in it."

"Today, yeah, but everybody knows everybody else in Ft. Royal. Dude was a local tourist type. He doesn't live there."

"Well, that's good to know, I guess," she muttered and heaved a giant sigh, scrubbing her face with her hands.

"You staying the night, then?" I asked when she had spent several minutes staring at her prone friend.

"Legit, I'm scared to leave," she said finally. "I know she's tough, but this has been her cross to bear for nine years and I know she's sad.

I know she's lonely and depressed, and I'm scared. I'm scared one of these days one of these incidents, it's going to be the straw that broke the camel's back. That she's going to give up, and that'll be it. I'll lose my best friend, just like that, because people can't not be judgey pieces of shit over shit they don't even know…"

Linny started to cry, her heart breaking for my little dark orchid in there and I didn't quite know what to say. I took a shot in the dark with the truth.

"I'm not going to let that happen," I said.

Linny gave me a withering look. "It's not like you can control it. Not like you can control what people think of her, what they say to her, how they make her feel…"

"No, you're right," I agreed. "I don't have control over any of those things, but might be I'm able to teach her the art of not giving a fuck."

Linny flubbed a laugh and shook her head. "I've been trying that for years," she said bleakly.

"You're also close, you two. Maybe she just needs it from an outside source."

"Maybe," Linny murmured, and let out a shuddering sigh.

"You kill my best friend, I'm going to kill you, but not before I come up with some real creative ways to make it hurt like hell." She gave me what I think was supposed to pass for a hard look but all it did was remind me of a tiny ferocious little kitten. Sure, the claws were needle-like, the fangs present, but they were far too dainty to make for any real damage.

Still, I tried not to laugh in Linny's face or hurt her feelings.

"I'm sure you would. You women-folk are crafty like that."

"Are you mocking me?" she asked, suspiciously.

Yes, maybe a little.

What came out of my mouth was my best southern boy, "No, ma'am." Respect. Simply for the fact I was addressing a lady.

"Okay. I'll call and check on her in the morning, then."

"Yeah, you go on and get some good sleep of your own," I said.

"Thanks for not bailing at the first sign of trouble," she said. "She might not know it yet, but she'll appreciate it too. Just be stubborn.

She's a good person. She would never give up on anyone, but they just keep giving up on her."

"Buck stops here," I told her. She nodded and descended the stairs. I wanted like hell to smoke a blunt, but if some shit went down at work and they had to piss test me? Yeah, I had to forgo it. I needed to remain gainfully employed.

I pulled in a deep breath and raked my fingers through my hair, locking them behind my head and letting that breath out in a rush.

"Ah!"

I'd never stayed with a high-maintenance chick for long, but of course this was different… While yeah, Ren was going to be some kind of high-maintenance, she was worth it. The fixer-upper part of her psyche wasn't damaged overnight, it couldn't be fixed with just a drywall patch and a slap of paint. This was deep. Structural. Dangerous territory for a noob like me to be poking around in.

I called Marlin.

"What's up?" he asked on the second ring. I could hear laughter in the background and I was glad the party hadn't stopped on our account.

"I may need a fuckin' pep talk here," I said.

"Damage pretty bad?" he asked.

"Yeah, not at all what I thought, but yeah."

"Trauma is trauma," he said. "Doesn't matter what the trauma was initially, the fallout from it is all the same."

"I don't want to fuck this up, dude."

"Tough shit. That's part of life, Stoker. You go in, you fuck shit up – it's what you do after that, that's what counts."

"Sure as fuck ain't here to fuck shit up and leave," I said.

"Attaboy, now you're talkin'," he said.

"Where do I start?" I asked.

"Well, you start by listening. Just remember, you can't talk and listen at the same time. Just. Listen."

"Okay, I can do that."

"She sleepin'?" he asked.

"Yeah, that Ativan knocked her the fuck out."

"Yeah, I gave you the horse tranquilizer dose."

"Thanks, man. And thank Faith for me, too."

"Anytime, brother, and Faith knows what it's like. She's been there. You ain't gotta thank her for nothing. She's pure goodness, my woman. If she can stop somebody else's suffering – she will."

"Yeah, I feel like Serenity is the same, you know? Just nobody's given her a chance."

"One man's trash is another man's treasure," he said quietly.

"Good way of putting it. Still want to curb stomp the motherfucker for littering, though."

"Ah, yup. I feel you there."

"Thanks, Marlin."

"No worries."

"Night."

"Night."

We disconnected.

I sighed and went in to be with my girl.

13

*S*erenity…

I woke to the sounds of Stoker shuffling around my apartment in the dark, his footfalls thudding dully against the kitchen tile. He was trying to be quiet as he poured a travel mug of coffee at my kitchen counter, but there was only so much he could do with steel-toed boots against a hard floor in the quiet wee hours of the morning.

The sun was making an effort to rise, but it looked like it needed some coffee of its own. I blinked, willing my eyes to adjust in the diffuse light and sat up sharply.

"Hey," he murmured, looking back at me over his shoulder.

I felt hungover without the pain. Whatever he'd given me to take had been a powerful drug.

"Hey," I whispered back, putting a hand to my head. "What did you give me?"

It was hard to think, like my head was stuffed with clouds and my thoughts sluggish. I was as relaxed as could be, but it wasn't a good feeling. It was like trying to think through thick molasses.

"Ativan, one of Faith's. Marlin said it was an elephant tranquilizer dose and it looks like he wasn't joking. You want some of this?" He lifted the coffee pot so I could see it and I nodded.

"'K, hang on. I'll get you fixed up."

He opened cabinets until he found the one he wanted and lifted down a coffee cup. He added creamer and poured the coffee, stirring it gently with a spoon, the sound the metal made against the inside of the ceramic cup sharp in the hushed quiet of my place.

"Here you go." He came over and sat gently on the side of the bed and handed me the cup. I wrapped both hands around it and breathed in the steam rising from it, trapping the sheet to my body, raising my knees beneath it for modesty's sake.

"What are you doing here?" I asked, and he put a hand on my knee, giving it a squeeze.

"I followed you," he said. "Found you on the side of the road with Linny."

I frowned. "I remember that, but what I meant was: why are you still here? Don't you think I'm a crazy person?"

He sighed and shook his head. "No, I think you maybe been through some shit. Linny filled me in a little, about the shooting…" he trailed off. "I was hoping you might be willing to talk it out with me."

"What is there to talk about?" I asked miserably. "You know now…"

"I know you were there, I know you were dating the guy that did it, and I know people have been giving you a ration of shit for it ever since – but the finer details? Not so much."

"I don't want to talk about it," I uttered, and hid behind my coffee, taking a drink.

"You know what?" he said. "I can respect that. You ain't got to talk about it. I mean, I'm still pretty new to you and I get it. I really do. Maybe someday, but today isn't that day."

I stared at him in open-mouthed disbelief.

"So, I guess that's it then?" I squeaked and he leaned forward and put his mouth against mine.

My eyes fluttered shut unbidden and I tried not to wish that this wasn't goodbye. I mean, what guy in their right mind would stick around for this?

"For now," he said, and my breath caught in my throat. "I've got to get to work, but I'd like to come back here tonight. Do something low-key, maybe watch a movie or something. Cuddle."

"You want to come back?" I whispered.

"Well, yeah." He smiled at me and I tried not to tear up.

"You mean it?" I asked.

"Yeah, Orchid… I mean it. I like you and I don't like to give up on the things I like just because of one outside sour taste, you feel me?"

"What did you just call me?" I asked, bewildered, wanting to pinch myself to make sure it was real.

"My pet name for you." He smacked a kiss on the end of my nose. "Deal with it."

"I-I don't know what to say, what to think…" I stammered.

"You don't have to say anything. What time are you off work?"

"Um, six, I think…"

"So way after me. I'll come by where you work to get your keys, and have dinner ready when you get home, if you'll let me stay."

He stood up and looked down at me, waiting expectantly for me to reject him but I couldn't. Not when I so desperately wanted him to be here, to stay with me… I was just shocked and amazed that he wanted to after…

"I'd like that," I answered him and he smiled faintly and nodded.

"Good deal, I'll see you at the mall. Just let me know what store."

I told him the name of the department store I worked at and what department. He gave a nod and picked up a tool belt that was slung over the back of one of my dining table chairs. I blinked stupidly and he picked up his travel mug. He came over to me and leaned down giving me another quick kiss.

"Sleep some more if you can," he said. "I'll see you this afternoon."

"Okay."

He slipped out and I watched him go, absolutely dumbfounded that I could have lucked out so completely. That he wasn't just going to ghost on me when he had every right to run screaming as far away from me as he could get.

I sat and wondered, my lips still tingling from his kiss.

~

THE DAY DIDN'T GET any better from there, but it did get considerably worse. At least, after I got to work. My department store had a new manager and it was already off to a rocky start. She lined us up and nitpicked our hair and dress, and then proceeded to move us all over hell and gone, proclaiming we'd gotten too comfortable in our given departments and that we needed to learn every one of the departments to a 'T'.

My first thought wasn't really so much a thought as it was a sinking feeling in the pit of my stomach. I prayed she wouldn't move me to a horror show of a department, but I had no such luck in that regard – she moved me from the familiar territory of the children's toy department to women's clothing.

I was crestfallen, but put on a smile despite it and followed my marching orders.

It was bad. The dressing rooms were a post-apocalyptic wasteland of discarded clothing and broken hangers. I sighed and set to work putting everything to rights while my co-worker Megan rang up customers at the cashier's stand for the department.

It felt like it took forever, but finally I swapped Megan out so that she could go to lunch. A little while later, Stoker came through.

"Hey, there you are. I've been looking all over the place."

"I'm so sorry, the new manager switched us all around to different departments the minute I got here and I haven't gotten a break yet to even give you the heads-up."

I felt stressed, waited for him to say something hurtful, about letting him down or annoying him, but all he said was, "It's cool, Orchid. You got the key for me?"

"Yeah, oh yeah!" I pulled my house key, which I had already taken off my ring, out of my pocket and handed it to him.

He held it up and gave it a shake send said, "I'll get out of your hair. See you when you get home."

"Okay," I murmured.

He winked at me, looked like he wanted to kiss me, hesitated a moment and finally settled for, "See you, Orchid."

"Later," I murmured.

I wrapped my black cardigan in front of me and hugged my middle, feeling a little bereft as I watched him leave. Wishing I was going with him. I was worried about fixing this... this thing that I felt hung between us now, while, at the same time trying to wrap my head around the fact that he was still here. I mean, if he were any other guy, I would have to guess he should have hit it and quit it by now – but he hadn't. As of right now, he was headed to my little studio to make me dinner.

How about that?

The women's department phone rang probably forty-five minutes later, just as I was returning from my first break. Megan said, "She's right here, she just got back," before holding the receiver out to me.

"This is Serenity, how may I help you?"

"Ah, sorry, Orchid, you could tell your landlady and this nice officer of the law that I have your permission to be here and to please not arrest me..."

"Oh, my God! Yes! Um, hand Mrs. Sedgwick the phone..."

I unsnarled the mess I made by not having the forethought to warn Mrs. Sedgwick I had company – which I never did, so I could see why she would be concerned. When I hung up the phone I turned around to our new manager standing nearby.

"What was that?" she demanded.

"I'm so sorry," I said. "I didn't think I was long –"

"So it was a personal call, then?"

"I'm sorry, yes, it was. It won't happen again."

"Right, Serena come to my office to sign your write-up before end of shift."

Shit, you've got to be kidding me!

"Um, close, it's actually Serenity, and yes, of course."

She gave me a pointed look and said, "I don't stand much for being corrected. Don't forget, before you clock out."

"Y-y-yes, ma'am."

Tears threatened, but not for what you might think. I mean, yeah, I was upset I was being written up, but she didn't stand for being corrected? When she got my goddamn name wrong? I was so angry, that helpless anger at being stuck, forced to endure because what else could I reasonably do? I couldn't quit. I couldn't punch her in the throat, or any of the people who harassed, bullied, or abused me for that matter.

I was so goddamn sick of it.

So I did the only thing I could do – I finished my shift, without taking a lunch because there was no one to relieve me when Megan was pulled to cover another department – and then I clocked out and went home. Yep, that's right. I conveniently forgot to get my further dressing-down and to sign my write-up for earlier. Of course, I was also half hoping that she would need me going to her office to remind her to write me up in the first place. Only time would tell.

If she fired me tomorrow, I was going straight to HR. Then again, I was betting if I tried to go to HR about earlier I would just be brushed off, told that it wasn't their job to deal with every little personality conflict, because how many times and in how many iterations had I heard that before?

God, I hated people.

Well, not all people. As much as it scared me, I really liked Stoker. I liked him a lot, and I needed to figure out what to do. It felt like investing in anyone was a recipe for disaster when it came to my poor, battered and abused, super-fragile heart.

I thought about all of that and more as I made the drive back home, and by the time I pulled into the garage beneath where I lived, I was pretty thoroughly miserable.

I felt doomed, in a way, because I already knew it was too late. I'd let my guard down; if I'd wanted to maintain distance, I never should have slept with him, because I absolutely could not keep emotional attachment out of sex.

I was afraid – I'd given Stoker a piece of my heart already, and it was a fragile thing - made of glass and there was nothing stopping him from making my heart go smash.

When I got out of the car, I could hear light music, the somewhat bluesy strains coming from the direction of Mrs. Sedgwick's massive front porch. I hit the fob to lower the garage door and walked up the drive to quite the sight.

Stoker was seated on Mrs. Sedgwick's top step, playing a guitar, the old woman rocking in her chair under the overhang of her covered porch. A little hibachi grill was set up at Stoker's feet on the bottom step and a grocery bag and a bunch of fixings for the hot dogs he was cooking was arranged to one side.

I had to laugh as I walked up the path to the porch.

"Oh, Serenity! I've made quite the new friend while you've been gone!" Mrs. Sedgwick called out to me.

"I can see that!" I called back. Stoker set aside his guitar and stood up, sweeping me into his arms and smacking a kiss onto my lips. I made a startled noise and jumped as he smacked me on the ass and winked at me.

"That was for giving your landlady such a fright," he said, with a grin that took any actual accusation or sting out of his words.

Mrs. Sedgwick just laughed and laughed. I was completely taken aback and mystified at the strange sort of friendship taking root in front of me, but it made my heart glad.

"Trust me, I've had all kinds of consequences for my thoughtlessness today," I said.

"What's that supposed to mean?" Stoker asked, and I sighed.

"Can I change first and put some food in my face? I didn't get lunch."

He scowled at that and said, "Yeah. You think you can bring down what's left of your pitcher of iced tea?" He bent and retrieved his glass from beside the little grill and shook the ice cubes in his otherwise-empty glass.

"Yeah, if you can give me a few minutes more, I'll make some more up."

"Whatever you need, Orchid, you got it."

"You've done good with this one, my dear. He's a good man, you should keep him." Mrs. Sedgwick was smiling happily at the two of us and I felt my cheeks flame vermillion.

"I'll be right back," I muttered and made a dash for my apartment.

I set the electric kettle on in the kitchen, took out my other plastic pitcher and got the tea bags out. While the water heated, I got changed into a pair of boot-cut low-rise jeans and a white, side-zippered cheater's corset top, aesthetically pleasing, without the inability to breathe in it. Hence why I called it a cheater's top.

I poured the boiling water from the kettle into the pitcher and dropped the bags in. I let them go, collecting the pitcher from the fridge and taking it with me. When I came back in, I would fish out the bags, add some honey and dilute what was sure to be concentrated tea with cold water before putting it into the fridge to chill thoroughly.

I refreshed Stoker's glass as soon as I got to him, and he held it out to me. I smiled, took it, and took a drink.

"Hot dogs?" I asked quietly and he laughed.

"I forgot to mention, I'm a pretty crap cook. I figured easy comfort food tonight."

"It's actually kind of perfect after the day I've had."

"What happened, honey?" Mrs. Sedgwick asked, leaning forward in her chair. I took the one on the other side of the little porch table that sat low between them and Stoker sat back down on the top step, turning the hot dogs on the grill.

I told them about the new manager.

"No, the fuck she did not!" Stoker looked halfway between aghast and ready to burst out laughing when I got to the part about my name.

"I'm not joking, she had the unmitigated gall to tell me she didn't stand for being corrected when she got my name wrong. My freaking name!"

"Well, I'll be," Mrs. Sedgwick tsked under her breath. "The nerve of some people!"

"Ketchup, mustard, relish?" Stoker looked to Mrs. Sedgwick first and I smiled, loving that he treated her so nice after she'd called the cops on him. He was being really understanding.

"A little mayonnaise if you please," she said and he and I traded freaked-out looks.

"Mayonnaise?" I asked incredulously. "On a hot dog?"

"Why, yes! I like it that way," she declared.

"At least it's not on your peanut butter sandwich," Stoker shrugged.

"What?" I cried.

"Swear to God, my grandma, all the time."

"That is so wrong!" I shuddered.

"Now, no, it's not!" Mrs. Sedgwick cried.

"Oh, no! Not you too, not on that one – if it's true, I don't even want to hear about it. That's so gross!" I made a face.

"No, it's not, it's delicious! Your grandmother had good taste!"

Stoker handed her a plate with a hot dog in a bun and some chips. I shook my head.

"No!" Stoker shook his head, drawing out the word while he fixed another plate. "No, she did not." He looked at me and arched a brow.

"Oh, naked, please."

"Naked?"

"I do ketchup sometimes, just not in the mood for it right now."

"As you wish, Orchid. Two naked hot dogs coming right up."

Dinner was nice. I helped Stoker clean up, the dread of impending confrontation tightening my shoulders and neck in a vice-like grip. He stepped up behind me as I stirred honey into the still-warm tea, the bags having been extracted in a soggy mess onto one of my saucers to one side.

His hands fell lightly to my hips, his nose buried in my hair behind my ear as he breathed me in. I expected him to ask, to want answers, the whole story, but he stood by his word when I said as much.

"I suppose you want to know about yesterday." My voice shook and he slid his hands up my back, thumbs digging lightly, trying to ease the tension. I gasped, half in pleasure, half in pain. He brought his lips to the side of my neck and kissed me, the pain from the careful kneading of his thumbs into muscles I couldn't seem to relax melting away under a tingling wash of clear, sensual sensation from his lips.

"I told you I do want to know, but only when you're ready. Not a minute before. I want you to trust me, Orchid."

His voice was low, and my eyes drifted shut at the warmth and comfort it held.

"I do trust you," I whispered. "I gave you the key to my house, didn't I?"

"Yeah, baby, but that's nothing," he murmured and I turned in his arms to look up at him. He rested his hands on the caps of my shoulders and smiled down at me. "It's the key to your heart that I'm after."

"Um, uh," I hedged, unsure what to say, my heart racing, tripping over itself to run to him despite my mind's best effort to hold it back.

He chuckled lightly and bent to kiss me, catching my lips as much as he'd caught the rest of me off-guard. I couldn't stop myself if I wanted to, my arms drifting around his neck, my lips wandering across his, tasting the sweet spiciness of my iced tea blend and the sheer maleness of him beneath it. My heart pounded painfully in my chest with just how much I wanted this even as he drew me closer to him with his hands on my ass, smoothing over the tight denim of my form-fitting jeans.

"When you're with me, you ain't got no worries, no cares," he murmured, drawing me back towards my bed.

"Okay," I whispered.

He stopped us just beside the bed and continued to kiss me, his fingertips sliding around my body, getting the lay of the land, so to speak. With a triumphant little chuckle, he gripped the zipper at the side of my top, lowering it gently. The thick brocade cloth sighed with relief in conjunction with my body as the restricting garment eased its hold on me.

I gasped, a slight moan escaping my lips, to be swallowed utterly by Stoker as his hand slid beneath the parted material on my side. I shuddered with anticipation, pressing myself closer to him, molding myself against the front of his body, my own hands pulling at the hem of his tee, trying to get beneath it to touch his warm skin.

"Stoker…" I whispered breathlessly when his lips moved from mine, along my jaw, before attacking that sweet spot on the side of my neck. I sucked in a sharp breath and arched into him, his hands drifting to my lower back, holding me tightly to him, possessive, protective, and I whimpered with the need to be skin-on-skin.

"I got you, Orchid. Doesn't matter how much you beg, just know that I've got you and we're doin' this on my time," he whispered, burying his hand in the back of my hair, his breath warm in my ear.

I couldn't form words, but I whined pretty spectacularly. He chuckled, low, dark, and deep, and carried on at his own pace, torturing me sweetly.

14

*S*toker...

I unwrapped her slowly, like a present that you were excited for, but already knew what it was. Her hair was thick, silky, and warm between my fingers where I held it at the back of her head, not to hurt her – no, she'd been through more than enough pain, but to give me that little inside edge of control. She responded to the hold I had in her hair, beautifully. Her body was taut, tighter than a guitar string, but so very still, as if she were waiting for me to pluck out a melody, and I had every intention to. One that had her arching off her bed, pressing into my body with that fine trembling that said I was frying every one of her synapses with a pleasure overload.

I had so many plans for my little orchid tonight, plans that would hopefully go off without a hitch and would leave her satiated and too exhausted to think anymore. Leave her in that good place with no worries or cares. Believe you, me, though, I had every intention of getting mine on this journey, too.

I went tit-for-tat on the clothing: her top, my tee, her jeans, my jeans, taking the opportunity to brush my palms over every inch of newly revealed skin with each article of clothing I removed. Her eyes closed as she gave herself over to the light sensations and I couldn't wait to lay her down, to replace my hands with my lips, to taste her skin, to increase the cadence of those soft, breathy little moans of hers.

I guided her to the bed, laid her down, joined her on top of the covers, pressing her down into them as I kissed her, holding my body just above hers as I moved my mouth down over her skin, traveling down, down, down, to my ultimate goal.

I raised my eyes to look up her body, between her full and perfect natural breasts, to meet her deep caramel gaze. Her chest heaved with slow, deep, unsteady breaths as I flicked my tongue gently against her clit. She gasped, her eyes drifting shut as her hips rose unbidden off the bed. I wrapped my arms around her thighs and pulled her against my mouth, breathing her in, relishing her womanly fragrance as I stabbed my tongue at her wet and wanting core.

She tasted divine. Salty sweet, the cooling breeze off the water on a hot summer day. Her body shuddered in my grip as she took the pleasure I gave her. I loved that about her; the fact she took what I gave, but not only that – the fact that no matter what I gave her, she managed this overwhelming sense of gratitude for it. It both turned me on and made me slightly angry for her – that she'd been deprived for so long that she felt the need to be so overwhelmingly grateful it was a palpable thing. That she ever had a reason to feel unworthy of this kind of attention, of feeling good, well, that shit chapped my ass and made me want to blow her mind just to make up for all the other motherfuckers who'd ever failed her.

She gripped the covers at her hips and tried not to writhe against my mouth, and I gotta tell ya, I loved her enthusiasm. She was shy and meek, sure, but only until the clothes came off. Then she was all in, letting all of her insecurities go for the time we were together.

She breathed heavily, the little moans at the end of each exhale music to my ears as I slid a finger up inside her, teasing her walls as they pressed around it tight, suckling at her clit delicately, carefully, trying to make her come for me at least once before I joined her.

God, I wanted to slide my cock up in her. I wanted to feel her wrap around me, warm and silken wet. I wanted her to ride me tonight, I wanted to feel the weight of her across my hips, her body pressing down on mine. I wanted to watch the play of expression through her warm brown eyes as she took her pleasure off of me and gave to me in return.

I wanted it all with my little orchid.

"Oh, God! Stoker!" she cried, and her body tightened around my invasive middle finger just that little bit more. She was so close. A few more swipes across her g-spot, another teasing lick or two and she cried out, sharp and needy, her lithe body arcing as though I passed an electrical current through it.

I didn't let her down easy, I kept her oversensitive body overworked until she cried out and tried to get away from me. I laughed and hauled her back my way, shrieking, laughing, pulling her into my arms and kissing her soundly, my cock brushing the velvet skin of her inner thigh. I groaned and snatched a condom I'd stashed earlier on her window sill above the bed.

"Let me," she murmured, taking the rubber disc from my fingers. I let it go and watched her, relishing in her hands on me as she smoothed the rubber down my length with her hands. I sucked in a sharp breath when she unexpectedly followed the sweep of her hands with her hot wet mouth.

"Oh, fuck, Orchid!" I threw my head back, breathless with the feel of her mouth on me. My own ponytail swept across my back, sending shivers across my skin, but I couldn't resist the siren's call of those eyes of hers looking up my body. She'd slid down the bed, and I put my hands to my lower back to keep from threading my fingers through her hair. I met her gaze and poured every bit of desire and trust I had for her into my eyes as she eagerly sucked my cock.

She was so beautiful in the dimming light of evening, her eyes sparkling with desire and determination, her back smooth and sweeping up into the perfect curve of her ass. She was like my personal goddess and oh, how I would worship her. She got me so close, right on that razor's edge, but there was no way I was going to go over, not like that. I wanted so much more.

"C'mon Orchid, I need to be inside you." I gripped her gently by her upper arms and helped her to her knees. She knelt on the bed in front of me and I kissed her. She kissed me back, following me as I lay back in the middle of her bed. She lay over the top of me and I palmed the outside of her thigh, above her knee, encouraging her to straddle me.

She did, our mouths clashing, tongues tangling, love and other natural drugs coursing through our bodies, a natural high.

"God, yes." I sucked in a long slow breath between my teeth as she basically dry humped me while we kissed. She reached between us and lifted me off my stomach, angling me to take me into her body. She slid down my length slowly, and I was treated to the most beautiful sight, her face serene, her perfect tits bracketed by her arms, her palms flat to my chest as she rocked her hips and rocketed us both right into the fuckin' stratosphere.

Her soft breaths, her moans, her feral little groans as I went over a particularly sensitive place deep inside of her – she took her pleasure and it was a pleasure to watch her let go, be real, and to make her feel so damn good. It was my honor to be here, to be her man, to witness it. To hold her, to be so deep inside of her, to love her...

She gasped and the sound was a different quality than the ones before it. I could tell by the sound, by the constriction of her body around my dick that she was right there, so close, it was only a matter of time or just that last little nudge of my thumb against her clit to send her over the edge, plummeting through that warm waterfall of orgasm.

"Oh, my God! Stoker, *yes!*" she cried and I decided to hold off, to see if she could do it. I wanted to know if she could come on my dick without my playing with her clit.

"That's it, Orchid," I encouraged her from between gritted teeth. God, she was so sexy, her energy so bright... I was so close myself, and I would be damned if I came before her second orgasm.

She cried out again, wordless, a sight to behold, her head thrown back, her perfect tits thrust out, her long thick hair tickling the tops of my thighs. I shuddered beneath her as she squeezed down around me tighter.

"That's it, baby," I encouraged, but I wasn't going to make it. I slid my hand between us, brushed my thumb over her clit and she cried out again, her pussy throbbing once around me, tightening just a little bit more. I was screaming internally, desperate for my own release, walking a fucking tightwire when she exploded into like a thousand points of light above me. I drove up once to meet her downward thrust, her pussy trembling around me, milking me fucking dry.

She could take it all. She could have whatever she fucking wanted, if only she would make me feel that way again…

She collapsed over me, her breath hot and even against the side of my neck as I held her to me. I chuckled, dark and deep, and murmured, "Look who's on top…" and she laughed. It was the purest, most musical sound I'd ever heard. Pure magic.

THE NIGHT WAS DEEP, insect song coming through the window. It was mild enough that the AC had been shut off and the windows thrown open. No need to use power you didn't need to when it was all money for somebody else's pockets.

Serenity was asleep against my chest, her arm across my body, curled like a contented kitten, adorable, and completely worn the fuck out. I absently stroked her silken hair while I stared at the ceiling, my mind spinning in lazy circles over the puzzle that was helping her heal. I didn't know what the fuck to do. I mean, the issues she had were big. Bigger than I'd ever seen and I'd seriously seen some shit – and until she was willing to trust me, to share, I wouldn't and couldn't know the scope, the magnitude, of her situation.

"I was in the library," she murmured, startling me. Thankfully, I didn't jerk, I just froze up. I thought she'd been asleep!

"The library?"

"Yeah, when the shooting started. I could hear it, all of us could, these loud pops and bangs. The library was huge in my high school, and the way it was arranged, there wasn't any place to hide, not really."

I kept my mouth shut and her voice died. I was hoping with patience, she would pick up the thread of this bedtime horror story.

"There was an emergency exit: go right outside the library doors, to the left, down the hall, another left. It was an access hallway, two doors. One was the emergency exit, one led down to the boiler room and the janitor's area. The librarian hustled us to the emergency exit, but somebody had chained the doors. There wasn't any getting out."

I held her a little tighter and kissed her forehead. Shit, I couldn't imagine. The fear alone, the terror…

"I didn't stay. I should have, but I needed to find Kyle – he was my boyfriend. I was so scared for him. I knew he was in the science wing, I just needed to get there. I went for it, down one hallway, the shortest route, cutting through the cafeteria." She gulped and shuddered against me.

"You ain't gotta tell me anymore if you don't want to, Orchid. I don't blame you if you're not ready," I told her.

"I… I found him in the cafeteria. He, uh… he died."

"Shit," I breathed. I held her tight.

"I didn't understand, at first. I mean, he was so gentle, and he loved me so much… he never said a thing to me. He never – I didn't know. I still don't know how he could have done such a thing." She sniffed and I felt a wet splash in the center of my chest from where a tear dripped off the end of her nose.

"It's okay," I whispered and held her close.

"That's just it," she said. "It's not okay, and it's never been okay since… right up until I met you. Now, it feels like –" She took a shuddering breath as if she needed to gather her courage. "Now I feel like there may be hope for some kind of a normal life for me and that scares me so much."

Because if I left now, if I ditched her… she didn't have to say it. It clicked. I got it, and I have to say, the fierce visceral reaction I had to the thought of leaving her cold, like this? *Not only no, but hell no. No way,* I thought savagely.

"I'm not going anywhere," I promised her.

"You say that now," she said with a cold, hollow laugh that held no happiness, no joy, just bitter disappointment that tasted of the same ol', same ol'.

I didn't like that, so I spit it out, figuratively speaking, with a derisive "Tch! I'm not going anywhere until you tell me to go, Orchid. That's a promise."

"Please, don't make promises that you can't keep," she whispered.

"I never do."

And I wasn't about to fucking start now.

People. They called us, the MC brotherhood, the savages... I was thinking I needed some help. Some advice. Good thing I knew just where to go for it.

I'd be making some calls in the morning.

15

*S*erenity…

I sighed, hanging my purse up on the coat rack. Returning to an empty apartment sucked, even after only having had Stoker here the two nights. I would see him again, Friday night. After I got off of work and headed to Ft. Royal.

I had the weekend off, so there was at least that to look forward to. Today had sucked, though. Sucked so hard, in fact, that Linny was coming over with the Margarita mix.

Taco Tuesday was about to go down with my best friend to lament the absolute horrid new working conditions at my store.

I heard her car pull up outside halfway into dumping the ingredients for the taco filler into my pressure cooker. She let herself in with a gusty sigh and demanded, "Where are the glasses and where's my blender?"

"Where they always are, bitch. Get it yourself!" I retorted.

"Some best friend you are!"

I rolled my eyes. "Please," I said. "I am way up on best friend points. Food will be ready in like ten minutes."

"You cooked! Okay, you are way up on best friend points. Food over drinks any day."

"Exactly," I said, as I went about setting up a taco bar on my kitchen counter.

She busted out the blender from the cabinet underneath, in the corner of the kitchen and I asked her, "Bring out the hand mixer while you're under there, will you?"

"Oh, hey, you got it." She dragged it out and set it up on the counter. I went for it and put the mixing blade attachment thingies into it, made sure it was turned off, and plugged it in for when the pressure cooker went off. Nothing shredded chicken, pork, or beef like a hand mixer, and in absolute record time.

Today's offering from the protein gods happened to be chicken, pressure-cooked in taco seasonings and salsa. I set to work on gutting two avocados to make some guacamole.

"You gonna do that thing with the mayonnaise?" Linny asked.

I snorted, "Always. What kind of unrefined savage do you take me for?"

"I swear to God, that is like the most ridic thing I have ever heard of but it works oh-my-God good."

"I told you!"

We bantered back and forth as I added some salsa and about a tablespoon of mayonnaise to the avocados, mashing everything together with a fork.

"So." She cut to the chase. "What is with this new manager of yours? Does she need to get laid or what?"

"Definitely, she needs a Stoker in her life," I said, and couldn't help but smile at the thought of him.

"Ahhh, now there is something worth talking about," she said, hitting the switch on the blender and drowning everything out. I rolled my eyes because, for once, I had something – or someone – exciting to talk about.

The blender died and I cut right in, "I am so scared I am dreaming and I am going to, like, wake up any moment when it comes to him." I said.

"Oh, yeah? He as dreamy in bed as he is to look at?" She turned from where she was pouring Margaritas into two pint glasses and bounced her blonde eyebrows lasciviously.

"More."

She laughed and held out a glass to me, I took it, and she clicked hers against mine. We drank and she said, "Okay, no holding out on me, I'm gonna need details."

"Oh, gawd! Linny! How detailed do you want?" I asked, maybe a little unprepared for this. I took a healthy swallow of my boozy drink to fortify myself.

"Uh, detailed. I feel like I spill all my tea to you and girl, you never have so much as a drop to give me. Well, now the tables are turned so, spill," she ordered.

I sighed. "God, where to begin?"

"Start with the good shit, talk about the sex."

I rolled my eyes.

"Best I've ever had, that's for sure."

"Nice!"

"Don't you want to know other things? Like what he does for work or...?" I left it open-ended and she laughed.

"Fine, give me the mundane details then." Talk about a melodramatic sigh.

I filled her in as I finished cooking, then filled her in some more over dinner. She sat back in her chair when I got to some of last night.

"Wait, he actually said that? You're not making that up. For real?"

"Yes! I told him I trusted him with the key to my apartment and he came right back and said it was the key to my heart he was after." I shifted uncomfortably in my seat, half afraid she would burst out laughing, that she would call it cheesy or stupid but she didn't.

"Awww!" she cried instead and put her hands to her chest. "I would kill to have a guy talk to me like that!"

"Right," I said nodding, the easy smile slipping from my lips as my anxiety and my fear rose to the surface.

Linny sighed, mightily, and looked me over. "Goddamnit, Ren," she said and I looked up sharply. "No! Not you specifically, more those fucking assholes. I swear to God, the more they fucked you over, the more afraid they've made you to be happy and you deserve it. To be happy. More than anyone I know." She covered my hand with both of hers where it rested on the table.

I pursed my lips and nodded at first, but finally shook my head.

"Augh!" The sound she made was so frustrated and I knew the feeling. "You make me so damn mad sometimes," she said. "You let these creeps live rent-free in your head, let them ruin things that they couldn't even touch without your permission first, and you give it to them."

I stared at her, open mouthed.

"I —" I didn't know what to say.

"I'm sorry, Ren." She pinched the bridge of her nose. "It's how I feel. You are so bright, so smart, so caring and funny and it is just tragic as hell that all of that is so wasted because you live in fear all the time that, what? Someone is going to have something to say about it?"

I couldn't look at her. I felt as if my happy, the good time I'd been having was being sucked down the proverbial tubes.

"Please don't look at me like that," she said, and looked, I don't know, scared?

"Like what?" I croaked.

"Like I just crushed you."

"Um, well." I gave a nervous laugh.

"Shit."

"You kind of just did," I said, and my eyes started to well.

"No, no, no, Ren I didn't mean it that way!"

"No, oh, I know you didn't but you know me… I, um, I think I just need to process."

She looked crestfallen, and I knew that feeling all too well right now.

"You want me to go?" she asked, meekly.

I nodded, not trusting my voice quite yet. I mean, not anymore.

"Ren, please —"

"I can't, Linny. Too much right now. It's just too much."

"Shit." She closed her eyes and her shoulders fell.

I needed her gone, I needed her to leave, I needed to be alone, to think, to process…

"Fine, um, okay," she said. "Can I call you tomorrow?"

"Sure," I said, following it up immediately with, "I'm sorry, I didn't realize I'd become so miserable to be around."

"It's not like that at all!" she cried.

"Please…" I stared at her and she stopped, getting teary-eyed.

"I don't want to ruin our friendship," she cried. "I've seen you completely cut people off for less than what I just said."

"Yeah, but they aren't you," I said. I hugged her, trying to figure out how to reassure her and get her out the door so I could feel the feelings that had the dam I kept inside bursting at the seams.

"Don't send me out there," she said and sniffed.

"I'm afraid to deal with anything right now," I said, my own tears coursing down my cheeks.

"I know, but I'm drunk, and I think you are too, and I don't want this to be the end of us or ruin us."

"I don't either," I said, and the overwhelming feeling of it all threatened to crush me.

"I just want you to be happy, Ren."

"I know."

I didn't get my alone-time, time to process, time to think… Maybe it was for the best, maybe not, I don't know.

All I knew was that I loved Linny dearly, she was my only friend, but that didn't mean I didn't sometimes need a break. I knew my filters for life experiences were broken and I had to work twice as hard at deciphering a person's intent as a result. I knew that Linny hadn't meant things the way I was taking them: *You're such a basket case, a doormat, a boring loser, and I'm sick of your broken.*

I understood it if that was the case. I understood it all too well. I wished I was normal. That I could just exist like everyone else. It seemed like they had it so easy moving through life without this extraordinary cross to bear… this weight of sins I hadn't even committed.

Talk about being crucified for the sins of your ex. My situation brought a whole new meaning to the common phrase.

"I want to be hopeful," I finally told Linny, when we'd finally cleaned up and had liquored up even more, after hugging and crying it out.

She nodded and sniffed; both of us were lying in my bed, facing each other, talking more. She had to stay the night, which had been the plan to begin with. It always was when we planned a night of drinking.

"I mean, you can't be the end all of be all's when it comes to being my friend, it's not fair to you."

"Have you ever heard me complain about it?" she demanded.

"No," I answered. "But I know it has to be hard."

"Not as hard as being you on a daily," she said, with an awkward smile.

I nodded and sniffed.

"Yeah, well…"

"At least the incidents are getting fewer and farther between," she said, sounding hopeful.

"The fact they're happening at all, still, after nine years, going on ten? That honestly just tells me that no matter how few, no matter how far between, they won't ever stop. Not completely."

"We can't control what other people do, babe." She tucked some of my hair that'd fallen into my face behind my ear. "We really only can do something about how we react to it."

Well, wasn't that some food for thought? I'd heard it all before, but for some reason, right here, right now, was the time that it really seemed to click. Probably because Stoker was in my life now, and I didn't want to lose him. I didn't want to give him any reason to be like 'Fuck this shit' and walk. I really liked him, and I wanted to be brave for once in my life and hold on to whatever it was that was budding between him and me.

I closed my eyes and breathed out, a stillness overtaking me with my moment of clarity and the decision made to work on myself in the very near future. It was going to be hard work, but I was hoping that I could try to fix some of myself. For me, but also for Linny and Stoker too. Maybe those were all the wrong reasons, but even if they were, the end result would still be better than staying the way I was now, alone and lonely, afraid all the time of what people said, of what they think of me.

I slept, but it wasn't a good sleep. It was full of bad dreams and haunting memories.

16

*S*toker…

"Stoker! What's up, man?" Marlin reached a hand down. I braced my boot against the side of his boat and hoisted myself up onto the deck. We did the guy-hug thing, clapping each other on the back before I eased off with a gusty sigh.

"Was hoping I could talk to you."

"Oh, yeah? Happen to be about that quality little brunette you found yourself?"

"One and the same." I nodded, stuffing my hands into my jeans pockets.

"Pretty sure we're gonna need a beer for this conversation, hold on a sec. Go ahead and have a seat."

I took a seat on one of the deck chairs set back under the boat's awning in the shade, while Marlin trotted across the back deck to one of the built-in coolers meant for the catch of the day. He opened it up and rooted around, almost shoulder-deep and extracted a can of beer. He reached in again, made a sound of disgust, discarded the can of soda he'd dredged up, and went back in for another beer, all while my teeth were on edge, dying to get out what I needed to get out.

Marlin bounded up and brought the two beers he'd retrieved out of the depths of the ice chest with him. He tossed me one and I held it out, cracking it open, the icy foam spilling over my fingers and pattering to the deck. I sucked some down as he dropped into the seat next to mine and asked, "So what's up?"

"I need to know how you did it, I mean do it, you know, with Faith."

He raised an eyebrow and said, "Well, I imagine it's the same way you do it with the hot little number from your show. I know you ain't unfamiliar with the birds and the bees, mate."

"I mean the trauma." I rolled my eyes from behind my mirrored aviators, glad he probably couldn't see it.

"She trafficked?" he asked, getting suddenly serious.

"Nah, man. This is a horse of a different color entirely." I told him what was up.

"Seriously? 'Murder Whore', that's what they got?"

"Yeah," I took another swallow of beer. "Let's hope these fuck-sticks keep it at just that. It's like a mob mentality that just won't fuckin' die."

"So the first thing, is when something trips her trigger like that, is to be the calm one," he said. "You seem to have that part down. You're cool-headed, unlike a lot of the rest of this crew. You do things from the heart, sure, but you think about it first. That's a point in your favor."

"Okay," I said evenly. "What else?"

"Everybody, every situation like this, is something different, man." He shook his head. "A lot of it is intuition, reading signals and staying in your lane. She rages and fumes, you let her. She pushes you away? You really gotta decide if it's the real deal or if you need to stay the course. Sometimes, you gotta lay off the throttle just for a little bit, back off and wait out the storm under an overpass or something, you feel me?"

I nodded. "So far, so good."

"I know you two are only a couple of weeks in, and I know those couple of weeks have been kind of intense… everything good?" he asked.

"Yeah, as far as I know," I said. "I mean, I don't know how anyone could think anything bad about my little orchid. She's – she's quiet, keeps to herself, doesn't bother no one. All she does is work and home. She reads, she cooks; she gardens out back of her place. She's crafty as hell, and a queen of thrift. One of those handy types that turns old things new."

"Sounds like an old soul," Marlin observed.

"I don't know about all that," I said. "I do know she hasn't gotten a fair shake and it's a damn shame."

"Lost soul?"

I nodded. "Like me. Like any of us."

"Citizens, man. You never know. You sure she'd be able to take the rough and tumble of a life like ours?"

"I think she's both stronger than she looks, and stronger than she thinks. I mean, unlike most citizens, she's still here. She hasn't gone bat-crap crazy, she hasn't tried to off herself, or tried to fight back."

"Yeah, you sure about either of those?"

"She's coming for the weekend, she'll be here Friday night," I said.

"Don't try and deep-dive her issues too soon."

"That your official recommendation?"

"Yeah, that and don't think you can handle this kind of shit on your own. Soon as you can – or are in a position to – get her some professional help."

I nodded slowly. "Might be hard to convince her she needs it."

"Eh, only if for whatever reason she's not ready for it. I think she might be, though."

"Yeah?"

"She didn't pitch a bitch, didn't kick you out or turn you away after the meltdown Sunday, did she?"

"No. No, she did not."

"Well, there you have it."

"So just keep doing what I'm doing?"

"Pretty much, man."

"I somehow figured as much, but I was still hoping you might have something else for me. Something I've been missing."

"How'd you figure out how to do what you been doing in the first place?" he asked.

"Watching you, and the captain, and Charity with Galahad."

Marlin chuckled. "Yeah, we are one ragtag fucking hell of a crew, ain't we?"

"Truth, brother, but I don't think any of us would have it any other way."

He grunted in agreement and we sat sipping cold beer, staring out over the water just over the rock wave-break of the marina.

"One last piece of advice?" He looked at me over the rim of his sunglasses.

"Lay it on me," I said.

"Open up right back. Don't hold back. You can't expect her to be an open book and not return the favor."

"I ain't got no secret pain, not on the level like she's got."

"Doesn't matter. Lead by example. Even if whatever she touches on hurts. Doesn't have to be tit-for-tat, but don't hold back, man."

"There are some things I can't tell her."

"Club things, yeah, I get that – but the explanation as to why you can't tell her those things ain't off limits. Be as open as you can, until you can't."

I nodded.

"Seems only fair." I let the comfortable silence fill in for a while, finally saying, "Thanks, man."

"Any time, brother. Any time."

THE DAYS SLID by in slow motion, stagnant, hot, muggy, and sheer miserable hell. I'd like to think it was just the joys that was working outside in Florida, but that didn't explain why the nights passed much the same when I was back in the air-conditioned confines of my house. I knew that as soon as she was here, it would be like a balmy breeze sweeping through the place. That was, of course, as soon as she got here.

I was with the boys from the band in the garage. The club meeting had gone by quick this week. The plan was as it ever was for me: club meet, band practice, and that's where it deviated. Instead of taking my ass back to *The Plank* or meeting up with the guys at the beach, I was staying home with my orchid.

I couldn't wait. I was jittery, almost worse than stage jitters, which was fuckin' weird for me, but I kinda liked it at the same time. Made me feel alive in a way I'd only ever gotten on the back of my bike with the open road in front of me, the wind in my hair, and no real destination in mind.

"Jesus Christ, man!" Gideon shouted. Rory quit it with the drums and Finn raised his eyebrows over the neck of his guitar.

"Sorry, my bad, guys."

"Dude, I've legit never seen you like this before," Rory called from behind his drum kit.

"Yeah, man. I mean, I fuckin' miss her. I can't wait for you all to really meet her. She's somethin' special."

"Look, just do me a solid, smoke a fuckin' bowl or some shit, mellow out, and try to stay on key."

"G! Man, take it easy. Maybe you should smoke a bowl and chill out." Finn scowled at him.

Gideon scrubbed his face with his hands and raked his long, dyed black hair back from his face. I'd quit dying mine black a while ago. It was just too much of a pain in the fucking ass when I was already a natural dark brown with no grays in sight.

"Let's take five, those who need to can take a piss or grab a toke and we can take it from the top. I'll get my shit together, I promise," I said.

"Fuckin' better man, I got better things to do than stand here jerking the mic stand like it's my cock in the middle of your busted-ass garage on a Friday night." Gideon was in a fuckin' mood again.

"What, Angela stop jerkin' it for you?" Finn asked, lighting up a cigarette, narrowing his kohl-lined eyes at our lead.

"Man, shut the fuck up!" Gideon snarled to a track of Rory's laughter as his sticks clacked and he got up from behind his drum set.

It was warm, but bearably so. I had the garage door flung open, as much to catch the salty breeze coming from the water as it was to be able to see my empty driveway, waiting for Serenity's little Toyota to pull into it.

I was just lifting my bass over my head to set it in its stand and to switch off the buzzing amp when she did just that. I was so glad to see her through her bug-splattered windshield my heart leapt into my throat and I straight up got choked up.

That's never happened before.

"Hey, she made it!" Finn cried.

"Fucking whatever," Gideon grumbled, and, yup – it was definitely that fucking little cockbite Angela that'd gotten under his skin.

"You be any kind of rude to her, I'm straight up punching you in the throat; you get me?" I stared him down and he blinked in surprise.

"Shit, so it's that way, huh?"

"Yeah, it's that way," I said and strode past my bike, tucked to one side of the garage, and out into the deepening Florida night.

She popped open her door and swung her legs out, her sandaled feet appearing below the door, touching down on the bright white cement of my driveway.

"Hey, Orchid."

"Hi," she said gently, smiling up at me. I reached down and she put her hand in mine and levered herself up out of her seat, groaning.

I laughed lightly. "A little stiff?"

"Oh, no… my feet are killing me. It was a long day on the sales floor."

"Shit. You need anything brought in?" I asked.

"Um, yeah." She smiled.

I asked a little eagerly, "You bring it?"

"I did," she affirmed. "Just point me in the direction of your kitchen and I'll make some up for you.

"Aw, you're the best!"

She opened the back door of her car and I shut the front. I picked up her overnight bag and the reusable grocery bag with the goods inside. I'd asked her to bring the stuff to make that killer tea of hers.

Had, like, four pitchers on my kitchen counter for her to fill, so I could have some all week. A taste of her, even when she couldn't be here.

"Oh, hi!" she said as Finn came up to her, once she crossed the threshold into the garage.

"Finn," he introduced himself.

"Serenity, my friends call me Ren."

"Nice to meet you, Serenity." He let go of her hand, and she smiled politely at Gideon and said "Hi."

"Hey, how's it going? I'm Gideon."

"Nice to meet you, Gideon."

"Nice to see you again, Serenity."

She blushed and said, "Oh, god. Were you on the beach last week?"

He laughed a little and nodded. "Uh, yeah."

"I met so many people, and I don't usually people so hard, so I sort of lost track. I'm so sorry."

"It's cool, you were kind of having a day, it looked like."

"Something like that," she murmured, blushing furiously.

"It's okay," I soothed as Rory popped out my kitchen door, skipping down the steps into my garage.

"Hey, she made it!"

"I certainly did," she said, laughing.

"Alright, break time is almost up," I said. "Let me get Serenity set in the kitchen and I'll be back out."

"Take your time," Rory said with a wink, and shot Gideon a teasing look.

I ushered Serenity into the house past Rory, and her shoulders eased slightly as soon as the garage door shut behind us.

"You okay?" I asked.

"Yeah, I'm fine. There's always a certain amount of tension meeting new people. It's me, not your friends, I promise you."

I set her overnight bag on the floor and the grocery bag on the crappy seventies dining room table and took her hand, reeling her in against my body.

"You do your thing, Orchid. I'll get through band practice and we'll have a low-key rest of the night, if you'd like."

"Sounds good," she said softly.

"Thought you might like that," I murmured, and closed the gap between our lips. I kissed her softly, and it was everything I'd been craving since I'd had to leave her on Tuesday morning.

"I missed you," she murmured, and her voice was uncertain as to how the confession would be received.

"I missed you too, baby."

"You better get back out there," she whispered. "I wouldn't want to keep them waiting."

"Naw, Gideon's being an asshole," I told her. "He can totally wait."

"God, just the thought of inconveniencing another person in the slightest gives me such a screaming case of anxiety, I don't know how you do it."

I laughed softly and told her the truth, "I can be an asshole, too. Two can play at that game."

"Ah," she made a sound of understanding, and I pecked another kiss on her lips before stepping back.

"Make yourself at home."

"I will," she promised, and I went back out into the garage.

I was just so stoked to have her here. God, I'd missed her, and now I had her for the entire weekend.

Fuck, yeah.

17

*S*erenity…

I let out a breath nice and slow and braced for the onslaught of sound from the garage. I wasn't disappointed. It was loud. At the same time, the vibration of it was some kind of soothing. I got into my purse at my hip, and I pulled the headphones out of the little pocket I kept them in and plugged them into my phone.

I had to turn my music up kind of loud, but it worked for me. Something about metal music, if I wasn't in the right mood for it, could completely set my teeth on edge. So, I plugged my music into my head and laughed at the four waiting plastic pitchers on Stoker's kitchen counter.

He really liked my tea.

I stretched and tucked my phone into the waistband of my layered handkerchief skirt, the black gauzy material shifting against my bare and freshly shaven legs. I wore it paired with a black, form-fitting, spaghetti-strapped cami and a pair of black, strappy sandals.

It was the height of my version of casual and made me look modern and chic. Probably it was the most modern-looking outfit I owned, aside from my work clothes. I sighed and went to the dining room table, and pulled out the two boxes of tea bags, and the milk-carton-style box of superfine baking sugar. I liked how it melted better in the hot water.

I rooted around in Stoker's kitchen and found the absolute bare minimum. Like, really, it was painful. He, at least, had a set of dry measuring cups and one wet. I found the three-quarter dry cup, four cereal bowls that would do, and set the tea kettle on to boil.

I worked to the sounds of Florence + The Machine, measuring out sugar, unwrapping an insane amount of tea bags and using the little binder clips I had to fetch out of the grocery bag to secure the bags to the sides of the pitchers so I didn't have to go fish.

I went through five kettles of water. Once the tea was set to brewing, I set a fifteen-minute timer on my phone and went to see if I had room in the fridge to put them all in when they were done.

I swear someone needed to be standing by with a camera to catch the look on my face when I opened that fridge. I started laughing, probably way harder than I should have, at the discovery I made.

The fridge was empty except for a few condiments in the door and some lunch meat and cheese slices in one of the vegetable drawers. So, yeah, there was plenty of room for the pitchers of tea – once I removed the brand new pressure cooker with the big red bow holding a note to it from the top shelf.

Hopefully having one here buys my sorry ass some cooking lessons.

It was hysterical, but in that way that told me I was ridiculously tired, and definitely needed a break from life. That was supposed to be what this weekend was all about: a break, from my life, and a further introduction to Stoker's.

I took the cook pot from the refrigerator and set it on an empty expanse of counter, plucking the bow and the note from the front of it. I still giggled about it. It was pretty funny. A light touch fell on my shoulder a moment or two later, and I jumped, shrieking, pulling the earphones from my ears.

"It's okay! It's okay! It's just me." Stoker stood in the middle of the kitchen, his hand pressed to his own chest as we panted in unison from our mutual frights and laughed nervously.

"Food's here," he said. "We ordered pizza, thought you might be hungry."

"Oh, my god, you're a lifesaver. I'm starving," I said.

"Figured that might be the case."

"Yo, man! We good?"

"Yeah!" Stoker called out, and the rest of the men from his band filed in.

"Oh, sorry, um, let me get that," I said hastily, and rushed to get my bags away from the four-person table.

"You're cool, we got it." Finn waved me down and winked one vivid amber eye at me. I hadn't looked too closely at any of their faces in the garage. He was handsome, his light brown hair in dreadlocks to his waist and held back by one of the ropes wound around the mass of them at the back of his neck.

Gideon looked perpetually dour, his long, dyed black hair shaggy around his face and in dire need of a cut, to lose the split ends, and a deep conditioning treatment, to deal with the uncontrollable frizz of damage to it. He had a deep, five o'clock shadow that shaded the hollows of his cheeks, making his already-sharp cheekbones into razors. He could be handsome, if he only didn't look so angry and miserable.

Rory looked the least 'rock star' of the four of them, his hair a nice and orderly business cut and a light brown. He smiled at me and gave a nod, setting the two extra-large pizza boxes on the table.

"Gonna put this in the bedroom," Stoker murmured, and hefted my overnight bag. I'd packed light – as in my lightest, airiest dresses and skirts – I was prepared not only for hot weather but also a ride if Stoker decided to take me on one. The weight of the bag was pretty much solely my jeans and a pair of boots that I had packed just in case.

I went and got plates and a roll of paper towels from the kitchen while the guys took seats at the table. I had planned to just get a slice and return to stand at the counter while the guys sat, but Stoker pulled me onto his lap instead. I laughed nervously, certainly not overly used to public displays of affection.

"Best seat in the house," he told me with a wink.

Dinner was pleasant. When the timer went off for the tea, I squeezed out the bags carefully, as they were hot, added the simple syrup to each pitcher, and then filled them the rest of the way from the cold tap.

"Any of that good to drink, now?" Rory asked.

"Um, yeah as long as there's ice."

"About the only thing I keep well-stocked in that freezer," Stoker joked, and he got up and helped me by filling glasses with ice.

One pitcher was gone between the five of us, and so I put more water on to boil; might as well refill it now while I still had the bags out.

"Holy shit," Gideon said, after taking a drink. "That's good."

"Thank you," I murmured.

"What is this?" Finn asked.

"Pear and ginger white tea."

"It's real fuckin' good. I thought Stoker here was batshit having you make four pitchers like as soon as you got here."

"Ah, yeah. He knows me pretty well, I guess," I confessed. "I'm happiest in the greenhouse or the kitchen. I asked him what I could do while you practiced and he asked for tea, and so, tea he shall have."

"And I surely do appreciate it," he said, and I smiled down at him. He puckered his lips and I felt my own split into a smile as I bent to smack mine against his.

"Mm." I chewed and swallowed a piece of pizza. "You guys going to be a while yet?" I asked.

"Probably another hour, why?" Gideon asked. "Want us to hurry our asses up?"

I shook my head. "No, not at all. I just wouldn't mind getting off my feet and I didn't know what the plan was." I looked at Stoker, who didn't look pleased as he stared at Gideon.

"We don't have to go anywhere tonight, Orchid. You do you, *mi casa es tu casa.*"

"Thank you," I said.

He smiled at me.

"If you're tired, you don't have to wait up on my account. You know where the bedroom is. Crawl in, get some sleep. It's cool."

"I think I might take you up on that."

"Long day, long drive, ain't none of us expect you to keep us entertained," Rory said with a wink.

"Last time I checked, we were the entertainment," Finn chimed in.

Gideon snorted. "Not if we don't practice."

"Well, don't let me keep you." I stood with a wince.

"Want me to tuck you in?" Stoker asked.

"No, it's fine. I don't want to keep you."

"You sure?"

No, I really wanted him to tuck me in, it sounded wonderful, but I was pretty sure Gideon would become murderous if I took him away from practice for any longer than necessary, so I tried to elegantly and graciously decline again.

"No, it's alright."

"Okay." He gripped my hand lightly and gave it a couple of squeezes, and I hoped like hell I hadn't hurt his feelings. I would die if I hurt him in any way.

"Good night," I said. "It was very nice to meet you all," I said, adding hastily, "Again."

"'Night," they chorused, and laughed a little. Even Gideon cracked a smile. I wandered through the little one-story rambler to Stoker's room and shut myself inside. Their playing started up a little bit later and it wasn't nearly as loud through walls and at the other end of the house. I could likely manage to fall asleep.

I slipped out of my skirt and took my bra off from under my cami. I wasn't comfortable being completely nude with the other men in the house. It just didn't feel right.

I set my bag from the bed to the floor in an out-of-the-way corner, switched out the light, and slipped between the crisp cotton sheets with a sigh, closing my eyes.

I couldn't fall asleep right away. I was terrible at it. Instead, I lay in the close dark of Stoker's bedroom, breathing him in, the bass thump and alternating hum of the muffled music through the walls lulling me a little bit more. I wished they would wrap it up, and immediately felt guilty for the selfish thought.

You should be grateful he pays any attention to you at all. It's a miracle you're even here. Funnily enough, the deriding voice in my head sounded an awful lot like my mother's. Imagine that.

I tossed and turned for a bit, but must have fallen asleep, because I didn't notice when the band stopped, or when the bedroom door opened, or when Stoker apparently got undressed.

The next thing I remember was him sliding up to my back, pulling me further into the shelter, the solidness, of his chest, an arm around my waist. He cuddled up to me, kissed the back of my shoulder and settled in behind me. I smiled, threading my fingers through his, and lo and behold, I went right back to sleep after only a few minutes.

I WOKE to his arms tightening around me, a hand up my shirt, kneading my breast, and to find myself subconsciously rotating my hips to rub myself against his erection. I moaned when he attacked the sweet spot on the side of my neck with his kiss, licking and sucking, sending cascading waves of sensation through my body. I pushed down my panties, pulled them off and dropped them off the side of the bed before reaching behind me, into the waistband of his boxer shorts.

He moaned against my neck when I wrapped my fingers around his length and encouraged him with firm, long strokes of my hand. We writhed together, like horny teenagers afraid to seal the deal and go all the way, until neither one of us could take it anymore.

"Fuck, Orchid, I need to be inside you," he whispered in my ear, his breath, hot along my neck, sending shivers down my spine.

"Please…" I begged, and he took his hand off my breast, from where he'd been deliciously pinching my nipple. He pulled it from beneath my cami and reached up above us, into the cubby of his headboard. Bringing out a condom, he tore the package open with his teeth and slipped the rubber disc free.

I wished I could lay still, but I kept writhing, his cock falling naturally in line with the crack of my ass, my fingertips drifting to my clit, teasing it gently while he rolled the condom down his length. Good Lord, I was wet and ready for him, dying to have him, however he would take me.

I didn't have to wait long at all. He hooked an arm around my thigh, just above my knee and lifted my leg, pressing the head of his cock along my sex, looking for purchase. He found what he was looking for, his head sinking into me, the length following as he moaned out like a man finally given relief. It was a sentiment I echoed as he filled me, the thickness of him filling me utterly, completing me.

"Stoker!" I gasped when he was fully seated, my pussy throbbing around him, just on the cusp of orgasm from the attention I gave my clit.

"Come on, baby, I want to feel it," he said, his arms going around me, holding me back against his chest.

I made myself come around his cock and it was everything, light and sound, fire and ice flitting through my veins, showering me from head to toe in delicate sensation. I gasped, and he moved, pulling back and thrusting forward hard. The roughness of it was a delicious contrast, something new to explore and I wanted it. I wanted him any way he would have me, so I cried out, "Yes!"

He fucked me beautifully, one hand on my throat, not squeezing, just holding me firmly, back against his chest, his other arm back up my shirt, kneading my breast with his big hand as he pounded into me from behind. It felt so good, but it was like he was just sort of missing the point, the one inside me that would take things from 'this feels so good' to 'oh, my fucking God what are you doing to me?'

I really wanted him to hit that point, but not enough to stop him, not enough to beg for it, not yet.

He slowed down, making long, slow, deep strokes into me that still felt just shy of the mark, while I gripped the wrist of the hand at my throat with both hands, just for a place to hang onto him.

"You good?" he crooned in my ear.

"Yeah!"

"You sure?"

"Don't stop!" I was desperate now, whipped into a sexual frenzy by the man whose body caged mine, invaded mine so sweetly.

"On your stomach," he ordered. "I'm too rough, you say so."

"'K."

He pushed me onto my stomach, gripped the hem at the back of my cami and stripped it off over my head, throwing it off to the side. I spread my legs and went to push off the bed to offer myself to him for doggy-style, but he pushed me back down, straddled the backs of my thighs and pressed my legs back together with his own.

He gave me a gentle, but still stingy, slap on the ass and my hips rose off the bed as I cried out, deep, throaty, the sound sultry and wild. I barely recognized the voice as my own.

"Good girl, Orchid. Stay just like that," he ordered as he pressed the head of his condom-wrapped cock at the apex of my thighs, questing for the entrance to my pussy.

He found it, sinking into it easy, crying out, "Oh, God!" as I purposefully clenched tight around him.

"Yeah, like that, baby. Just like that, keep that pussy nice and tight for me."

I gripped fistfuls of the sheets near my shoulders and hung on as he pulled back and drove into me and, holy fuck! That was almost too much, too hard, too tight, too powerful, too everything. I gasped and opened my mouth to ask him to go a little easier, when he surged into me again, only this time it hit all the right things.

My voice emanated in a cry for more rather than a cry of protest, wordless, yet carrying the intent I wanted it to just fine regardless.

He gripped my shoulders and pulled down on my body as he surged forward, and I slid across the sheets just the tiniest bit and felt my eyes roll into the back of my head. The friction against my clit — oh, God. Holy shit. I could come like this. I could totally come like this.

"Oh, God, like that! Just like that! Harder!" I begged, the anticipation winding to a fever pitch, driving me wild and right up the wall, right along with up his bed.

"Yeah? You like that?" he demanded through gritted teeth, his breath panting, his voice dark and husky, his tone soft, his inflection hard as iron as he mercilessly drilled me into the mattress.

"Oh, God, Stoker," I gasped, my voice breathy.

"Yeah?"

"I'm gonna come, keep doing that, I'm gonna come," I warned him, I begged him, and he kept fucking me just like that, and to no one's surprise, I came. I came so hard around his cock, so suddenly, so fiercely, it was like a goddamned hurricane making landfall. I screamed, he cried out, and he drove into me so hard and with such finality, I just knew he'd come too.

I had never come practically in unison with anyone ever before. I honestly didn't actually think it was a thing.

I came back to myself with the weight of Stoker's body on top of me, pressing me into the sheets. Both of our bodies were dewed with sweat, though mine was somehow cool to the touch. We panted, both of us trying to breathe, my pussy throbbing pleasantly and occasionally with these wonderful little aftershocks.

Stoker was still inside me and every time my pussy twitched from within, he made a little surprised, "Ah!" and shuddered above me, his cock still oversensitive. I knew the feeling, I didn't want him to withdraw from me yet, a little overwhelmed and just not quite ready to feel anything else yet.

He kissed across the back of my shoulders, sweeping my hair out of the way so he could kiss the back of my neck and I melted, my eyes drifted shut, and I shuddered with a head-to-toe wave of post-coital bliss.

"God, you feel so fucking good, Orchid," he whispered in my ear, before sucking on my earlobe.

I cried out, my body's sensitivity turned up past high, every touch rocketing along nerve endings, using them as a superhighway to reach the parts of me still on fire, throwing gasoline on the flames.

I could totally stand to come again. I wanted it. I needed his body on mine.

"I want more," I finally gasped out.

"What my lady wants, my lady gets." He reached between us and held the condom on himself as he pulled out and oh, man, that felt so fucking good, but it wasn't enough. I turned over on my back and sat up, reaching for him, grabbing him by his bearded cheeks, pulling his mouth to mine, feeding at him, drinking him down, my soul parched for his affections.

He kissed me back, pulling the used condom off his cock and tying it off without looking, dropping it somewhere off the side of the bed. I heard it hit plastic, like the rustle of a grocery sack, and smiled and giggled against his mouth even as he reached for another one.

"Shit," he gasped against my lips. "Gimme a minute, babe. I need a bit more recovery time."

"Mm, just don't stop kissing me."

"Never," he swore, before plunging his tongue past my lips and capturing my mouth, ravaging it with the same intensity he'd just fucked me with, stoking the flames of my desire even higher for him.

It only took a few seconds and he was tearing open the next rubber and rolling it on.

"Your turn to fuck me," he murmured against my mouth, and he twisted, lying down beside me. I straddled his hips and faced away from him; reverse cowgirl was always more taxing, more demanding, but I just wanted it. He gripped my ass in both his hands, squeezing it as I lifted his cock and situated it so I could slip it inside me.

"Oh, yeah." His voice was like a caress, soft and breathy. "That's so hot."

"I'm glad," I whispered, and rolled my hips, bracing my hands on the bed, between his calves.

"Take your time, Orchid. Make yourself feel good. It's gonna be a while, I think, before I can get off again, and honestly, I don't want to rush it this time."

"Mm." The noise I made may have been noncommittal, but I

slowed way down, taking him slow, taking him deep, the angle so good, the heat of him sliding through my wetness so perfect.

I don't think I ever remember being so turned on in my life which was, in its own way, kind of sad, but there wasn't any room to be sad. Not today. Not with waking up in this gorgeous man's bed, his hands on my body, his cock in my cunt, and all day ahead of us to fuck until we were both satisfied.

18

———

*S*toker…

Somehow, I'd woken up with a tiger in my bed. She'd let this incredible wild woman out to play with me, out of nowhere, and I gotta say… I was in seventh heaven over it. There was nothing more erotic, more sensual, than watching her perfect ass rise and fall, the skin soft beneath my hands. Watching my cock disappearing into her hot, wet, little cunt. Her pussy lips gripping me as she tightened up around me, her silken flesh sheathing me so perfectly.

It was like I was the key to her lock, and I hoped like hell that carried over into unlocking her heart as well. I wanted so badly for her to let me in. I wanted to play in the secret gardens of her thoughts and memories. I wanted to be the man she needed, because she was damn sure the woman I wanted.

I know, I know, it'd only been a couple of weeks, but I finally got it now. What they meant when the guys talked about their women. When they said to me, 'You just know.'

I gripped her hips and smoothed my thumbs over her lower back. She was so beautiful, so pure despite the taint she felt she carried because of her past. I don't think she got that all of us, every damn one

136

of us, had one. Almost all of us had something unsavory in those pasts, too.

I know I wasn't a saint.

I came from a home as broken as the next guy. Mom hooking up behind my dad's back. My dad drunk as fuck, until she finally died.

I'd been an angry kid. Angry as fuck. My dad didn't know what to fuckin' do with me, until, when I hit my teens, he'd given up on me too. My mom's parents, the grandparents I'd gotten this house from, they were the only ones who seemed to want me. It was a refuge from my dad's insults and fuckery, coming out here during the summer. I was all too glad to get the fuck out of Louisiana and move here permanently.

I tried dropping out of high school to do it, but my granddad wouldn't hear of it.

I moved my ass here, and he put my ass right back into school. It was his only condition on my sticking around. School, and then trade school, like him, like my dad.

I had my own dark secrets to share, but I was a chicken-shit. I knew I'd feel a lot better opening up when I was sure my little orchid could open up to me, that she would understand, that she wouldn't judge.

"Turn around," I told her.

I wanted to gaze into those eyes of hers. I wanted to watch those perfect natural tits bounce. I wanted to fill my hands with her soft flesh and listen to her moan my name, watch the look of ecstasy cross her face, feel the ends of her long, lightly curled hair sweep across my chest.

I didn't want to let her out of my sight, out of my bed. I wanted to keep her here all weekend and have both of us head into the workweek seven different kinds of sore from our exertions.

I wanted us to need a weekend to recover from our weekend.

She managed to turn around completely without my dick slipping free of her body, which was kind of amazing, a feat unto itself.

She gathered up her hair, holding it off of her neck, and rose up on her knees just slightly, and rolled her hips like a dancer.

Shit, that was hot. I smoothed my hands up her body and pinched her perfect peach nipples between my thumbs and the side of my hand, putting just a little tension on them. She bit her bottom lip and closed her eyes, giving herself over to feeling and she looked like a goddess above me. Her chest heaved in slow, even, gasping breaths that ended in a soft, sultry little moan that curled my toes.

"That's it, baby. Take your pleasure," I encouraged, and it was a beautiful thing when she felt like she had permission to be herself. She let go and it was the only time I saw her be free, saw her smile without any lines of tension, saw that beautiful sparkle in her big brown eyes.

I wanted to capture that feeling in a jar for her, let her sip from it any time she started to backslide into being a nervous wreck over something some dipshit had to say, when it didn't matter what any of those motherfuckers thought.

I let her perfect tits go and slid my hands down her body to her hips, my fingers digging lightly as I thrust up to meet her downward stroke.

"Ah!" Her mouth opened in a tiny 'O' of erotic surprise and I smiled up at her and did it again, ramping the energy between us back up, turning up the heat, taking the simmer we were at back to a rolling boil.

"Stoker!" she cried, and it held an edge of uncertainty as she collapsed over me, bringing her mouth to mine. I gripped her ass, held her up off of me just enough, and took over from beneath her.

She held onto me as I fucked her from below, our bodies slapping together, making my bedroom sound like we were in the midst of a porn studio – which could be hot in its own right– but I digress. My gaze was fixed on her beautiful face, pinched with that look she got when she was totally in the moment, drowning in the feels, and getting super close to her climax. Her eyes were unfocused, hooded with plea-sure, as if she were both here and not-here at the same time. As if she listened to music only she could hear.

I murmured to her, whispered her pet name, whispered her name, told her she was beautiful, told her just how good she made me feel, and I think she desperately needed to hear those things, not just from me, but from any human being, because her eyes misted and when she closed them, there were tears gathered on her dark lashes like crystalline stars in the deep night sky.

I held her to me, whispered soothingly, and let the emotion crash over her, swirl through her, and drag just a little bit of the negative bullshit she carried out into the ether. She didn't crash, she didn't sob, she didn't break down on me or weep to a point the sex was ruined – in fact – she gasped into my shoulder, "Please don't slow down. Please don't stop."

"Wouldn't dream of it, baby," I whispered and kissed the side of her head, renewing my cadence, picking up the rhythm of our bodies coming together.

When she came this time, it was a lighter, gentler orgasm. Her breath fell from her lips in a satisfied sigh, washing over my shoulder and chest as she pushed herself up to kiss me. I kissed her back, and I wasn't even close to mad or upset I didn't get my own. I was so wrung out from my first orgasm that I may have been hard, but I wasn't ready to come again. Not anytime soon, anyway.

I held her tight to my body, her breath washing over the side of my neck as she tried to catch it.

"You okay?" I asked after a bit.

"Oh, my God, yeah," she got out between her pants.

"Good," I said. "Kiss me."

She pushed up once more on shaky arms trembling with exertion and kissed me sweetly. I smiled against her mouth and murmured against her lips, "You are too perfect."

She laughed nervously and I smoothed some hair out of her face and locked eyes with her.

"You are. No arguments. I get you aren't used to compliments, but you'd better get used to hearing them from me... you're perfect, Orchid. You're my kind of perfect, no matter how deeply flawed you think you are."

She bit her bottom lip but it was too late, I'd already seen it tremble. I smiled at her and let her fling herself down onto me, let her wrap her arms around my neck and bury her face in the side of it. Let her laugh, let her cry, and let her feel all her feelings. I gave her the space to just be her and it felt good. It was like I felt and watched her grow in that moment, and the genuine happiness on her face and in her eyes made me feel ten times over like a real man.

"Breakfast?" I asked her after a bit more kissing.

"That sounds wonderful," she murmured. "I'm starving."

"I can make pancakes."

"Ohhhh, that sounds so good!"

"Pancakes it is, then."

I gave her a slap on the ass and she yipped in surprise before laughing.

I loved that sound.

I loved the way she smiled, and the light in her eyes; I loved the way she swept her hair over her shoulder, her lips swollen with my kiss, exuding that glow. She wore the freshly-fucked look like a crown and she was definitely my queen. She just didn't know it yet, and I didn't want to swear fealty here and now and freak her the fuck out. It could wait. Patience. *All good things come to those who wait...*

"What are you thinking so hard about over there?" she asked, slipping back into her panties, sitting on the side of my bed.

I pulled on a tee with the sleeves cut out, leaving gaping holes from shoulder to hip. I was still feeling overheated, so it worked for me.

"Just how much I like you," I said, which wasn't far off the truth.

"Oh, yeah?"

"Yeah."

"What else?" she asked, and I smiled.

"How much I'm looking forward to tonight."

She nodded and some of the shiny came off. We were supposed to hang with my club, either at the beach or *The Plank*, depending on the weather.

"Nervous?" I asked.

"And a little embarrassed," she confessed.

"About last weekend?" I asked. She nodded silently. "Don't be." I shook my head and pulled on a pair of jeans while she slipped back into the same skirt she'd arrived in last night.

"Ugh, I totally freaked out in front of everybody." She pressed her fingertips deep into her eye sockets, over her closed eyelids, the rest of her hands covering her face as she flamed bright red.

"Listen," I said, going around the bed and pulling her arms down, putting them around my waist. I flipped her hair over her shoulders to trail down her back, smoothing my thumbs over her jaw on either side as she looked up at me. "All of us have some kind of a fucked-up background or history. Some of us worse than others. It's not about that with these guys and gals, though. It's about finding common ground among your chosen brothers and sisters, and the understanding that who we are now is what matters. We all got a past, Orchid. You, me, the next guy down the line… history is in our rearview, baby. Whole road is open in front of us. Question is, what do you want to do?"

"Eat pancakes," she answered finally, and I threw back my head and laughed.

"A good starting point," I agreed, and ushered her in the direction of my bedroom door. She went into the bathroom and I went into the kitchen to get breakfast started.

Serenity...

For someone professing he wasn't much of a cook, he certainly knew how to do pancakes real well. Fluffy, flavorful, and an absolute delight, I wanted to know his secret. He wouldn't tell me, though.

"I tell you somethin', Orchid. I'll use whatever I've got to keep you coming back for more, so no-can-tell yah."

I rolled my eyes so hard I swore I caught a glimpse of my own brain matter.

"You don't have to hold a recipe hostage to get me coming back. I love the time I get to spend with you," I told him frankly.

"See, that's just one of the things I love about you," he said, leaning back in his chair. "You're honest. As real as they get."

"People usually just bitch at me that I'm blunt or that I'm rude."

"Honesty has a way of making some folks real uncomfortable," he replied.

"So how come it doesn't bother you?" I asked.

"Suppose it's because I ain't got nothin' to hide to begin with. Also, the fact I have no fucks to give what anyone but my people have to think about me."

I dropped my eyes to my plate, my fork still and all but forgotten in my hand as I turned his words over and over like a shiny penny in my mind.

"You care what I think," I cautiously whispered, half-expecting him to laugh at me for being so bold as to suggest such a crazy thing.

He smiled at me, that charming smile of his, and cut a bite of pancake.

"Guess that makes you one of my people," he said.

"I really like the sound of that," I said with a smile, and his grew bigger.

"Yeah?"

"Yeah."

"You may have just made my day." He winked along with those words and it warmed me down to my toes.

We finished breakfast and showered together, dressing casually for the day, to ride. The weather looked a little suspect to me. Overcast and muggy, threatening rain, with thunderstorms possible later in the day.

I had no idea where we were going. Stoker wouldn't tell me, but I didn't care. It was enough that we were together and I delighted in the rushing pavement and the hot wind as we skimmed over the sizzling pavement.

He pulled into a lot not more than an hour away, full of greenhouses, a nursery that had me perking up behind him. It was a place I had never been yet always had wanted to go: Sunfire Orchids.

"You're sure?" I asked him when he cut the engine.

"Absolutely."

"Are you really sure?" I asked with mounting excitement. "We could be here for hours."

"If I wasn't sure, I wouldn't have brought you, Orchid," he said, laughing.

I squealed and threw my arms seround him, squeezing him with enthusiasm. He laughed and patted my knee and I got off the back of his motorcycle. He got up and leaned it onto its parking stand, holding out his hand to me. I took it, and we went into the first greenhouse, which was acclimatized and held the checkout stand and some friendly employees who welcomed us in.

He let me spend hours poring over everything they had to offer, and I was so excited. I had to look at everything twice and some things a third time before I made any selections, and, me being me, I had to then decide what I really wanted above all else with the meager amount of money I had in my pocket to spare for such luxuries such as indulging in my hobby. I didn't have much, and as much as I would have loved to buy another new-to-me variety of orchid to raise, I just couldn't afford that at all. So, I settled on a ten-dollar small tub of orchid fertilizer.

"Gonna hit the john before we leave," Stoker told me, pressing his lips to my temple. "Wait for me out at the bike?"

"Sure," I said with a slight laugh. I couldn't believe he even had to ask. I mean, we had just spent close to three hours looking at everything and he had to be bored to death, but he hadn't complained once, tried to rush me, or made the slightest indication that he was over it already and ready to do something else.

I was grateful, and so I took my prize and sat against the saddle of his bike and read the container, waiting for him to come out. I also had taken some pamphlets on the orchid varieties they offered, both here, physically at the nursery, and through online ordering. I was just beginning to wonder what was taking Stoker so long when I looked up to see him coming out the door, a four-inch pot with a Dendrobium Enobi, or Purple 'Splash' orchid in his hands. It was a beautiful flower, the white burst from its center splashing out against the purple edges.

"Oh, my god! What did you do?" I asked, open-mouthed.

"Bought my woman some flowers. I hear chicks dig it when they get flowers," he said, and I couldn't help but smile.

"How are we going to get it back to your place?" I asked. "The wind…"

"It's small enough it'll fit in one of the saddlebags," he said.

"Really?" I asked, taking the pot from his hands and smiling appreciatively as my gaze wandered over the line of buds arching out into delicate blooms.

"Pretty sure. Gonna need to move some things around, maybe tuck a towel around it to keep it upright, but should be okay for the hour or so until we get there."

He didn't waste any time, insisting I just stand by and enjoy my new pretty while he shifted things around in his hard-sided saddle bags to make a nest for it. He carefully tucked both the orchid and the plant food I'd bought inside and equally carefully closed it up.

I went to him and hugged him, kissing him soundly and murmuring, "Thank you," against his lips.

"Do anything to make you smile like that more often," he murmured.

I felt myself blush.

"I don't deserve you," I mumbled, and he smiled down at me.

"Disagree," he said softly. "I'm just sorry we didn't meet each other much sooner, but everything happens for a reason, in its own time, right?"

"Right," I whispered.

He kissed me one more time before sighing and saying, "Let's get this show on the road."

I laughed softly, and we headed back to Ft. Royal.

Stoker wanted to take me to lunch, but I felt guilty with the idea of him spending so much money on me so I tried to reason with him and have him take us to the grocery store so I could cook, instead. It was, perhaps, on par with eating out expense-wise, but cooking for him would make me feel better, in that if I couldn't contribute financially, I could at least still contribute to the meal somehow.

He wouldn't hear of it, declaring that this weekend I was his to spoil, and the sentiment behind his words caused the stricture of guilt to ease from around my heart. He asked me to change into something cooler, answering his phone as I headed back into his bedroom. I slipped into a short white fluttery skirt along with the white corset top I'd worn earlier in the week. I loved this top; paired with a skirt or a pair of jeans, it was so versatile. To complete the new look, I slipped my feet into a pair of sandals before I stepped back out into the living room, where he was still on the phone.

"Yeah, we'll be there. Uh-huh." He grinned. "Aye, aye, Captain." He disconnected the call on that note, and I smiled at his almost-excited look.

"Where are we going?" I asked.

"*The Plank*, later tonight," he answered.

"What's *The Plank*?"

"A bar at the leading edge of town and our de facto clubhouse when the weather is shit. It's almost guaranteed to rain tonight, so the captain called off the bonfire on the beach and is having the club convene at *The Plank* for drinks and some pool and maybe some darts."

"Ah," I nodded.

"You look great," he murmured.

"Cooler, that's for sure," I said, my smile growing, and drifted over to the dining room table to look over my new orchid plant, checking the stem and leaves for tears and breaks, happy to find all of the blossoms still intact.

"I'm going to grab a change of clothes myself and then we'll take a walk to the boulevard and find some food." He raised his eyebrows, silently asking without words my opinion of the plan.

"Sounds good," I said, and with a nod, he went back to change himself into something cooler, too.

When he came back out, he had on a pair of olive green cargo shorts, frayed just at the knee telling me they'd once upon a time been a pair of pants. His leather vest, he'd shrugged back into over his bare chest, and I admired the way it framed his drool-worthy physique, my eyes roving over the colorful patches on the front.

One caught my eye and made my lips part into a wide smile, pulling a laugh through them like a fish on the line.

It was a red flag, slashed upper-left corner to lower-right corner by a white line — the universal maritime flag for 'diver.' What made it funny though, was 'MUFF' written in all capital bold black letters across it.

He looked down at what I was looking at and laughed too, shaking his head.

I bit my bottom lip and giggled out, "Classy."

"Sassy, and a little smart-assey," he agreed.

"What'd you do to earn that particular merit badge?" I raised an eyebrow, not entirely sure I wanted the answer, but the genie was out of the bottle and there wasn't any putting it back.

"Past is past," he evaded lightly, pulling me into his arms. "I'm living for the here and now, with you."

"Slick," I said, offering up my lips to his. He kissed me lightly.

"You will be, later tonight." He gave me the devil's own grin and I bit my bottom lip to try and keep my smile under control.

"How do you know I'm not already?" I asked, equally playfully and he gave a delightful little growl and attacked the side of my neck with these wonderful little love bites that left me squealing and squirming from the ticklish sensation he wrought.

We walked, hand in hand, down the sidewalk through air thick with heat, humidity, and the electrical charge that promised thunder and lightning. It was quiet out here, the threat of nature's fury a hairs breadth from making itself known with a maelstrom of rainfall, angry growling skies and the clash and riot of light and sound.

I loved the moments right before a storm, the minutes leading up to the sky's cathartic weeping, the rain sweeping the sidewalks and streets clean. The only thing I loved more than these quiet moments before the storm was the shining purity that came after, when everything sparkled wetly under the sun and the very air seemed cleaner somehow, the smell of wet, green earth left hanging on the air and the light chasing back the memory of the ominous clouds.

I kept pace with Stoker, our walk brisk as the sky let out its first rumble. I shuddered and picked up my pace beside him, my hand tightening around his.

"What's up?" he asked his voice cautious.

"Nothing," I lied. "I just don't want to be caught by the rain."

It was only half a lie, I told myself. I really did hate being anywhere and stuck in wet clothing, but what I really feared was the thunder. The crash and rolling bass through the sky echoed back to shotgun fire echoing through the corridors of Rachel Alice Morgan High School.

You know its thunder. You know what it is, I reminded myself and in this particular case, knowing really *was* half the battle.

20

Stoker…

She was shy, nervous, and half-hiding behind me when we went into my favorite dive, right there on the edge of the beach. They had good food and a clean atmosphere that appealed to the tourists, but the place was all dive bar when it came to the food, and cheap when it came to the well drinks. Not as cheap as *The Plank*, but definitely way better food.

Rory looked up from behind the bar and called out, "Sit anywhere, man! Hey, Orchid, that you hiding behind him?"

She peeked out from around me and smiled, calling back, "Yeah!" and it was the most adorable thing. She held my hand between both of hers and dared to come out a little, like, now that she'd been called out, she had to face the room, and I kind of got that about her. She was content to be a wallflower but once she was seen or remarked on, she realized she wasn't invisible and came out in full bloom.

Go big or go home, right, baby? I thought to myself as we threaded through occupied tables and found a seat in a close two-seater booth along the left wall at the end of the bar, just before the short hall that led back to the bathrooms.

Rory came to the corner of the bar nearest our newfound seats and asked, "You know what you'll have to drink?"

"Ah, I'll take a beer," I said and looked to my little orchid.

She pondered the drinks menu a moment and finally asked, "You got any cider?"

"Sure do, by the bottle. Dark Horse Cider, from up there in Washington State."

"Is it dry?" She made a cute little face that screamed 'dry' was definitely not what she wanted.

"Eh, middle of the road," he said, waffling his hand back and forth.

"I'll try it," she said with a smile, and he was a bartender on a mission, off after a stiff nod of approval to grab us our drinks.

We both perused the menu, even though I practically knew the damn thing by heart, until Rory came back to this end of the bar and set down two bottles for us. I got up and threw him some chin as thanks, bringing them back across the short expanse of open floor between the end of the bar and our table.

"Need a minute, or you know what you want?" he called from behind the bar.

"I'm ready if you are." Serenity smiled and I could never do anything but smile back when she smiled at me that way.

"What looks good?" I asked her.

"I'm feelin' the fish tacos," she said with a wink, and I laughed.

"Fish tacos for the lady, and I'll go with my usual."

"Fish tacos for the lady and the surf-and-turf special for my dude, sub salad for onion rings – got it."

"Thanks, Rory."

"You bet," he said, using a knuckle to punch in our order into the system.

I turned back to my little orchid watching me.

"What?"

"Nothing," she said lightly. "I just like looking at you."

I gave a slow grin and almost felt like I was the one blushing. Her words were nice to hear. Dudes just didn't get complimented like that very often. It didn't surprise me that she would. She was the most fearless, afraid person I'd ever met. Contradictory, in all these fascinating little ways that I couldn't get enough of.

We had a nice lunch, talking and laughing over random things. The conversation was a light sparring match in places. I was struck by just how much I loved the way her mind worked, and at how she made my mind work overtime to keep up. She was beautiful, alluring, intelligent, and we were so in tune with one another.

The woman was quickly becoming my best friend, and it felt good. Like I was a puzzle that'd been missing a piece, she just fit, so nicely, like she'd been cut specifically to fit that missing space, and the picture on top spelled out 'Love.'

I was falling in love with this woman and the realization had me grinning like a fool in the middle of the packed bar and grill my band-mate worked at. The thunder was muffled in here by the din of conversation around us, but it'd started to pour out there and the occasional strobe of lightning through the windows would leave a lull in those conversations. It was one of those flashes and lulls that gave me away.

When we were out like this, she kept her head down, her gaze fixed nowhere in particular, but studiously away from anyone else's, including mine. It was like, she tried so hard not to draw attention to herself that it made her glaringly obvious, and I didn't know how to tell her or work with her on it to help her.

I digress, though.

Because, when the lightning flashed and the crowd at the tables out on the floor sucked in a collective breath, she looked up, and locked eyes with me. Her expression changed to surprise before softening to something else, something that said 'secretly pleased' and she asked, "What? Why are you looking at me like that?"

"It's nothing," I said lightly, turning her own words back on her. "I just like looking at you."

She laughed and shook her head gently, and dropped her eyes back to her plate, her cheeks painted in a faint blush of pleasure.

By the time we were finished eating, the thundershower had mostly petered out. It was still a steady drip from the sky, but the atmosphere had lightened, and while it would be a damp walk home, it wouldn't be a soaker, or completely miserable. It would, to my delight, be just enough for us both to want out of our clothes, and I was totally okay with that.

I paid Rory, up at the bar, for our food, clasped hands and tapped shoulders, and my little orchid and I were out. We went to walk back to my place but, secure with me, hand in hand, she surprised me and asked to have a gander through some of the shops along the boulevard.

I'd be lying if I said I wasn't disappointed, but at the same time, I wasn't about to deny her heart's desire anything. If she wanted to window-shop, I was down. If anything, it would give me a better understanding of the things she liked so I could be sneaky and gift some things to her later. If I was lucky, and she was down for it, I had birthdays, and Christmases, and a lifetime of 'Just because I felt like it' ahead of us.

"Oh, wow," she murmured, stopping outside the town's jewelry place, *Hidden Treasures*. One of their bigger claims to fame was a bevy of reclaimed sunken treasure that'd been fashioned into jewelry, old pirate and Spanish coins made into pendants or hanging earrings. It also boasted a bunch of fresh- and saltwater pearls in just about every color they came in. It was super expensive shit. She had good taste, but she was also just looking.

It was way above my paygrade in a lot of ways, but definitely something I'd be willing to shell out for if this were going to be the forever kind of thing. So, I watched her carefully for that spark of desire over that one thing that was so strong I could say to myself, *That's it, that's the piece I'm buying for her.*

She didn't spot it at first, but I did. It was a necklace in one of the cases off to the right as you came in the door. The chain was fine white gold, the pendant looked like hand-hammered white gold, too – at least the petals of the orchid –the center bits were a regular gold setting holding a precious stone that I couldn't identify, but was a light blue in color, like a drop of dew or whatever.

The piece was striking, gorgeous, and screamed out at me that it was the one for her. Her sharp intake of breath when she spotted it all but sealed the deal.

"That's so beautiful," she remarked and I nodded.

"Was just about to point it out to you," I lied.

"You like to see it?" the girl behind the counter asked.

"Oh, no, probably far too rich for my blood," Serenity said with a light, but uncomfortable laugh.

"No, come on, let's get a closer look," I said. "If you don't mind?" I addressed the shop girl with the last.

"Not at all," she said brightly.

She pulled the necklace and I helped Serenity into it. The shop girl held up a mirror for her and Serenity traced just below the pendant, which lived beautifully in the hollow of her throat. I mouthed over her head at the girl, *I'll be back for it*, and she nodded.

"Thank you for letting me try it on," Serenity said and went to take it off with a reluctant sigh.

I helped her with the fine clasp and checked the price tag.

Shit. I'd be back for it. But in a couple of installments. This wasn't going to be a one-and-done purchase at that price, but I happened to know the place took payments and when it was paid off? The piece could go home with you.

I knew it'd only been a few weeks I'd known her, but this was no impulsive thing. I really wanted to do something for her, something meaningful that would make her happy, that would let her know she was loved without saying it outright this soon – I didn't want to scare her, or give her second thoughts. I wanted her to hold onto this easy and comfortable feeling we had when it was just her and I.

We left the shop and went into a few more random little places, an easy stroll down the boulevard that ate up time and the distance between us and *The Plank*.

"Ready to head back?" she asked. The sun, though not visible with the remaining cloud cover, was giving its last, the dark creeping out from between buildings and wrapping around my little town.

"Actually, we're closer to *The Plank* than the house at this point and by the time we reached my place, we'd touch the doorknob and have to turn back to make it on time."

"Better early than late," she said with a smile.

"My thoughts exactly." I gave her hand a squeeze and she wrapped her other arm around mine, leaning into me as we turned the corner to the line of bikes parked out front of the little bar.

The captain was here; looked like Hope had ridden on her own; and a bunch of the other guys' bikes were parked out front. I spotted Marlin's, Atlas', and Radar's. Pyro's was out here, too.

I felt weird arriving on foot. It wasn't something I did, but we were already here, so it was whatever.

I held the door open for my little orchid, and it was like I held my breath along with it. I mean, this right here felt like she was really stepping wholly into my world for the first time. At least, for a no-holds-barred look into it.

Citizens weren't always welcome at *The Plank*. We kept it club as much as we could. The only real exception to the rule was the VFW guys we let in here when the town's VFW Hall burned to the ground. Cutter, being a veteran of a foreign war, brought it to the club at an emergency meet, and he'd posed it as bringing a little legitimacy and respectability to *The Plank*. At least enough to keep law enforcement from getting any wild hairs. Not that we had any trouble from Ft. Royal's four-man police force. They were firmly in our pockets.

I stepped in right behind Serenity, dropping my hands to her bare shoulders and pressing my thumbs lightly in between her shoulder blades, where her tension rode.

"Back in the back," I told her, as she nervously looked around at some of the old-timers giving her curious looks. A couple of them were wary until they spotted my cut. A few of them gave me a chin lift, a nod of respect. I threw some chin back at them as we passed, and I herded my beautiful woman past them thinking to myself, *Yup, look at what I got, motherfuckers. All mine.*

"Hey," Cutter crowed as we stepped into the club's section of the bar. He was draped in his electric chair, Hope sitting on one arm, looking up at us with his greeting. Her face went from serious to a stunning smile in an instant and I relaxed.

"Hope we're not interrupting," Serenity's musical voice came from just behind my shoulder.

"Not at all." Hope's smile grew bigger.

"Welcome in," Cutter agreed. "Pull up a chair, there, Stoker."

I pulled up a chair as directed and dropped into it, helping my little orchid into my lap. She put an arm around my shoulders to steady herself and perched prettily on my knee.

"We were just talking about you, actually," Hope said with a wink.

"Oh, no. I can't tell if that's good or not." Serenity's laugh was a tad forced, her nerves on full display.

"Nah, it's nothin' bad," Cutter said. "We was just sayin' you could probably stand a weekend away. Get out of Florida for a minute. Head up north with us where nobody knows you."

"I don't follow," she said and chewed her bottom lip.

"Lake Run?" I asked.

"See, I knew you'd pick up what I was puttin' down." The captain winked at me and I smiled.

"Actually, I'd forgotten all about it. Thanks for the reminder," I said.

"Okay," Serenity said. "What is this?"

Hope grinned. "We, and by 'we' I mean the Kraken, are friends with another club up north in Kentucky called the Sacred Hearts," she said. "They were a little before my time, but they're a great group of guys and girls, and every summer we meet them halfway for a weekend at this lodge. Camping on the grounds, drinking, swimming, a little fighting all in good fun, and general fuckery. It's a blast, and really good for the soul."

"You should come as Stoker's guest," Cutter said, and I was touched that they would include her.

She looked a bit apprehensive and a little overwhelmed by the idea so I cooled things off with, "We can talk about it later."

She shook her head. "It's not that. I would love to, it's just, when is it? I have a hard-assed manager and I would need to know at least a month in advance to get the time off, and even then it's no guarantee I'd be able to afford to take it off or anything. She really doesn't like me, and could drop my hours or..."

"It's six weeks from now, Labor Day weekend."

Serenity nodded. "I can try. Holiday weekends usually get the time-off requests filled fast, and there's no guarantee even if I get it, that I won't be called in last minute."

"That's some bullshit." Cutter raised an eyebrow.

"That's retail with Stalin as your manager." She rolled her eyes.

"Tell us about him," Hope encouraged.

"It's a 'her', and I don't know…"

"You're among friends, baby. Get it off your chest." Cutter took a run at getting her to open up. I kissed her shoulder, a press of lips and she sighed.

"She just took over. I don't know what happened, but she showed up and…"

Bitch sounded like a real piece of work. Serenity got done describing this new bitch's first day in and I wanted to punch the cunt manager in the face – woman or not.

"Should find a spot without cameras and punch her in the face the next time she talks to you that way," Hope said decisively. "Pop her in the mouth once, they tend to watch it after that until they need a reminder down the line."

I chuckled and Serenity blushed furiously. "I don't know that violence is the answer," she said, cautiously.

"Dog-eat-dog world out there, beautiful," Cutter said, taking a pull off his bottle of beer. "We learned a long time ago the rules were made to keep us down and so we decided fuck the rules, right, boys?"

A rowdy cheer went up and I laughed; it was true. We mostly colored inside citizen lines to keep it peaceful, but we weren't above a little mayhem or retribution for things. Depended on how high the disrespect ran, and it sounded like my little orchid was taking it in spades where she worked.

"The problem nowadays is that no one expects to get punched in the mouth for their disrespect. You don't close it for them, they just think they can keep on keepin' on runnin' it." Cutter said.

"In my experience," Serenity countered, "the more you try to fight back or argue poor treatment, the worse it gets…" She trailed off and wouldn't look at any of us. I gave her a light squeeze and she bit her lips together. Hope and Cutter exchanged a glance with me, and I gave a slight nod.

That was enough for now. I didn't know, if we pushed it any farther, how she would react. I'd try getting more out of her later, but I wanted her to enjoy tonight.

"Citizen's folly," Cutter said, then added directly, "I think we can just leave it at that, how about you?"

"Agree to disagree?" she murmured.

"Something like that." He winked and she smiled.

"So, you going to try and get that weekend off?" Hope asked.

My little orchid nodded. "I'll try."

"Excellent! We'd love to have you," Cutter said.

"Okay," Serenity agreed and I nipped her shoulder. She gasped and looked down at me from where she was perched on my knee. I smiled up at her and encouraged her with my eyes to kiss me.

She leaned down and did just that, and I was happy.

21

*S*erenity…

We drank a little too much, but we were having fun. At least, I know I was having fun. Stoker's hand was on my waist as we stood around the pool table, laughing and talking with his club's vice president, Marlin, and his woman, Faith.

She and I bonded a bit over our mutual anxiety and post-traumatic stress disorders, but her story? Vastly more tragic than mine. It was a bit easier, opening up about mine, knowing how much worse her tale was, but I still didn't go into great detail. I also didn't expect her to. It was enough to know the damage was mutual, the symptoms of our disorders an almost perfect match.

It was nice to know I wasn't alone, when I had been for so very long.

Stoker missed his final shot and straightened, crying, "Ahhh!"

Marlin laughed and said, "Can't win 'em all, buddy. Rack 'em up and I'll let you redeem yourself."

Stoker bowed his head, chuckling and shook it saying, "Nah, man. It's getting late. I think I'm gonna take my lady home for the night."

The way he said it, what he called me, 'his lady', sent a shiver of delight through me, which was quickly chased with a shot of desire for

158

him. I smiled happily and hopped off the bar stool I was perched on, handing him my pool cue. He racked it alongside his on the wall and held out his hand to me.

"You sure you're good to ride?" Marlin asked, and I giggled.

"We walked, so yeah, man, we're good."

"The fuck, over? You walked your happy ass here when you got a perfectly good bike to ride in on? Somebody needs to pull your man card.

" Radar was laughing, wandering over from the dartboards. Stoker tucked me into his side and mock-laughed at Radar.

"You're not funny," he said, deadpan, and Radar laughed at him in turn, for real this time.

"I'm fuckin' hilarious."

"And we're fuckin' outta here, so we can fuck," Stoker shot back, and our section of the bar went up into a rowdy cheer.

I blushed and hid my face against his leather vest as he steered us a bit unsteadily towards the door. He pulled it open and we walked out under the overhang – to a wall of rain.

"Well, shit," he declared and I started laughing.

I started laughing, and I couldn't stop, and pretty soon, both of us were slain by a giant fit of giggles, that turned into kissing, that quickly turned passionate as he lifted me, my arms around his neck, his hands around my back and stepped us out into the downpour.

I howled and laughed, full-bodied and filled with joy as he spun me around while we were soaked to the skin in seconds. I locked my mouth to his and he sat me on the trunk of a nearby car, his mouth feasting at mine, nipping my lips, his hand copping a feel of my left breast which made me groan into his mouth.

"Hope you don't like these," he grunted, and before I knew it, his hand, that had drifted up my leg beneath my skirt, had tangled in the G-string panties I was wearing beneath my skirt. With a sharp jerk of his fist, the seams popped and the panties gave way on the one side.

"Oh, my God!" I gasped and he took the hand from my breast and ripped the other side of my panties.

"You're not going to fuck me right here, are you?" I asked, and barely could hear myself over the dull roar of the rain falling around us.

"Yep," he grunted, going for his belt, pulling me to the edge of the trunk with his other arm.

I was surprised to find my blood heat with want, the desire rising and boiling over in an effervescent rush of gooseflesh down my arms.

I pulled him against me and asked mid-kiss, "Condom?"

"Mm, grabbed one from the fishbowl on the way out," he murmured and I laughed. I had noticed the fishbowl of condoms on the end of the bar right beside the door, but I hadn't seen him grab one. He was crafty, and slick, and I loved that about him.

I edged closer to him and we resumed kissing fervently, the rain pattering around us warm and full of life.

"Not afraid of getting caught?" he asked.

"I'll just hide behind you, and not really, not if we hurry it up."

"What if I don't want to hurry it up? What if I want to take you long and slow?" he asked, a teasing and seductive edge to his melodic voice.

"Long and slow is for back at the house," I said breathlessly, shoving myself against him as he stroked his cock between us, between my thighs, making himself ready. "Now shut up and fuck me," I demanded, and he threw back his head and laughed.

When he tipped it forward, he brought his mouth back to mine as he worked the condom he'd snagged out of the bowl out of its wrapper and rolled it on. I wiggled so my ass was half-hanging off the edge of the trunk of the car and he shoved his cock inside me, sharp and deep, my body not quite ready, stretching around him to take him in with an unhappy aching throb of protest.

I moaned, my arms going around his shoulders, holding myself close to him while he gripped my outer thighs and practically pulled me onto him with every thrust. The passion was real, reacting and burning hot like we were made of potassium, coming in contact with the rainfall around us.

The orgasm that happened was incendiary and heightened by the risk that some old-timer, or one of his club could come outside any moment. Or, better yet, the owner of the car we were fucking on could come out to go home and…

"Fuck, yes, Orchid!" Stoker groaned, and he shuddered against me, his fingers gripping my thighs with bruising force as he filled the condom inside of me.

I groaned too; if I could have just held off for two seconds more, we could have come in unison.

Damn.

I would have liked that. For some reason, I would have liked that a lot. The intimacy of it appealed to me like no other. I would love that with him. God, I was pretty sure I just loved him at this point, the emotion strong as he held the condom on himself and pulled out. He stripped it off his softening cock and flung it down a storm drain while I pulled my skirt down over the tops of my thighs, the light material sticking to me and having none of it when it came to cooperating with me.

I shivered, which had nothing to do with the temperature and everything to do with just how achingly unfulfilled I was feeling. I wanted him to take me home. I wanted to spend the rest of my night in his bed having sex every which way it was intended. Hard, soft, dirty, sensual… I was a glutton for it, all of a sudden.

"You okay?" he asked, helping me down off of the car once he was, ah, put away.

"Better than okay whenever I'm with you," I confessed.

"Right on, I like it!" His chest swelled with pride and he put an arm around my shoulders as we set off in the direction of home. Well, his home… I didn't want to get ahead of myself but who knew? Maybe someday.

THE WEEKDAYS DRAGGED and the weekends flew by and I was so close to the long weekend, the trip with Stoker and his club, that I could taste it. It was my Friday, we were supposed to leave as soon as Stoker picked me up from work, and the second hand seemed to be ticking over like it was the minute hand on the clock.

I was sweating bullets. Our manager had been by squawking a few times about the schedule and I just knew she was about to screw me out of my already-approved time off.

Not today, Satan, I thought at her. *Not today.*

Oh, but it was going to be today…

"Serena," she called out, and she had never, not once, gotten my name correct since I had initially corrected her. In an attempt to just not make waves I had never bothered to correct her again. I ground my teeth and plastered on my most genuine looking fake smile.

"Yes, Lydia?"

"You're going to have to come in tomorrow," she said, with a nasty little smirk.

"I'm sorry," I said in an attempt to stand my ground. "I can't. I'll be out of state; you approved the vacation time over six weeks ago."

"I approved it, yes, but now I'm canceling it."

I opened my mouth to protest, but it wasn't my voice that spoke.

"You can't do that, and if you do, she quits and we sue."

I blinked and craned my neck way back as Stoker's hands fell onto my shoulders.

"Hey, Orchid."

"You don't show up tomorrow, you're fired, and that's final," Lydia glared at me. "And just who are you?" she demanded.

"Stoker, and 'Lydia Farminger' isn't the name you started out with, is it?" Lydia's mouth dropped open and Stoker gave her a nasty little smile. "Ah, yeah. Didn't expect anyone would do any digging on you, did you?"

"What are you doing?" I asked.

"Just watch," he said, low, for my benefit only, his thumbs digging gently into my shoulders.

I swallowed hard. I couldn't play fast and loose with my job, it was the only one I had and what if I couldn't get another right away? I couldn't do that to Mrs. Sedgwick. I lived paycheck to paycheck and barely managed to keep a couple hundred dollars in savings. What was he doing?

I stood frozen as a few of my co-workers drifted near and Stoker tore my manager to shreds.

"No, you got married. Your real name – or maiden name if you like, is Lydia Caruthers. Your sister was Caroline Caruthers."

I jerked slightly in his grasp and he firmed up his grip on my shoulders.

Caroline Caruthers had bullied me all through junior high and high school… She'd made my life a living hell and looking at Lydia now, I could see the resemblance. A lot of the things Caroline had done were so cruel I'd blocked them out. She'd been one of the first killed in Kyle's rampage and despite how poorly her sister had treated me, despite how her sister was attempting to treat me now, my heart went out to Lydia. Were it not for Stoker calling her out, I probably never would have seen it, guessed, or known.

"How dare you," Lydia seethed.

I shook my head. "I don't want to get you in trouble," I said. "Far from it. I would, however, like to go on my vacation, that you approved, and when I get back, I would like to see if we can come to a working arrangement that we can both live with."

"Nah," Stoker said. "You're going on your vacation, an email's already been sent to HR. Let them deal with her. We'll send another when we leave, I'm tired of bitches like these taking shit out on you that was outside your control. Come on, Orchid. Let's go, you're off work."

I didn't know whether to be mad or relieved that it was out of my hands… I'd always secretly wished someone would take it out of my hands, would stand up for me and give me the breathing room I needed, but at the same time, I felt like I should have been careful what I wished for. I tried to be kind, and this was no exception – what Stoker had suggested he'd done sounded cold, calculating, and borderline cruel.

It was hard standing there watching Lydia glare at me through angry unshed tears, but Stoker was right – I hadn't done anything. I hadn't known, so why was I still being punished for it all at every turn? I just wanted to live my life, make ends meet, and carve out the tiniest bit of happiness for myself.

"Clean out your locker," Lydia said coldly.

"I'm sorry, but I'll do that if and when HR tells me to," I stated.

One of my co-workers crowed, "Alright!"

Megan rushed forward and thrust my purse into my hands, and Stoker murmured, "Let's go. We'll sort it out when we get back."

I was sort of shell-shocked and nodded my head, feeling a little bobble-headed as he turned me and, arm around my shoulders, led me out of the store and out into the mall. As soon as I stepped out of the giant archway into the high-ceilinged thoroughfare of the mall, I let out an explosive breath I hadn't realized I'd been holding, and the trembling started.

Adrenaline. The adrenaline is wearing off.

I think it was the first of any kind of confrontation I'd been in where I felt I may have just come out on top. Usually I lost, and lost badly, even though I never instigated anything. A good confrontation had always just left me emotionally wrecked and in tears. A bad one had left me on the floor in various stages of broken or bleeding.

This was different, but my body and mind couldn't seem to handle it, and the tears and emotional wreckage were threatening to wash in with tsunami force.

We needed to leave. I needed to go outside, and I couldn't let anyone see.

"Hang on, Orchid. Almost there," he crooned as we walked briskly out to where my car was parked.

"Were you being serious about the emails?" I asked.

"As a heart attack, baby. I had Radar hack your shit and Hope helped write it. I knew this bitch was going to try something after everything you've told me these last few weeks. My timing was fucking impeccable today, though. Coming up on you right as she tried to spring it."

"I am so going to lose my job," I said shaky.

"No, you're not, and if you do, who fucking cares?" he demanded as we breezed out the doors into the oppressively hot Florida summer day.

I stopped, rearing up short.

"I care!" I cried. "I lose my job, I'll lose my home, and Mrs. Sedgwick depends on me and —"

"Stop, baby. Easy, now." He pulled me into his arms and I gave a panicked, broken little sob.

"I love you," he murmured and I froze.

"What?" I jerked back in his grasp and looked up at him. "What did you just say?" I couldn't believe that I'd heard him right.

"I said, I love you… and I'm not going to let anything else bad happen to you if I can help it. I'm sick and tired of people handing you this raw deal and yeah, I'm even a little mad, a little disappointed in you for just taking it but, babe, I think that's honestly because no one ever gave you the notion that you actually could stand up for yourself, let alone taught you how."

"You love me?" I whispered in awe. I was thoroughly stuck on that one point, and for me, it was a really big one. I couldn't remember the last time anyone other than Linny told me those three little words, let alone meant it as fervently as Stoker did. I mean, I could see it in the depths of his kind liquid dark eyes as he smiled down at me and smoothed some of my dark hair out of my face.

"I do," he said, and I bit my lips together and tried very hard not to cry for a very different reason.

I lost, and Stoker, chuckling, pulled me in and held me tight against his chest as I sniffled against his vest in the bright sunshine and oppressive humidity surrounding us.

"Come on, everybody's waiting outside your place to make this ride," he murmured, and I nodded and got myself together. He followed me home, and sure enough, when I went to turn into my garage, my street was lined with motorcycles and several of the men and women of the Kraken were sitting on the steps or standing around on my landlady's front porch while she poured them all glasses of sweet tea and they chatted.

I was floored and my heart melted at just how pure all of their smiles were and despite the rough appearances, the decidedly 'outsider' vibe they all threw off in every direction, I realized they also radiated kindness, the like I'd never seen from a group of "citizens" before.

At least, not in my own personal experience.

"Hey, Orchid!" Hope called from the porch as the door to the garage trundled down and I stepped into the driveway.

"Hey, Hope," I called softly.

"Everything alright?" Cutter asked Stoker.

"Just peachy, Captain!"

"Ah-huh, looks that way," he said, eyeing me.

I plastered on a smile and said, "I'll be right down, just let me go change really quick. I'm sorry I'm holding you all up."

"No hold-up, honey," Atlas called. "As road captain, it's my responsibility to keep us all on track and on time, and we got plenty of it. You go on and get cleaned up, wash your face, we got your landlady to keep us company!"

"Oh, my!" Mrs. Sedgwick cried and laughed with a blush. I smiled and Stoker put a hand to my lower back and guided me from behind up my steps to where I could unlock my apartment door.

Faith and Charity bounded up the steps after us and Faith called, "I want to see your place!"

I smiled and said, "Come on in."

My bags were packed and by the door, my clothes for the ride laid out on the bed. I just needed to change, braid my hair, and we would be good to go. I was stopped by Stoker's hand catching mine.

"Give us a minute," he told Faith and Charity, and shut my front door in their faces. I felt my jaw drop and stared at him agape.

"Stoker! How rude!"

"Hush, they understand," he said reeling me in. "I need to talk to you about something."

"What? Did I do something wrong?" I asked. I was forever worried I was screwing something up in a big way. The lives the club led, the rules they followed, they were so different from anything I was used to and I was constantly afraid of misstepping, of doing something offensive, or of angering someone. Even unintentionally, it would be devastating for me.

"No, Orchid. Never. I just need to ask you something important."

"What?" I asked, half afraid he was about to ask me to marry him or something. I mean, we were good together, and I was so very afraid that I loved him too, and what that could mean for him… I was already afraid for him loving me and what kind of trouble that could cause, but this was Stoker, and I had no real reason to worry for him. He was so confident and brave compared to me, so self-assured.

"I was wondering," he said, "if…" He reached behind him, under his jacket and vest and brought out a folded package, wrapped in an orange bandanna, the four corners tied together in a short knot, the package flat and square and holding something leather.

"If?" I asked, cocking my head.

"If you would wear my rag, make it official and be my ol' lady."

I stared up at him and blinked, stunned.

"You're serious," I whispered.

"Yeah, babe. Already told you, I love you. I want to keep you safe, and part of that is declaring you mine before any other dude either in my club or one up north gets the wrong idea."

"Wrong idea, how?" I asked, mouth suddenly dry.

He explained it, how women wearing the 'Property of' vests were considered off-limits to other men's advances. I listened carefully as he explained the biker's definition of 'property' and it was quite literally everything I had always ever wanted and feared I would never have.

"Yes," I whispered, a sharp, healing ache throbbing once in the center of my chest with the word. "I'll wear it, if you're sure. If you're really sure you want me in that way."

"Little Orchid, I want you in that way for always, but I get that always is a really long time and a scary prospect, so I want to give you my rag and tell you for sure I want you that way for now, until you decide you don't want me, okay?"

The mere thought of my ever not wanting him sent a lance of agony through me. I took the package from his hands and put my arms around him and we held each other like that in the air-conditioned hush of my apartment while the men of his club laughed below and Faith and Charity waited outside my door. I felt guilty about that, but I indulged myself for just a touch longer than I felt was polite because this moment held weight. This moment was so very important to me, for us, and I didn't want to rush a thing.

"We should let the girls in," he murmured finally, and I nodded against his chest and took a reluctant step back.

He smiled at me and opened the door, and the first question out of Faith's mouth was, "Did she say yes?"

"Yes, I said yes!" I said, and sniffed and with a soggy little laugh said, "I need to call Linny, but later."

"Come on," Charity urged. "Let's fix your makeup and get you dressed to ride."

"Oh my God," I said horrified. "My makeup!" I'd forgotten all about it and I must have looked like a real horror show scream queen!

"You go do that, and I've got these," Stoker said, hefting my single gym bag and my purse. He'd said to pack light, and I'd done my best. I was thankful he seemed satisfied and didn't ask me to change anything.

I went into the bathroom and scrubbed my face while Charity and Faith stuck around and commented here and there on how much they loved this or that little knick-knack on one of my shelves.

I washed my face completely, changed clothes, and redid my makeup from scratch out of the meager half-dead supply that I hadn't bothered to pack.

Faith braided my hair without asking, which I found to be nice, while I applied my face and Charity held out the bandana that had come wrapped around my new leather vest. She'd folded it into a wide swath, and Faith fixed it for me, around my head.

"When you start to sweat in all that leather, you'll be glad for it under the helmet. Keeps your makeup from running and the salt out of your eyes," Charity explained.

I stepped out into the rest of my neat little apartment and Stoker held out the vest, already over my jacket, for me. I smiled at the 'Property of Stoker' emblazoned across the back and he turned it around for me to shrug into. The name patch on the front read 'Orchid.'

I liked that he called me that. I liked that everyone seemed to naturally fall into calling me that. I loved it even more how they all cheered for me when I stepped out onto the little landing and wrap-around porch, and I felt like a badass Cinderella as I went down the stairs.

It was the first time I ever felt like I fit.

22

S toker...

The ride was the longest she'd ever taken with me, at pretty much a straight shot. We'd been taking long weekend rides, but no matter where we went, it wasn't the haul from south Florida to the lakeside lodge the Sacred Hearts' guys owned. By the time we'd ridden halfway, and stopped for snacks and something to drink, I could tell she was seriously starting to feel it.

At the lodge, we pulled down the steep drive to a line of bikes already parked and waiting for our arrival. We lined up and backed in, filling the little parking lot and drive loop out front the rest of the way out.

My little orchid got off the back of my bike and immediately put her hands to the top of her ass and pressed, arching back to alleviate her lower backache.

I heeled down the kickstand and shut off the motor, and asked her, "Doing alright?"

"Yeah! I think I'll feel better once I've gotten a shower, wash the grime off – you know?"

"Absolutely, I do, and I'm right there with you – that is, if we got a room. If not, we're camping."

"You got a room, I set it up ahead of time for you," Cutter called over. "Any man with a woman has a room unless she was dead set on campin'. We're getting too fuckin' old for tents and ground-sleepin'."

"Speak for yourself," Charity said as she walked by, with a wink. Galahad laughed and followed along behind her, their tent in his hands.

"Watch it, Blossom!" Hope warned her, and I had to chuckle. They had their Power Puff Girl's names embroidered on their rags, and it suited them.

We greeted the guys from the other club and chatted amicably while we waited for the front desk to sort us out with keys for our respective rooms. Some of the SHMC women were talking to Orchid and Faith off to one side, and it felt good that despite the fact she was thoroughly a citizen with a citizen's upbringing, she was taking pretty well and pretty quickly to our way of life.

It didn't hurt that she was unerringly polite. It just was who she was. She only dared to be sassy when it was just me and her alone and when she did bust out the sass, it was pretty spectacular. She could be funny as hell, when she wasn't so self-conscious and paranoid. It was something that, the more miles we'd poured on between us and Florida, she'd shed like a cloak.

"Hey, man! What's up? Long time, no see!"

Nox came striding over with his twin in tow and held out a hand. I clasped it and we tapped shoulders.

"Hey, Orchid. C'mere a minute!" I called.

"No shit?" Rush asked, when she headed our way.

"No shit," I affirmed with a reckless grin.

"What's up?" she asked lightly, tucking herself into my side.

"Want you to meet the twins. This is Nox and this is Rush, they're Sacred Hearts."

"Hi," she murmured timidly, and I could understand why. While Nox was tall and had a wiry build, Rush always looked like he was about to fuck something up. He was just an all-around built dude.

"Nice to meet you..." Rush trailed off so she could supply her name if she wanted to.

"Oh, it's Serenity," she said, taking his offered hand and shaking it lightly. "But everyone calls me Orchid now."

"Nice," Nox said. "How'd you come by that one?"

She smiled and said, "I raise them. I have a little greenhouse at home. Took a class in high school, horticulture, and fell in love with it. I've been growing them ever since."

She'd told me about her Horticulture teacher in the school they'd transferred her to. How he would let her hide in the greenhouses at lunch, let her disappear from the rest of the student's cruelty. Let her be herself, and taught her extra about the plants and about orchids specifically. He had been a spot of kindness, a light in the otherwise dark of her teenage existence.

I wanted to find the man and buy him several rounds of beers.

"Nice, mine was wood shop," Rush said and she smiled. "Build my own furniture and other things as a side gig now."

"That's awesome." Serenity smiled big.

"You guys got your room yet?" Nox asked.

I shook my head. "Not yet."

"You do," Charity said, sidling up and handing over a key. She winked at me and wandered back off. I hadn't even seen her come in from outside. It was supposed to be officers-only put up in the lodge, and I realized that she and Galahad had probably given up their room so we could take it. There were way more Sacred Hearts here than just their mother chapter. Every chapter from across the states were here, and I'd even heard they might be going international.

"Cool, thanks, Blossom!" I called out.

"Don't mention it!" she called back over her shoulder with a little wave.

"Staying inside, huh?" Rush asked.

"Yeah," I nodded.

"Let's go grab your shit," Nox said, and we did just that, packing in mine and Serenity's bags, giving her a chance to grab a quick shower and a change into some cooler clothes.

"Fancy a swim in the lake?" I asked, and she looked at me dubiously. I laughed and said, "No gators up here, Little Orchid."

"Leeches?" she asked.

"If there are, we've never encountered 'em," Rush said.

"Before we do, let's check and see if Maren and Bailey want in." Nox gestured for us to follow.

We went out of our room, didn't bother to lock the door, and left the key inside. We didn't have to worry about our shit being stolen with this crowd. No one wanted to be out bad for anything we'd brought with us.

We went out to the lake, found Nox and Rush's two women, and said hello to Trigger, Reaver, and Dragon along the way.

"Check it out, we got a blob this year!" Reaver crowed and sure enough, they were getting the giant inflatable going across the lake to where there was a high enough cliff face to jump off onto it from.

"Nice!" I called back.

We settled in on some giant, round inflatable air mattresses that were big enough to fit four or more people, with a well in the center for ice and cans of beer. The edges held built-in pillows to lean back into. I helped my little orchid down into one and she cuddled up against me as Rush and Nox pushed us out into the lake.

Maren cuddled up with Nox like Serenity cuddled into my side, and Rush and Bailey took up the other two slots as we bobbed out into the open water.

"Let the relaxation and good times commence," Rush declared, as 70s rock blared out over the lake from the back deck of the lodge.

"Fucking fantastic," I declared.

"So, how long you two been official?" Maren asked.

I looked down at my little orchid with her big, black, bug-eyed sunglasses covering most of her face and she answered, "Um, well, we met a few months ago at a show."

"What kind of show?" Bailey asked.

"My band was playing a 'Battle of the Bands' as a lead up to the main act," I said.

"My best friend Linny dragged me out. It ended up being a total shit show, except I got to meet Stoker."

"Nice, but when did you become *official* official?" Maren pressed.

"As in, my Ol' Lady, is what she's asking, babe."

"Oh!"

"Right before we hit the road to come out here is when I asked," I told her.

The twins exchanged a look and a silence fell over the raft. Orchid's hand tightened around mine.

"You know what happened ain't ever going to happen again, not with the likes of us, right?" Rush asked.

"Rush…" Nox cautioned his brother.

"No, it's all good, Nox," I said easily. "No disrespect meant or even implied, boys. I swear on my mamma's grave. This was what was right, what I wanted more than anything." I clutched Serenity into my side and dropped a kiss against the top of her hair. She sighed out happily, tension draining from her lithe small frame, and the boys visibly relaxed.

"Okay," Bailey said when the tension had dissipated almost completely, "so what made your first meet such a shit show, then?"

"Oh, God!" Serenity covered her face with her hand. "It was awful!"

I let her tell the story, because yeah, it had been awful, but it'd put her in my path. It'd put me right where I needed to be to score a chance with someone as selfless and beautiful as she was and as a result, I wouldn't change that night for anything except to maybe take away her pain… like she'd needed any more of it.

We drifted out into the lake, enjoyed some cold beers and soda from the raft, and chatted with Hossler, Lightning, and Reaver's boy when they paddle boarded by.

When the dinner bell rang, the three of us guys paddled us back to shore with the paddles strapped to the sides of the raft, tying up at the smaller dock over by the littler, fairytale-looking stone cottage on the property.

Serenity paused outside of it while the other two couples forged ahead and said, "It really needs a trellis and a climbing clematis vine there." She pointed to a too-empty expanse of cobblestone wall and I nodded.

"That'd be real pretty," I agreed. She sighed and I cocked my head. "What's wrong?"

"Nothing, I'm just not used to people-ing so hard, you know?"

"Let's get some food and if you want, we can always head back to the room, just you and me, anytime."

"I don't want to be rude–" she said, and I stopped her with a hand on her shoulder. I turned her to face me and gripped her shoulders lightly.

"Hey, look at me," I murmured. She looked up and chewed her bottom lip nervously.

"You want to go back to the room at any time tonight, you just squeeze my hand three times like this." I gave her shoulder three rapid but firm squeezes. "I'll make all the excuses. You just let me know. It's all good, baby. I want you to enjoy yourself, and part of that is not letting you get too overwhelmed."

She smiled and nodded. "Thank you. That honestly makes me feel loads better."

I figured it would. One of Marlin's pro-tips when it came to dealing with trauma – always have an out. He'd told me it was important for Faith to never feel trapped. After some of the things I'd gotten from Serenity, I realized that even though her situation was vastly different from Faith's, that it translated the same.

She couldn't handle feeling trapped or ridiculed, feeling put on the spot was bad juju and I couldn't blame her one bit. So… 'Always have an out.'

"I didn't think I'd gotten this bad," she confessed, her arm around my waist, mine around her shoulders as our flip-flops and sandals scuffed along the dirt path to the steps leading to the upper back deck of the lodge, where the food was.

"You're fine, I promise. I know it probably feels like you aren't, but it's not as bad as you think or as it probably feels – but how you feel is perfectly valid, given your circumstances."

She stared up at me and asked, "How are you so patient?"

I laughed a little. "I don't know. Ask anyone, it's never really been my strong suit. At least, not when it comes to the little shit that don't matter. You? You matter," I said, and bent to kiss her. She kissed me back, her lips curving into a smile as she melted into me and I loved that I could have that kind of effect on her.

We ate at a giant picnic table, the SHMC crew knocking it out of the park with some down-home country barbecue. Our table was a healthy mix of Kraken and Sacred Hearts with me and my woman and the VP, Dray, and his ol' lady taking up one end of the table.

The laughs were plenty, the jokes dirty, and the sun was well on its way down. Dusk settled over the party, the citronella tiki torches getting lit, and the bonfires down at the lake starting to smoke and catch.

"Thank you so much for all of this," Serenity told Dray when she found out his position in his club. She was gazing out toward the lake, past the winking flames of the citronella candles and torches along the paths and staked out in the flowerbeds.

"It's our pleasure," he said, and he sounded so much like his dad, the SHMC's president, I couldn't help but smile to myself over it.

We ended up by the fire, in a circle with mostly SHMC and their women. Dray and his woman, Everett. Trigger and Sunshine, along with Reaver and Doll. Reaver's son, Nox and Maren, and her little brother Sage. Of our crew, Cutter, Hope, Galahad, Charity, and Faith were there and I was just about to ask about Marlin, when my acoustic bass was passed in front of my face.

"Ha, ha! Yeah," I took it and Marlin stepped over the log my little orchid and I were leaning against.

It was cooling off, and Data came by with a stack of plaid throw blankets.

"Anyone need one?" he asked as I tuned up my rig.

"Yeah, man. Can you give one to my girl?" I asked.

He handed one down to Serenity, who took it with a soft thank you and wrapped it around her shoulders. She cast a grateful look in my direction for speaking up for her. I winked and Marlin put his cig between his lips and strummed his guitar.

"Lay somethin' down for me," he said, and I gave a nod, and heard someone say from the other fire "Oh, no shit? They gonna play?"

"Ya shut up, we will!" Marlin called out.

Truth be told, these times around the random fires, late at night, playing with Marlin or even just by myself were my favorite.

Don't get me wrong, I loved playing with my band but metal wasn't always my scene. These quiet moments were something else. Something good for the soul. Thrashing it out on stage was a great way to let off steam, to belt out some anger, let it out barreling into the world with all the force of a fuckin' freight train – but when I finished one of those shows I was exhausted, like I'd spent so much of myself.

This kind of playing, this music, did the exact opposite. This type of playing, this music, put something back.

"Ready when you are," he said and I nodded and knocked against the side of my rig, tapping out a pattern between knuckles and a slap of my fingers against the glossy black wood. I laid down some chords and kept at it until Marlin figured me out and could lay over my bassline.

The melody poured from us both, an impressive array, but him and me? We'd been doing this kind of shit for a while.

Pretty soon, people were laughing, suitably surprised or impressed, some body rockin' going on in their seats, and even some claps to keep the rhythm. What I wanted to see was what my little orchid thought, and that sight? Well, that was something else. Her eyes were closed, her face slack and at peace as she listened. It catapulted my heart straight into the stratosphere, I'm telling you.

We drank around the fire, played long into the night, and by the time we decided enough was enough, my little orchid was sound asleep, leaned back against the log, cuddled in her blanket.

"Hey, somebody take this and follow me up so I can take her?" I asked.

"Yeah, brother. I got you." Trigger got up, and Sunshine rose like her namesake from the ground, her sunny disposition a little ragged around the edges.

"I'll meet you back at the cabin if that's alright, baby?"

"Yeah, yeah!" he said and kissed her quickly. "Have Reaver walk you along with Doll," he said.

"I got 'em, bro," Reaver said, helping his woman to her feet.

"Thanks."

Trig reached out and took my bass from me and I gave a nod. Serenity sucked in a sharp breath and jolted, her arms going around my neck and shoulders as I lifted her. She was barely a buck and some change, and I was used to holding up more on the regular in my line of work. Still, I couldn't do it forever, and I was glad the lodge wasn't too far.

I set off in that direction and she laughed and said, "Put me down before you hurt yourself."

"Not on your life, babe," I said and I meant it.

I would never let her go.

23

*S*erenity…

I slept like the dead, safe and warm and loved in Stoker's arms, and the next morning, at breakfast, the Sacred Heart nicknamed Reaver and his wife approached us, along with Cutter and Hope.

"Hey!" Reaver dropped down onto the bench beside me and I slightly leaned away from him into Stoker. There was something about him that bothered me, and something more that made me immediately feel guilty about it. I mean, he was a genuinely nice and funny guy. Just, something about a coldness in his gaze told me there wasn't something quite right with him and I'd glimpsed scars on him when he'd been wandering around shirtless, in just his leather vest, the day before that told me he was absolutely no stranger to violence.

"What's up?" Stoker asked him over my head.

"Heading on out for a ride to go check out some waterfalls," Cutter said. "Wanted to know if you wanted to come along."

"That sounds wonderful, actually," I said looking forward to a slight break from all of the people.

"Excellent!" Reaver crowed and tousled my hair. I jerked back from under his hand with a slightly offended laugh and he bounded up. Stoker smiled at me and I smiled back, and he gave a nod.

"Just give us a bit to finish up our breakfast and change clothes and meet us out at the bikes," Cutter said.

"You've got it, Captain."

"I'll have Contessa pack us up a picnic lunch," Doll said.

"Ooo! Good idea, baby!" Reaver kissed his woman, Hope winked at me over her sunglasses, and the four of them melted off into the crowd while I finished my sausage, eggs, and fruit a bit more quickly than I should have.

"Slow down there! They'll wait fer yah." Dragon, the president of the Sacred Hearts mother chapter was kind in his admonishment, but I still blushed.

"Too late now," I said, smiling. "I'm done."

He chuckled and tapped the filter of a fresh cigarette against the rest of his pack. "Keep the shiny side up, my friend," he told Stoker, and Stoker gave him a nod.

"Will do, thanks."

I was kind of in awe. If only our leaders and politicians acted like the leaders of these clubs who clearly cared about every individual, the world would be a much better place.

We went in and changed, I braided my hair over my shoulder, and Stoker smiled over at me as he pulled on his scuffed motorcycle boots and adjusted the cuffs of his jeans over the top.

"You ready?" he asked.

"Just about."

I sat down on the edge of the bed beside him and pulled on my own boots, a pair of laced boots I'd had in the back of my closet and not nearly as well-made as the riding-specific boots he owned, but service-able. I laced them up and tied them tight so the laces wouldn't come loose and stood up. He got up and held my jacket – again a much cheaper knock-off – with my new leather vest over it. I shrugged into it all and turned around, running into a surprise kiss.

"Mm, what was that for?" I asked.

"Because I love you," he murmured.

I smiled. "I love you, too."

"Glad to hear it, baby. You ready now?"

"I am."

"Okay, let's go."

We spent the day on a sunshine-filled ride, the wind whipping all cares or worries away. Hope rode double with Cutter this time as we wound our way on scenic highways and byways on a loop of waterfall exploration.

Let me tell you, these weren't anything like the waterfalls in Florida. The waterfalls in Florida were barely a trickle by comparison. We picnicked on a big blanket near one of them, which is where I learned about Cutter and Reaver's propensity for knives as well as that the entire trip had been staged for my benefit – that part of the fun for these guys was target shooting back at the lodge, and rather than place me near the gunfire, they'd opted for this day-trip so everyone could be satisfied.

I couldn't be upset about it. In fact, I couldn't believe they had gone so far out of their way for my benefit. I may have even teared up a little.

"Aw, don't cry!" Doll had hugged me and Hope had shaken her head a bit ruefully.

"You've got a family now, Orchid. Better get used to it."

It was more than a bit of a foreign concept.

I'd been a mistake. My mother had, for the most part, been a working-poor single mother. I'd been a welfare baby, had been mostly in charge of taking care of myself starting when I was seven. I mean, from seven to nine I was a latchkey kid while my mother worked shifts at the local WalMart.

Then she met Daryl. He'd moved in, and let me tell you, he'd never had a problem telling me what a drain, what a waste I was.

I left school bullied and generally beat down, only to go home and suffer through it some more. I was living proof that words sometimes could hurt more than a rock or a fist. I don't honestly know how I held my shit together, how I hadn't attempted suicide or something.

Yes, you do.

Kyle.

Kyle, and then Linny.

"As long as it's how families are supposed to work," I said, "then I'm on board."

Cutter shook his head and asked me, "Just what happened to you, anyway?"

"Shitty home life," I said with a shrug. "Shittier school life. Kids are assholes," I said and didn't want to expand much beyond that.

"It's cool," he said. "You ain't gotta tell us shit. We all got our pasts and secret pains. Just know that with us, you ain't gotta hide it. You really do just get to be you."

"I am," I said with a smile. "There's really not much to me."

"Now, that is a damn lie," Stoker said and pulled me into his side, smacking a kiss to my forehead. Everyone laughed and I laughed too, but I honestly didn't see it or understand it. There really wasn't anything to me that I saw.

"Someone mentioned you were in a school shooting, that's why the little road trip – what was that like?"

"Reaver!" Doll slapped him in the chest, but he didn't move, just kept that unsettling, still gaze on me.

"Awful, and no offense, it's not something I talk about," I said shifting uncomfortably.

"I'm sure Reave didn't mean anything by it, sugar. What I think he meant to say was if you ever need to talk about it, any one of us is around to listen. Doesn't do well to bottle things like that up," Cutter said, stretching.

"He's right, on all accounts," Hope said.

I nodded.

"No, I know, I just don't talk about it and would really rather not – like ever, if I can avoid it. It's too painful."

"Alright, you guys," Stoker came to the rescue.

Doll jumped in to help.

"It's totally time for a change of subject," she said, and just like that, the subject changed to the fights that were supposed to happen that night.

As in fist fights between the guys. I was pretty sure Hope was the only female just as enthusiastic about it. I understood things like boxing and televised MMA fighting, but just randomly beating the crap out of someone that was supposed to be your brother?

"See, I don't get it," I said, laughing. "Maybe it's lost on me because I never had any siblings."

"Probably," Reaver agreed, bobbing his head like a bobble-head doll. I laughed and he winked at me. I could recognize a certain kind of broken in him. He had a driving need to be liked by everyone around him and used comedic action to that end. I recognized it, because I felt the same driving need to be liked, I just went about it a different way. By being useful, by trying to remain unobtrusive.

I had a lot of food for thought on the ride back to the lodge. Stoker checked me regularly in the side-view mirror, reaching back to squeeze my knee affectionately. I smiled for him, but I would like to talk… to him. It was no offense to anyone else in his club. I was just far more comfortable with Stoker, which considering how intimate we were, only made sense.

I took a long time to warm up to people, to trust them. While I loved Faith and Charity, I was intimidated by Hope, and to some degree, Hossler, too. Everyone with the SHMC I just plain didn't know well enough to spill my deepest darkest secrets. That, and merely talking about them seriously felt like complaining, and I had learned early on, complaining about things didn't get you anywhere, so why do it?

When we got back to the lodge, it was just as dinner was about to start. Lunch had been a while ago and I could eat, so that's precisely what we all did; went in and changed into cooler clothing and went out to the back deck to load some plates.

Everyone was in good spirits when we returned and there was a bunch of chatter about Trigger 'doing it again', and a bunch of guys from both clubs congratulating him for it.

I just ate quietly beside Stoker, my mind still turning thoughts and interactions from earlier in the day over and over.

I mean, I knew I needed intensive therapy. The only problem was any mental health services I would need were too far out of reach for me. It'd helped, the times I'd gone when the services had been available right after – well… right after. But, then I'd been transferred, and those services were for Rachel Alice Morgan students at Rachel Alice Morgan… I wasn't *at* Rachel Alice Morgan anymore, so I had slipped through the cracks.

My family was working poor and didn't have the luxury of medical insurance. Nor did I really have the luxury of it now. I mean, I lost a good portion of my wages to have it, but the deductible was so high on it, it wasn't like I could ever really use it. In fact, it would have been cheaper to incur the tax-time penalties every year than have it. At least for a while.

I was in that subsection of Americans that suffered rather than benefited from the Affordable Care Act, but I couldn't fault the government that had implemented it. They really were trying to help, at least I liked to think so, and I also liked to think that someday they would come up with something better that worked better for people like me.

Again, there wasn't any use complaining about it. It just was what it was, had to be accepted, and I had to move on and make the best of what I did have.

I was a pro at that, or so I thought.

I was in the kitchen of the lodge, bringing in one of the big, mostly empty potato salad bowls, trying to be useful and bring things in from outside when it happened.

Boom!

I froze, and it was like a scene from a movie inside my own head. The kitchen wavered, the expensive tile floor, the no-slip matting shifting and disappearing, replaced by flat linoleum that sparkled with polish under the overhead fluorescent lighting.

I heard it again – *Boom!* Only this time I wasn't at the lodge anymore.

My mind had taken me right back to Rachel Alice Morgan's halls. To people running, the emergency exit chained shut – fuck! I panicked. I took a deep breath, then another one before the first had been completely exhaled. The urgency there, the flight instinct in full swing.

Okay, out. I have to get out.

But I wasn't there, and somehow in the back of my mind I knew I wasn't, and even though, in my memories my feet traveled forward, I felt myself sink to the floor in this cognitive dissonance of both being aware and totally unaware at the same time that you're not really there.

I couldn't stop it, though. My mind had me trapped on this hellride of having to bear witness to everything I tried to keep locked away in the overflowing vault of bad memories, and bad waking dreams of 'shit I lived through.'

Down the hall, through the open fire doors, take a left, down the next hall – Boom! Was that closer or further away?

I picked up my pace, I was running now, running even though it felt like someone held me still. Terrified tears ran down my face as I made the worst decision and even though my mind screamed silently, no, no, no, no, No! Don't go in there! I did... I went through the doors leading into the cafeteria and froze.

She was lying on her side. Caroline. Caroline Caruthers, in the midst of all that shiny linoleum, the dark stain of her blood seeping across it. Wrong all wrong. Her blue eyes sightless and staring, her face gore-flecked from the blowback of the gaping wound in the center of her chest where her heart should be, but was just raw meat.

I retched and looked up into the ice cold gaze of...

"Kyle?"

I whimpered.

He smiled at me, and his gaze warmed and I couldn't understand... He racked the sawed-off shotgun between his hands and I jumped. He smiled at me like he held all the power, and he did...

"I did it for you," he said, and he looked so little-boy-proud at his accomplishment.

He stepped toward me and I stepped back, asking, horrified, "What have you done?"

"Made it so these fucksticks know who's in charge! Made it so these fucking animals can never hurt you again!" he shouted, and I cringed.

I couldn't keep the horror, the terror, off of my face and Kyle's face pinched in anger as he screamed at me, "Don't look at me that way!

You're supposed to be happy! I did this for you! I did this all for you! Come on now, Serenity!"

He took a step forward, I took a hurried step back, and his face contorted into a sort of agony.

"Kyle, don't," I begged, but it was too late, he pressed the barrel of the shotgun under his chin.

"Kyle, don't!" I screamed and BOOM!

Oh, my God, his face! His face vaporized into near-nothing, his body falling as I fell to my own knees, screaming, screaming over and over, wordless, panicked, soulless as everything I was was hollowed out of my center, splashed across the linoleum floor along with Caroline and Kyle's blood which seeped into the holey knees of my jeans as I crossed my arms over my chest and tried to hold myself together.

24

*S*toker…
   Boom!

"What the fuck?" My head jerked up from the table we were sitting at and I exchanged a look with Nox and Rush.

Boom!

"Fuck," I swore. "Serenity, where's Serenity!" I cried.

Hope called out, "I saw her head towards the kitchen."

"Somebody get those assholes to stop!" Rush bellowed, and I practically vaulted the picnic table and crossed the stone patio in two long strides, my feet barely touching the ground. I batted the screen door aside and flung myself into the downstairs of the lodge, going for the stairs.

"Kitchen!" I screamed, and one of the staff busboy and kitchen-prep guys pointed, his eyes wide.

I got into the kitchen to a goddamned mess. Contessa, the woman who ran the place, was sitting on the floor, holding onto Serenity who was terrified, her eyes wide, her face slack and stunned as her dark eyes saw what wasn't here.

"Shit," I muttered, and got down on the floor in the midst of broken plastic bowl and potato salad, snapping my fingers in front of her eyes.

"Orchid?" I asked, and she didn't even fucking blink.

She just said in a dreamy, disconnected voice, "Kyle?"

She struggled in Contessa's grasp, but Contessa had a good hold of her as she said with urgency, "Kyle, don't!" and a second later, more forcefully, "Kyle, don't!" and then all hell broke loose.

She collapsed on herself, screaming, and it was as if someone had reached into her chest and she'd had her heart ripped out. I'd never heard anything like it before, and I never wanted to hear anything like it again. Contessa struggled with her as Serenity thrashed and thrashed against the floor, kicking her legs out, sliding in the spilled food, the smell of mustard sharp as I reached for her and ordered Contessa over Serenity's shrieking, "Give her to me!"

Contessa let her go and Serenity flopped but not before I grabbed her wrists and pulled her tight against my chest, slipping in the potato salad, going down hard on my ass, pulling her between my legs, wrapping my whole body around her as she screamed and screamed, her heart breaking in real time from something that'd happened ten years ago.

Flashback, this had to be a flashback, and rescue came in the form of Doc, the SHMC's on-call physician with his old-school medical bag, thrusting his way through kitchen staff onlookers and ol' ladies that'd been helping with the dinner cleanup.

"Hold her good, now!" he yelled over her screams and brought out a needle and a vial.

"What is that?" I demanded.

"Benzos," he replied, drawing up a dose. "Put her right out for some hours, keep her from hurting herself."

He raised her skirt and shot her right in the butt with it and she almost immediately calmed.

"S'okay, baby. I got you, baby," I murmured into her hair and she whimpered ineffectually.

"Come on now, let's get you both up," he said.

The silence in the kitchen aside from our labored breathing was so bizarrely loud. I don't know, it was the only way to describe it. We got

Serenity up between us and over to a spot it was easy for me to pick her up.

"I'll come help," Faith murmured and she looked heartbroken for my woman, which made sense. I knew what it was the instant I'd seen my little orchid thrashing on the ground. I'd seen it before, knew what it was, thanks to Faith. She had her own set of triggers and had gone into a flashback of her own at one of our beach parties at something a tourist had said to her. Some kind of phrase he just happened to utter the right – or wrong – way had set her off.

"Thanks, Doc," I said, and he shook his head.

"Go on, now. You take care of your girl while we take care of our own." He scowled and I had a feeling somebody was going to get their ass beat and Doc would be doing a different type of needle work in the next couple of hours.

"Don't hold back," I called over my shoulder, adding, "and don't feel like you need to wait on me." I had better things to do than handle the justice side of things for this level of disrespect.

I'd told Cutter that I'd planned on taking Serenity for a ride, had told him we didn't want any special accommodations, just to let me know when the shooting was supposed to begin and I'd get us out of there before it started. He'd reached out through Data to Dragon to make sure I was set, and when Dragon had learned the why of it, he'd taken it upon himself to be a good host and put a moratorium on shooting this go. It was supposed to only be between the hours of X and X, and somebody had defied him. At the very least, there was going to be a major ass whoopin'.

Faith helped me clean Serenity up; she was limp as a rag doll, but conscious. Sort of. Her dark eyes leaked tears, the occasional whimper escaping her lips as the drug worked its way through her system.

"She gonna be okay?" I asked, worried, and Faith smiled, petting her hair as I wet a washcloth in our little bathroom to start working on getting the potato salad off her feet and legs. Faith nodded and sat on the floor with Serenity's head in her lap.

"She'll be okay. She'll sleep, and wake up feeling like shit, but she'll be alright. Embarrassed more than anything, I'm sure." She hung her head and hid behind her blonde hair before saying, "I always am."

I opened my mouth to tell her she didn't have anything to be embarrassed about, but that's when Marlin stuck his head in the open door to our room and said, "There you are, everything good?"

Faith smiled at her man and nodded. "It will be, given some time," she said softly.

"Need some help?" he asked.

I shook my head.

"Naw, I got it, man. What happened?"

"Drunk motherfuckers from the Alabama chapter," he answered.

"Why's it always gotta be 'Bama?" I asked rhetorically.

"At least it's not Florida this time," Faith said with an impish smile and a roll of her eyes and I cracked a grin. In that moment she looked so much like her youngest, but most responsible sister out of the three of them, Charity.

"Be my eyes and ears, man?" I asked Marlin, and he threw me some chin.

"You got it, bro."

That's what I loved about our club. He may have been the VP, but I was the wronged party according to most club's charters. So, in this moment, it wasn't out of pocket for me to ask someone considered my superior in the hierarchy to hook me, and help me out with something a citizen would perceive as menial or bitch-work that I should be doing myself.

I had more important things to do right now, which is exactly what I thought, looking down at Serenity as we got all the potato salad off her skin and I got her out of her slaughtered clothes and into one of my tee shirts to cover her. We got her tucked into the bed, and Faith sat with her, my woman's head settled onto a pillow in Faith's lap, while she smoothed back my girl's hair, almost petting her, comforting. Something a mother would do for her frightened child.

Faith was honestly the expert in this arena, having gone through it more than any of us.

"Go," Faith murmured. "I know you want to stay, but…"

"Yeah. Respect," I muttered.

It was all right for Marlin to hold my place and be my eyes and ears for a while, but Serenity was my woman, my property, and so I needed to go out there and see this through. Not just for her, but for my own club. Respect is earned, not given, among our kind, and the outlaw code must be upheld. I needed to get out there and deal with these assholes myself. Or at least be a part of the proceedings.

I went to her, caressed her cheek and kissed her brow. She was out. The drug had taken effect quickly, sucking her under and into the temporary peace of oblivion.

I hurt for her. I had some guesses as to what her words and actions had summed up to back in the kitchen and I didn't like it. I didn't want to jump to any conclusions, but it gnawed at my insides just the same.

I went out to deal with what I could; the stupid asshairs that'd caused her distress. Once they were dealt with, I could have a beer, calm down myself, and wait for her to come out of it so we could talk. If she would talk. I hoped she would. She couldn't carry this burden by herself anymore and she shouldn't have to. Not after this long.

I went out down to the lakeshore where Dragon, Cutter, and, I think, the president of the chapter whose boys had fucked up, were arguing.

"Who damaged my property?" I demanded, and the presidents all three looked up and over.

"Well, there you have it," Dragon said.

"Come off it, D! –" The man whose cut read 'Toe Beans' shut up when Dragon raised a hand indicating he didn't want to hear it.

"His property, his call, Beans."

"I want their asses whooped, question is who's doing it? Me, his crew, the enforcers…" I trailed off and waited expectantly for an answer.

"All you, buddy," Cutter said. "Figured you'd want a personal touch."

"Damn right I want to put the personal touch on this," I grated.

The two dumbasses, Retch and Baltimore, stood nearby, a little glassy-eyed from whatever drunk or high they were on. Retch smirked at me, which just served to piss me off more.

"Look man, no disrespect was intended. Are they dumbasses? Sure. Did they fuck up?"

I didn't let him finish. "Oh, hell, yeah, they most definitely did."

"What's your bitch's problem, anyway?" Retch asked, swaying on his feet.

"No disrespect, huh?" I asked, arching a brow at their president.

He sighed, his shoulders sagging, and he looked at his two men.

"I tried, but you fuckin' knuckleheads just couldn't keep your damn mouths shut, could you?" he demanded. He grunted in dismay and turned back to me. "They're all yours."

Dragon was taking Toe Beans aside and saying, "Listen, I can appreciate you going to bat for your boys, but sometimes only lesson to be learned is a lesson learned in blood…"

And ho boy, I was gonna make Retch, at least, bleed. Baltimore wisely kept his mouth shut and didn't have fuck-all to say except, "I'm sorry man. I didn't know it would go down like that."

'Like that'… not 'like this'. It wasn't lost on me he was genuinely sorry for my little orchid's suffering, not worried about his own. Still, by the look in Cutter's eye, there wouldn't be any going easy on either of them. We had a rep to uphold; the Kraken weren't soft when it counted.

"You boys take your ass-whoopin' now. Trig, Reave, get their hands."

Impressive. Dragon wasn't fuckin' around. This wasn't a fight, this was a lesson, so handcuffs came out from somewhere and they hooked up Retch and Baltimore behind their backs so they couldn't throw down. They just had to take what I was giving.

Baltimore, I let off easy, with just a few punches to his face. Enough to bleed him and get him off his feet. Enough to leave a reminder any time he looked in a mirror for the next couple of weeks.

I beat the shit out of Retch. Not only would he have a reminder every time he looked in the mirror for the next week, he'd be fuckin' feeling that reminder every day of it, too.

Their chapter buddies hauled them off to their tents, Doc trailing along behind to help get 'em cleaned up and stitched if they needed it. I busted Retch's eyebrow open pretty good, he might need a stitch or two. I think Baltimore fared better, but he was bleeding pretty good from his nose.

"Good job," Cutter said with a nod, clapping me on the back. "Let's grab a beer and some ice for that hand." I nodded and shook the offending hand out, the knuckles scraped and bloody, two of them swelling. Gideon was gonna be pissed if it affected my playing. I needed to ice it, and keep it from getting stiff with some practice.

Faith appeared at my elbow as I was wrapping a bandanna full of ice from one of the coolers around my hand.

"She's out," she murmured.

"Thanks for sitting with her," I said.

"Sure, anything else I can do, just let me know."

"Actually, can you grab my bass from the room for me?"

"Sure." She drifted over to Marlin for a quick kiss before she floated off in that way she had to do what I asked. I raised my beer in his direction, a salute to his woman, and he threw me some chin.

Later, two beers in and chilling by the fire, I was silently walking my battered hand through chords to keep it limber.

"Sounds to me she's got some real issues. You sure you're game to handle all that comes with?"

I stared at Dragon, who had spoken from across the fire and kept my trap shut. From what I gathered, he was the kind of guy that, when he spoke, you should listen. I was listening.

"She ain't a puppy, or a new pet. She is as her name implies," he said. "Orchids take a lot of care, the right conditions, to grow and bloom proper. Are you sure the MC conditions, that this life, has what she needs to thrive?"

I raised my eyebrows as I let my fingers continue to walk up and down the frets on my acoustic bass. Cutter looked from Dragon, to me and waited me out.

"I know that after today, it may not seem like it," I said with a heavy sigh, "but, hell, yeah. Citizens been letting her down for her whole life. We're something different. We understand loyalty, we get brotherhood and we don't give up. If I give up on her now, how am I any better than any of the people that have come before? Short answer is, I wouldn't be. So I'ma stay the course."

"My man." Cutter nodded and glowed with pride, and I gave him a nod.

"You got a good man, there," Dragon said, nodding in agreement.

I could see I'd passed whatever test. I didn't much like being tested. I wasn't a fuckin' hang-around green recruit. I wasn't a fuckin' prospect. I'd earned my goddamned patch a long time ago. My indignation was tempered, though, by the fact that, clearly, my captain, and Dragon and his crew, had my lady's best interests at heart.

"Thank you kindly, Dragon," Cutter replied and he looked back at me. "I surely do."

I threw my captain some chin and he inclined his head. I was about to say thanks, but Serenity's melodic voice permeated the dark outside the ring of light thrown by the campfire.

"Stoker?"

"Oh, shit, hey, babe." I handed my bass off to Marlin sitting nearby and he took it from me, no questions asked. I got up as she stepped slightly more into the light where she could be seen. She looked small in my oversized tee, wrapped in the throw from yesterday.

"You doing okay?" I asked, cupping her elbows.

"Can we talk?" she asked timidly, her dark eyes troubled, a storm of emotion behind them.

I nodded. "Yeah, come on." I took her gently and steered her back in the direction of the lodge. When we were alone, walking back to our room, I asked her, "How are you feeling?"

"Awful," she replied, and the way she held herself was stiff as we walked down the carpeted corridor.

"Can you expand on that a little?" I asked, and tried a gentle smile on her.

She looked up at me, a quick, solemn glance and said, "Head feels funny."

"Doc put a sedative in you. He's a real-life doctor and has helped Faith in the past, so I trusted him to do right by you, or I wouldn't have let him," I said.

"I-I-I don't know what happened. One minute I was in the kitchen, and the next thing I knew I was back in the school, in the hallway, hearing the booms and running…" She trailed off and stopped outside our room's door, gazing up the hallway helplessly.

I waited her out, waited to see what she would say or what she would do next and when nothing came for several strings of silent heartbeats, I broke first.

"Talk to me, baby," I breathed quietly into the hallway.

Her dark eyes, so full of pain, flicked to mine.

"He was in the cafeteria… I watched him die. He killed himself because of me."

Her face crumpled and she broke down. I pulled her tight against the shelter of my body and smoothed a hand over her back, crooning into her dark hair.

"Shh, it's okay. I've got you, now."

"It's not okay," she cried. "It will never be okay. It's all my fault. I couldn't pretend, I couldn't keep the horror off my face and he saw it and he killed himself right in front of me. Turned the shotgun on himself and – oh, God! I loved him so much and I didn't know! I should have known, but I didn't know!"

What do you do when the person you love the most let's out a piercing cry like that? When she lets out the sound of their heart disintegrating, right in front of you?

I didn't know what to do, all I knew is that I hurt for her. I hurt with her, and I didn't know what to do either, but I ran on pure instinct. I held her. I let her cry, and I let us both into the shelter of our room to keep her away from any curious onlookers coming to see what the noise was, or who might be heading for their own rooms.

I shut the door behind us and took her by the arms, taking a step back, making her look at me.

"Nothing he did was your fault," I spoke clearly.

She shook her head violently. "He said he did it for me…"

"Be that as it may, just because somebody does something for you doesn't mean that it's your Huckleberry, Orchid. He did it for him, he did it in spite of you. If he'd asked if it was what you wanted, what would you have said?"

"No!" she cried.

"Exactly," I gave her a little shake. "I love you, babe. I love you, and I'm telling you, you've gotta let that shit go. I know, it's easier said than done, but you can't carry the responsibility of his monumentally shitty actions on your shoulders anymore."

She sniffed, and stared at me with wide dark eyes, her tear-stained face lovely in the muted lamplight from the room's bedside table.

"It's not your fault. It's super shitty, it sucks hairy balls, but it was never your fault."

"It still hurts," she whimpered, and I nodded.

"I know. I get that." I pulled her in and held her close and sighed. "I want to help you, but I don't know how," I said.

"I don't know either," she said brokenly.

"We'll figure it out," I promised her and she sank into me a little. I guess it was the right thing to say, and to be honest, it was the stone-cold truth. I would help her figure it out. I would work on the problem with her until the end of our fucking days if that was what it took.

"I don't want to drag you into this," she said thickly.

"Into what?" I demanded.

"This," she said, stepping back and bringing my scraped and swollen hand up between us, cradling it gently between her own. She shook her head and murmured, "Where I come from, in my experience, fighting back and standing up for yourself only makes things worse."

"Yeah," I whispered, swallowing hard. "I bet you never hit 'em, though, did you?"

"No, I'm not a violent person."

"I'm not either, babe. Believe me. There are just some things you cannot let pass in this life. Disrespecting my property is one of them." I cradled her face in the palm of my hand, smoothing my thumb against the soft skin of her cheek.

I took a breath, paused, and finally said, "This? This was only half you. I had no problem beating the brakes off of one of them – the other I let off easy. This, is mostly my life, the MC life. This is how you settle things with violence. Honorably. You don't pick up a gun unless it's necessary. You don't blow away women or innocent bystanders because of some words. You punch them in the mouth, make them swallow their hate and you walk away. I guaran-damn-tee they won't fucking do it again."

I swallowed hard when she didn't say anything right away. Her eyes flicked up to mine then back to my hand, and I made her a vow. "Anyone wants to fuck with you, they have to go through me, and by extension, the rest of the club. They aren't so tough when they realize someone'll beat their ass for it. Just… just don't give up on us yet."

She gasped and lifted her eyes from my injured hand to meet mine.

"I don't want to give up on us. I'm terrified you won't want me anymore. When my problems get to be too many, when defending me gets too tiresome – what then?"

"Never," I said, and I didn't let anything about the single word leave room for argument. Not my tone, inflection, nothing.

I kissed her then, sealing the deal. When words failed me, actions spoke loudest and I poured every ounce of commitment to her that I felt into that kiss. She made a surprised noise against my lips and I pulled her closer. She came to me willingly, dropping the throw she'd had around her shoulders to the floor, her arms going up and around my neck. I gripped her ass beneath the hem of the tee I'd put her in and pulled her against me harder. She gasped at my erection pressing against her stomach through my board shorts, the sound killing me with desire.

"I need to love you," I growled against her mouth. "Please say yes, that you're good for it."

"Yes," she gasped breathlessly as I trailed my mouth down the side of her neck.

Awesome.

I lifted the hem of the tee and she let me go just long enough for me to pull it over her head and off her arms, dropping it to the floor. She came back to me, pressing herself against me, her kiss desperate, and her touch demanding as she went for the drawstring on my shorts.

While she worked that, I slid out of my cut and gave it a gentle toss to the chair in the corner of the room, eyeing it carefully, satisfied when it pooled in the seat and didn't slip off to the floor.

I went back to kissing my woman as she shoved my shorts to the floor. I stepped out of them and my thongs as she pressed herself against me with a strained half-whimper, half-moan.

She tore her mouth from mine and gasped out, "Condom?"

"Always. I got you baby," I murmured into her mouth and it struck me – every time we had sex, she asked for one. Every time, without fail. I filed it away for later and snatched a condom out of the drawer of the bedside table, smirking that I'd put them on top of the typical hotel room Bible.

Sacri-licious, I thought to myself as my ol' lady practically climbed my body like a fucking tree to get close to me.

"You good to ride me?" I asked, tearing the plastic wrapper open with my teeth.

She plucked the condom free and stroked me with her other hand.

"Yeah," she breathed.

"Yeah?"

"Yeah," she affirmed, and I smiled as she rolled the condom down my length.

I shuddered. It felt so damn good already. Her hands on me, the rubber slick and smooth against my flesh. She made rolling on a rubber a damn sensual thing, but I craved the sensuality that was watching her lower herself onto my waiting cock. I craved the silken pleasure of my hands on her warm flesh, guiding her up and down over the top of me, my cock driving deep into her wet heat.

I lay back with anticipation as she lowered herself onto my cock, her hands behind her head, holding her thick dark hair off of her neck in an artful pile as she rolled her hips and took us both on a natural, pleasure filled high.

"That's it, Orchid. Oh, so good…" I encouraged her softly, my eyes closing as I gave myself over completely to just feeling her body wrapped around mine, weighing me down, a comfortable weight, one I was glad to have in my life.

"Stoker," she gasped and I smiled up at her, watching her take her pleasure above me.

Such a beautiful sight.

25

*S*erenity…

I felt like I was on some invisible edge, but not the kind that would send me into the shining fall of orgasm. That was some ways off yet. No, this edge that I rode was made up purely of my own mind playing devilish tricks on me. It was whispers in the dark that made frightened children hide beneath their blankets – though these whispers were of some very adult fears.

He's lying, he's going to take you back home and he's going to make every excuse not to see you again. He can't love you. You can't even love yourself… this is over before it even got started.

He felt so good inside me, and all I felt was raw. I was emotionally blasted open, the fragments of my heart still raining down from the violent re-visitation of my worst trauma. I would do anything to erase it, even for just a little while. I was desperate to feel something, anything, other than the angry throbbing hurt of losing my first love and my utter guilt at my inability to stop loving him, even after what he'd done.

I wanted to feel something, anything, other than the fear that, just as I had dared to fall in love again, Stoker might leave me. That fear stung like cold fire against nerves I didn't even know I possessed.

"That's it, Orchid. Oh, so good…" He moaned and his eyes fluttered shut. I couldn't help but smile, my eyes roving his face, his shoulders and chest, memorizing this moment, the sight of him in silent supplication below me, his hands urging me to roll my hips the way that I knew we both liked. The way that touched that spot deep inside me and urged me high enough to reach the stars.

I wasn't ready to come yet, though. I wanted to make this last. I wanted it to last forever. I never wanted to go back to the girl I was. I wanted so badly to escape the suffocation of my life before Stoker, but I didn't want to suffocate him in turn. I was so twisted and torn, and I didn't know what to do and I didn't want to think about it – I shouldn't be thinking about it. Not now, not while I was so emotional, but it was just about impossible to think about anything else.

His hands drifted up my body, cupped my breasts, squeezed my nipples between forefinger and thumb, pulling on them gently, stimulating me further. I dropped my long thick locks and put my hands to his chest and rolled my hips like we both liked. My body felt lit, sparks of light and sexual energy surging, kindled low in my belly, just below my womb and swirling up through me, reaching for the sky.

I rolled my hips again, and my emotions rolled with the motion, roiling and swirling in a somersault, as though they were a drop of ink dripped into a glass of water, slowly dispersing, coloring my insides, becoming less concentrated the more the fire built inside me, seeping out of my pores, slicking my body with sweat, the air cooling my skin, the hurt evaporating with every slow arduous roll, with every deepening thrust of his body into mine.

It was as if the higher I went, the more I came down. Stoker's touch, his love grounded me, giving me a safe place to stay, encouraging me to stay.

His eyes said 'Trust me', his hands told me, 'I'm here', and his soft gasp as I loved him begged me not to go anywhere, begged me to stay with him, and lent me the strength and determination to do just that. To stay, to fight, to take a stand, and to believe that my life could get better, that the past could be let go.

"God, Orchid, you feel so good. The things you fucking do to me…" he whispered, and I glowed from the praise. I felt invincible in these moments, impervious, like the love we created between us acted as a shield, and the hurt, the constant sorrowful ache, subsided within me and fell quiescent.

He calmed me. He grounded and centered me, and I only wished that I did something for him in turn, but I could never be certain.

I bent and kissed him, his hands going to my ass, holding me tight as he thrust his hips up and took over for a while, letting me rest but leaving me breathless.

"Don't stop!" I begged when he paused. He sat up abruptly and I yelped in surprise, but he wasn't done with me. Not yet. No, he was just getting started. He rolled me onto my back, my thigh bone feeling like it would surely break for just a split second, when he turned me. His arm an iron cable across my lower back, he laid me into the softness of the bed, his hands going to the outsides of my knees, hauling them up, encouraging me to wrap my legs around his lean hips.

His fingers found the spaces between mine, curling over the backs of my hands as he played his lips softly against mine. He pressed his palms against mine, my hands into the bed and rolled his hips, carefully withdrawing and surging forward, and I fell.

I fell far, far away, down, down, and further down, dropping from the starlit sky clutching the ethereal stardust that was Stoker to my breast. Stoker, who stroked his long, lean body against mine, into mine. Stoker, who made me hope so dangerously that my life could, would, change and for the better.

"I love you, Serenity," he whispered in my ear and a new, fresh set of tears sprang to my eyes, but there was no pain where they came from. When I was like this, when we were like this, there was no pain. There was no bad here…

A short time later, after we were both sated and when my tears had dried, we lay quietly in each other's arms, drowsing under the light of the moon pouring through the bedroom's window.

He had turned out the light, and come back to bed and I was almost lulled to sleep completely by the comfortable silence when unexpectedly, he asked me, "Why do you always ask me to put on a condom before we have sex?"

I paused and thought about it. I mean, really thought about it. I hadn't realized I did.

"Do I?" I asked finally, frowning, not wanting to believe it, worried I had been doing something off-putting.

"Every time," he affirmed, hugging me close, pressing a kiss to the top of my head.

"I didn't realize I was doing that," I said, honestly.

"Why do you think you do?" he asked, and it deserved an answer. He deserved everything just for staying with me.

"Control, maybe?" I hazarded a guess.

"Interesting conclusion," he said, and sniffed, clearing his throat. "Why'd you land on that one?"

"I don't know," I answered, but I think, at least instinctively, I did. "Maybe because I don't feel like I really have much. Or, I really haven't had much. I mean… I don't know!" I laughed nervously.

"No, that's good," he said. "If you're uncomfortable and don't want to confront the reason why, that means you're on to something."

"You think so?"

"I do." He nodded, I could feel it in the way he shifted beneath me.

"Do I really ask every time?" I asked again.

"You do."

"Does it bother you?"

"Sometimes. I mean, only insofar as it doesn't feel like you trust me."

I sat up sharply and looked down at him, my eyes boring into his.

"I do trust you," I told him. "Implicitly."

He brought up his hand to caress the side of my face and smiled, brushing his thumb lightly over my lips.

"I, maybe, needed to hear that," he whispered, with a slight smile that bespoke a vulnerability of his own.

"I trust you," I told him again. "Please, don't ever think that I don't."

"No offense meant, baby. No disrespect. I can't really expect you to share how you feel, what you think, with me if I don't open up first."

I shook my head, "I trust you," I repeated. "I love you... I guess I'm just scared. Sharing my feelings... what I think? I guess it's never really gone over well in the past, and it's just my natural default to keep it to myself."

His eyes left mine and roved over my face as if he were memorizing every bit of it. Like he'd stepped into the *Louvre* and was gazing upon a piece crafted by one of the masters. The defenses that had started to go up around my heart at his probing questions softened and backed down with that look.

"You can tell me anything, Orchid. I promise to not judge. I promise to listen as best I can. To help you however I can."

"That means a lot," I whispered.

"You mean everything," he whispered back and I dropped my forehead carefully to his, wrapped in the comfort and security of this moment.

"I've never talked about Kyle. To anyone. Not even Linny," I whispered.

"You loved him," Stoker said matter-of-factly. "His death hurt you, deeply. I can't imagine what you went through, seeing him die like that."

I dropped my eyes to his chin, not wanting to look him in the eyes when I made my confession.

"I still love him, at least, a part of me does. I still loved him despite what he did. I know he's a monster, so loving him even after he killed all of those people, for me... what does that make me?"

He tipped my chin and my eyes flicked to his. "A better fucking person than the rest of the human stain on this fucking planet, babe. To love unconditionally like that is a rare feat. It makes you strong, not weak. It makes you an unbelievably amazing woman."

"I guess." I swallowed hard, my throat growing thick with emotion. "I guess I'm afraid to love like that again."

"It's okay," he murmured. "I get that. I really do, and I'm here to tell you, you ain't gotta love me like that. I'll take whatever you're willing to give, Little Orchid. I'm here for whatever you need, and I'm all good with whatever you're able to give me. Moment by moment, minute by minute, mile by mile."

I nodded carefully, my eyes leaking, and he smiled at me, pressing my head back to his chest. I sighed out, a shuddering breath, and closed my eyes, listening to his even breathing. Then he started to sing, low and softly, and it was a soothing sound, bittersweet like dark chocolate, a song I'd never heard before, but it didn't matter. I lay quiet in his arms and just listened as he smoothly sang me to sleep.

~

THE NEXT MORNING, I faced the day with trepidation. My hands trembled as I buttoned my swimsuit's cover up and Stoker watched me from the edge of the bed.

"C'mere," he said, low and gentle. I went to him and he unbuttoned what I just buttoned and said with a faint smile, "You missed a button, you were all crooked."

"Oh," I stammered out a nervous laugh.

"Talk to me, baby. I'm right here, and I can't help with whatever it is if I'm not in on what you've got going on in there."

"Oh, you know." I feigned lightness. "Just epically humiliated about losing my shit and about to go out there and face everybody. No getting around it, but it's only like – the worst."

I swallowed hard and he swept my face with his gaze and probed at the smarting wound gently with, "Remind you of high school?"

I let out a shaky breath and said, "How did you guess?"

"I hate to admit it, but I was one of those fucking shits. Picked on other kids to make myself feel better. More powerful. Was just hiding my own pain and passing it on from my old man. He was kind of a dick. We get along okay, now. Mostly because we got states between us." He sighed.

I shook my head. "I can't believe you were ever as bad as some of the bullies in my school," I murmured.

"I don't know," he said ruefully. "I was a pretty fuckin' miserable shit. I know that now."

"And therein lies the difference," I murmured. "You changed. You wanted to change. I still run into one of my tormentors from time to time and they're still just as cruel, just as shitty as they were back then. Maybe even worse since…" I trailed off. I had only just wrestled it back into its vault, and I couldn't be sure I had the door secured all the way. At least not yet.

"Let me tell you something, Little Orchid," he drawled finally. I cocked my head and considered him as he continued, "Most of the people out there? They had it rough comin' up. One way or the other. Some of 'em, not so much, but they ended up going through some serious shit. Everybody we got outside that door is some kind of broken from something. Each and every one of them have lived through something or other embarrassing. Every one of 'em have either shown their ass at one time or another or had a meltdown like yours."

"Is this supposed to make me feel better?" I asked with another nervous giggle. I wiped my sweating palms off on my cover-up against my thighs.

"It is," he said solemnly. "Maybe I'm just going about it the wrong way. The point is, they ain't got any room to talk where you're concerned and if any of them do, I'll either dredge something out into the light of day to embarrass the shit out of them or barring that…" He raised his bruised and scraped fist and pumped it a couple of times lightly.

"You'll punch them in the face?" I asked. "Just like that?"

"We're bikers," he said with a blasé shrug. "We love a good brawl."

I laughed, genuinely this time, and said, "Surely not before their first cup of coffee?"

"You'd be surprised," he said with a wink. "Besides, it's before noon. Ain't a lot of 'em even going to be up; most of 'em are still drunk, and the rest are going to be too hungover to give a fuck."

I laughed again, for real, and let him stand and take my hand. He opened the door to our room and stepped out into the hall looking first this way, then that.

"All clear," he said, and I smiled and followed suit.

When we emerged on the lower patio where the picnic tables were, there were very few people up and having breakfast. A lot of them I didn't recognize from our club or from the Sacred Hearts' mother chapter. There were a few exceptions, though.

Radar, from our club, stepped onto the patio from the stairs leading up to the big, back deck where the food was set up. He gave me a nod and raised his eyebrows in a silent query of 'Are you alright?' I managed a weak smile and gave a nod of my head, and his tense posture eased and he moved toward an empty table.

"Come on, Orchid. Let's get some food."

"'K," I answered lightly and we went for the stairs.

It was a gentle re-introduction, thanks to the hard partying and it was nice that everyone seemed genuinely interested in how I was doing at first, before dropping it altogether. No one pried, no one made fun of me, or made it into a big thing.

The doctor came over, checked me out and declared me all good.

The rest of the day was spent on the lake. We took advantage of the big four-man yellow relaxation raft and even spent time swimming, and jumping on, and being launched off, the blob they had set up.

By evening, I was worn out, but was feeling mostly back to my old self, grateful that Stoker stuck with me and didn't act or say anything about be being too clingy.

We were sitting around one of the fires and cuddling when Reaver dropped in beside me over the big rock we were using as a backrest, scaring the shit out of me. I had both hands over my heart while a few people had a good laugh over it, while a few more wore pinched expressions of worry.

"You scared the crap out of me!" I cried, breathless.

"I heard that about you," he said with a grin, and he looked like a kid at Christmas – if the kids were clearly drunk and possibly high off of marijuana. He smelled faintly of both the low-key drug, a faint earthy scent, and alcohol, a sweeter, almost fruity overtone.

"People been bothering you?" he asked.

"Not here," I answered honestly with a slight smile. I was leaning into Stoker who had his arm around me, and I felt like I was facing down a dangerous predator, looking at Reaver. Like he was a tiger in our midst and nobody, bizarrely, seemed any kind of concerned over it.

It was an incredibly strange feeling, but at the same time, though I was thoroughly intimidated, I still knew I was safe and Reaver, despite his glee at having scared the shit out of me, still seemed to want to make me his new best friend. He had a hell of an odd way of showing it, though.

"Now, this here, is my very favorite knife," he said to me, flicking open a switchblade that he'd made materialize from seemingly nowhere.

I jumped at the little mechanical snick it made as the blade leapt free, and he grinned like the maniac I was quickly figuring out he was. A bunch of the people around the fire from his own club chuckled and I leaned further back into Stoker, who laughed slightly and said, "Easy bud, I know you get off on fear, but my lady's had a lifetime of it."

"Exactly!" Reaver crowed. "Which is why I am now gifting you my very favorite knife, Little Orchid." He closed it up, turned it on his palm so the hilt was pointed at me and bowed his head gallantly.

"I wouldn't even begin to know what to do with it," I said.

"Somebody bothers you, you pull it," Reaver said, like he was confused he even had to explain how this works.

"I'm a lover, not a fighter, so I wouldn't know what to really do after that." I laughed a little as I said it. The whole exchange was strange and completely laughable, really.

"Pro-tip," he said. "They get close?" He leaned in, and in a conspiratorial tone, whispered loudly, "You stick 'em with the pointy end."

The people around the campfire lost it and he grabbed my free hand and turned up my palm, slapping the folded blade into it with one hand and curling my fingers around it with the other. He leapt up, scrambled up and over the rock and disappeared into the dark with everyone wiping tears from the corners of their eyes, they were laughing so hard.

"I don't know just how many 'very favorite knives' Reaver has given out to women over the years," Dray said from across the flames.

"It pretty much means he likes you," Irish, Dray's woman, chimed in.

"I guess it's better than marking territory like pissin' on a tree," Doc said, and more howls of laughter ensued. I looked up at Stoker who was smiling down at me. He gave me a wink and I felt my shoulders lose some of the tension they were holding.

"You have some strange friends," I whispered.

He chuckled lightly and kissed my temple, murmuring in my ear "In case you hadn't realized it yet, Orchid, they're your friends too, now."

Oh.

26

Stoker…

    The ride back on Monday was glorious. The sun was shining, it wasn't too hot, and when we got close to Serenity's exit, Cutter gave me the hand signals that I was good to break off from the pack and take her home. I saluted my captain and my crew and gave the handlebars a light twist to take the off-ramp into Ft. Lauderdale, and Serenity to her little studio apartment.

I didn't like it one bit, either. I wanted so fiercely to take her home, my home, away from the fucksticks in this area, to turf that was more familiar to me and a sort of fresh start for her.

Wasn't going to happen, though. At least, not today.

I pulled up to the curb out front of her landlady's house, Mrs. Sedgwick waving at us from the front porch where she always seemed to be, watching the world go by.

"Hi Mrs. Sedgwick!" Serenity called, waving. She went over to talk to the old woman while I worked on getting her bag out of my saddle bag. She exchanged a few pleasantries.

I waved from where I stood and caught Mrs. Sedgwick telling my little orchid, "He's such a nice young man."

Serenity came back my way and we went upstairs, where she sighed and left all of the crazy at her door. It was something else, watching her cross the threshold, and I realized that my girl's home truly was her sanctuary and that she'd peopled pretty hard over the long weekend and was glad to be home.

"Should I take off and leave you to it?" I asked, and she turned and smiled at me, hanging my rag on her coat rack and shrugging out of her cheap leather jacket, off some bargain rack somewhere.

I needed to get her better protective gear if she was going to keep riding with me. Half-assing it wouldn't do.

"I wish you didn't have to," she told me. "But I know you have work tomorrow. Meanwhile, I get to find out if I even have a job." She rolled her eyes and the unhappiness was back.

"You trust me?" I asked, going to her, pulling her to me by the belt loops of her jeans. She instinctively leaned away but didn't resist coming to me too much. I think it was just ingrained habit from her background.

"Of course, I do," she said, frowning at me like I'd said something stupid, but I had a crazy notion and I wanted that to be in the forefront of her mind when I asked her what I was about to ask her.

"What would you say, if I said, my house was just too fuckin' big for me? That I'm tired of rattling around in there on my own."

"I'd ask you, what would make it better?"

"You, moving in with me," I said, and she gave me a sad sort of little half-smile. I rushed on with, "Ain't gotta make up your mind right now, but I want you to think about it."

"Oh, yeah?"

"Yeah. I think it'd do you a lot of good getting away from this area."

She was quiet, staring past me, off into space as the cogs and gears of her mind clicked and whirred, running through the possibilities, weighing out the pros and cons.

"I would feel bad leaving Mrs. Sedgwick in a bind," she murmured and I nodded.

"Is that the only thing holding you here?"

She smoothed her lips together and looked up at me. "Linny."

"Who is more than welcome to come visit any time she wants. Got a room for your bed, could make it our bed or the guest bed…" I trailed off.

"What about my orchids?" she asked.

"I'm a carpenter, I've got a truck. I could disassemble your green-house, load it up and take the whole damn thing with us." She laughed a little and I smiled. "Could even make it bigger. My backyard is pretty sizable. I'd build you whatever you want, Serenity. Work benches, stools, planter boxes."

"What about a job?" she asked.

"You could call up where you work right now, tell Lydia to fucking shove it, and I could walk you into any place on the boulevard back in Ft. Royal and have you hired on in the first five minutes we were in town."

She looked wistful. "Just leave all of this behind, just like that?"

"Just like that," I agreed, and rocked her gently back and forth in my arms. I could see she was sorely tempted.

"God, I want it all so bad," she murmured.

"Yeah?"

"Yeah, I really do," she said softly.

"I can be back here tomorrow with a load of boxes right after work," I said.

She rolled her eyes. "You're working closer to Ft. Royal now. Nowhere near here."

"I'm no fuckin' stranger to a commute, Little Orchid," I reminded her with a laugh.

"Can I think about it?" she asked softly.

"You can take as much time as you need, baby."

"You're really serious?" She stared up into my face, searching it, trying to see if I was yanking her chain at all.

"As a heart attack," I affirmed.

"Even after…" she trailed off and I knew what she meant.

"Maybe even because of it, a little," I told her truthfully. "I don't feel like I'm as here for you as I should be, as I could be, even with only a couple of hours of distance. I feel like you, being here, so close to where it all went down is like a poison for your soul. The people, the hate that they give, it's not allowing you to do the kind of healing you need. You should be somewhere that you can find peace."

"What if… what if you find out after living with me that you can't actually stand me?" she asked.

I gave her a look like, 'Don't be ridiculous'. "Is that your insecurities talking, or really you?" I asked her.

"Fair point, well made," she said, her voice husky as I stepped closer and lowered my mouth to hers.

I kissed her softly, and failed at keeping it light. I really did have to go, get back to Ft. Royal, and get my shit together for work the next morning.

"I love you," I murmured against her mouth, when I was finally able to give her up.

Not forever, just for now, I told myself resolutely but it was still damn near impossible to tear myself away. I missed her already, and she was standing right here.

"Moment by moment, minute by minute, mile by mile," she whispered, and I smiled.

"That's right," I told her.

"I'll think about it," she said, and I felt a tightness loosen in my chest. I knew her, and the tone of her voice, the inflection she gave it, the gravitas of those four little words told me I definitely had her on the line, but I wasn't about to push my luck.

"Lock up behind me," I said, and she sighed unhappily, but nodded.

"I miss you already," she said, holding open her front door for me and I had to smile. Her words were the very echo of my thoughts just a moment before.

"I'll see you soon enough."

"Promise me you'll message me when you get home," she said.

"This is my solemn vow. I will message you when I get back to my place."

"Thank you," she said with a smile, and she let me go.

I sighed and went down the steps to go back to my bike, pausing to look up at Mrs. Sedgwick on her front porch.

On impulse, I went to talk to the old woman.

"How you doing, Mrs. Sedgwick?" I asked.

"Oh, I'm fine, I'm fine! How was your weekend?"

"It was good, real good. Say, let me ask you something."

"What's that?" she asked.

"Would it be a terrible hardship if I took Serenity to Ft. Royal to live with me?"

"Oh, how wonderful!" She clapped her hands together and laughed, delighted.

I guess that answered my question.

"I don't think she should stay around here," she said. "People have a funny way about 'em, you know? She won't find happiness around these parts with her past hanging over her head like it does."

"I couldn't agree with you more. I've asked her, but I don't know if she'll say yes. I don't want to pressure her none."

"I understand," she said, waving me off. "If she comes to me, I will be more than happy to encourage her. She's a good girl and I'll miss her, but I always knew this wasn't going to be forever. You know how it is."

"Yes ma'am. You have a nice evening now," I told her.

"Oh, I surely will. You be careful riding home, now."

"Always." I gave her a wink, and she shooed me, laughing.

It was good to know I had the keen old woman on my side in this. If there were any holdouts in my little orchid's mind, that would have been it. Just Nellie Sedgwick and her best friend Linny. If there were going to be any hurdle at all, it was really going to be Linny.

I would just have to see what side of the coin landed face down on that one.

I rode back to my place and it was a pretty uneventful ride, except for the weight I carried, the heavy sensation in the center of my chest that I'd left her behind and just how *wrong* it felt.

I was never more sure of anything in my life than I was about

Serenity and her place in mine. She belonged with me, and I only hoped that she could look past her fucked-up programming and past her damage long enough to let herself grab onto the happy I knew she had with me.

I called her just as soon as I pulled into my garage and shut off the bike.

"Hey," she murmured, and I smiled.

"Hey, you doing okay?"

"Mm-hm, took a shower after you left and was just lying here waiting for you to call."

"Listen, your bitch manager tries to give you any grief tomorrow —"

"I actually had an email from HR waiting for me, sent Friday afternoon."

"Oh, yeah?"

"Yeah, just a generic one." She put on a fake-official sounding voice and said, "We will look into this matter and get back to you as soon as possible."

"Oh, yeah," I said, not surprised.

"I mean it," she said softly. "I'll think about your offer."

"You just let me know what you want, baby. I'm here for it. I mean it. Whatever you need."

"You are far too good to me."

"Just making up for lost time. You deserve the world. I may not may not be able to give you the whole world, but I'd do just about anything to make you happy."

"I love you," she whispered softly, and I smiled.

"I love you, too."

"As much as I hate to —"

I cut her off with a slight laugh. "Ah, hey, yeah. I get it. Get some good sleep and ping me tomorrow. Like I said, I wanna know what happens."

"Alright," she said.

"Bye for now."

"Good night."

I ended the call and let out a shuddering sigh, trying like hell to shake it off, the feeling like I should turn right back around and go get her.

It was her decision. I respected that. Now I just needed to wrangle my Neanderthal brain into submission.

27

*S*erenity…

Work was an absolute fucking drag. Lydia was a bitch, but she kept a lid on it now that HR was up her ass, but honestly, what made it a total drag was the seed Stoker had planted. The one that was growing at a phenomenal rate that said 'You don't have to do this anymore if you don't want to. You can move away from here, get a new job, someplace smaller; someplace where it's not so full of these entitled monsters who don't care about you. Who don't care what you've even been through…'

Stoker cared. The rest of his motorcycle pirate crew cared. I was becoming friends with Faith, giving Linny a break from being the only one I could lean on.

Speaking of Linny, if I broke for lunch now, I might catch her on hers in the food court.

"Timothy, am I good to take lunch?" I asked my co-worker. He looked up from where he was secretly browsing on his phone like we weren't supposed to and gave me a nod.

"Yeah, sure, go ahead."

"Cool, thank you."

I clocked out from the terminal and got my purse out of my locker, ghosting past Lydia's open office door behind her back like she was an angry T-rex, like I was trying not to trigger her visual acuity or something, and stifling a giggle at the image it conjured in my mind.

I found Linny waiting in line for food at our favorite joint to grab salad at.

"Hey, you! How was your weekend?"

I rolled my eyes slightly and said, "I don't know that I'm going to be able to fill you in on the whole thing in one lunch half-hour," I said.

"So gimme the highlights and make me dinner tonight and fill me in on the rest." She stuck out her tongue to one side biting it gently between the perfect, straight white teeth her parents had spent a small fortune on in high school, getting them straightened. She raised her eyebrows and looked strikingly like that blonde actress that played that female super-villain in that one movie.

Problem was, Linny could never be any kind of villain. She was both too vanilla and pure goodness. It was the only explanation I had as to why she was still my friend through the endless string of disasters that pretty much comprised my life until Stoker.

"One, you're adorable, and two, I don't even know where to begin," I said.

We paused to order our food and paid for it, stepping aside to wait for them to make it up.

"Start at the beginning, and like I said, just gimme the highlights."

"Okay, um, first day great, second day also great, second evening went to hell in a hand basket but Stoker fixed it – because he always does, and third day was awesome. Then, last night, Stoker said I should quit my job and move with him to Ft. Royal and that's the part that gets me and the part I need your help on, because oh, my God – I really want to, Linny!"

"Whoa, whoa, whoa! Back it up! Did you just say what I think you said?"

"Uh-huh."

She stared at me, stunned, for several moments, silently just searching my face as our order number was called out. We went up and got it and went to find seats, and she sank into hers like she wasn't really all the way here. I knew the feeling. My brain had been in Ft. Royal, on Stoker, turning over and over what a life there would be like. Like a bit of sea glass, worn smooth and beautiful by the waves and the sand.

"So, are you going?" she asked, and I crumpled a little.

"I don't know! I wanted to talk to you first!" I said.

She sank back in her seat and shook her head gently from side to side and I swear to God, if the wheels in her head turned any faster, they'd start to smoke.

"You're right, there's no way to process this in a half an hour," she said finally.

I groaned. "I know, you totally hate the idea of me leaving," I said and she shook her head spearing some of her salad on her plastic fork.

"Actually, from the few pro's and con's I've weighed out, it's just the opposite. You know I love hanging at the beach, and here, the beach is getting too crowded and way too full of entitled male douchebags."

I laughed and said, "Okay, so for just a second can we focus on the pros and cons for me?"

She gave me a flat 'Bitch, please' look. "Honey, Sugar, Sweetie Pie – there aren't any real cons that I can see. You have needed out of this area for a while, and while, yeah, it seems like really soon after only knowing Stoker a few months, I see how he looks at you. The way he takes care of you. You two are practically fucking made for each other. It's crazy how good you go together, and to be quite honest, I am more than a little jealous."

"You, jealous of me? We really are in the up-side-down, aren't we?"

"Not hardly," she retorted. "This has been a long time coming for you, babe, and I really, really hope you throw a little caution to the wind here, and you go for it."

"Really?" I asked, surprised. I'd fully expected Linny to be the voice of reason here. Unless... what Stoker had proposed was legitimately totally reasonable.

'Is that you talking, or your insecurities?' he'd asked me at one point over the weekend, or at least something akin to that, and I'd paused then and thought about it. Just as I paused now and thought about it again.

Why did I honestly do anything that I did?

In order to be safe. In order to feel safe.

It was my first thought, so it must be true, and what else was true is that I never in my whole life had ever felt safer than when I was in Stoker's arms.

"Okay, I know that look," Linny said, interrupting my thoughts.

"What look?"

"The one that says you've totally just made up your mind. Need me to scrounge my store's backroom for some boxes?"

I looked at my best friend over our salads and sighed. "I think I should probably double-check with Stoker and make sure he's sure, don't you?"

She rolled her eyes.

"He's sure. That boy is totally sprung where you're concerned, and who could blame him? You're a treasure, my love. I'll bring you what I can find tonight. What's for dinner, anyway?"

I laughed and shook my head and asked, "What do you want?"

Linny and I had dinner, talked in depth about our weekends, and spoke more about the idea of my moving, which became less of an idea and more of a plan, the more we talked.

Now that she'd gone, I wiped my sweating palms on my comfortable black cotton skirt and stared down at my phone charging on my bedside table.

I'd never been nervous about calling Stoker before, but I was now.

I had picked it up and poised my finger to unlock it when the screen lit up with his smiling face and it started buzzing in my hand.

"You have got to be kidding me," I mumbled, and answered the phone.

"You have impeccable timing," I told him.

"Oh, yeah? How's that?"

"I literally had the phone in my hand and was about to call you when the screen lit up and it's you."

"It's me, alright. You doing okay?"

"Yeah, why?"

"Haven't heard from you all day, it's not like you."

"Oh, um, I just had a lot to think about, and Linny came over – she just left, actually."

"Oh, yeah?" He sounded cautious.

"Yeah." I sank into my reading chair.

"What'd you guys talk about?"

"Our weekends, and the move," I said carefully.

"Wait, what'd you say?" he asked, sounding surprised.

"You know," I said, my cheeks heating. "The move. My moving. In with you…"

"You serious?" he asked, and his voice held suspense, like he was expecting me to pull a Lucy and the football on him a la the old Charlie Brown specials that played on television when I was growing up around the holidays.

"If you still want me," I said softly.

"Holy shit, you're saying yes. Please tell me you're saying yes right now."

"I think I'm saying yes," I said with a nervous laugh.

"Alright. Okay. Um, your job, have you quit your job?" he asked.

"I suppose I should put in a two weeks' notice…" I trailed off.

"What? No. Fuck no. Fuck that fucking ho," he said, and I smiled and rolled my eyes.

"She was on her best behavior today," I said.

"She fuckin' better be."

"Look, as wretched as she's been the last couple of months, I wouldn't be turning in two weeks for her sake, the company –"

"You aren't seriously going to tell me the company's been good to you, paying you a sub-standard wage, refusing to pay you overtime when you worked overtime hours… come on, baby. You're better than that place, and if you're gonna be a rebel, you might as well start somewhere."

He was teasing me now, gently. I laughed and said, "How's it going to look on my resume, not giving notice and just ghosting like that? Doesn't exactly inspire confidence with any future employers, now does it?"

He made a dismissive noise on the other end of the line. "You're gonna be just fine, Orchid."

"Well, be that as it may, I am still putting in my two weeks tomorrow, and then that will give me time to pack this place up and weed things out."

"Sounds like a plan, baby. Want me to come that way Friday after band practice?"

"Would you?" I asked softly.

"I would do anything for you," he said, and I closed my eyes and savored the notes of his voice as he said it.

I believed him.

"Okay, well, it's getting late. I know you need to be up early, and so I am going to let you go for now."

"Shit, I hate it when you're right," he said softly and with feeling. "But when you're right you're right, so I guess it's bye for now."

"Just for now," I murmured.

"Moment by moment, minute by minute, mile by mile, Orchid."

I sighed and closed my eyes. "Thank you, that helps."

"I know this is a big step for you."

"I haven't lived with anyone since my parents kicked me out, expecting I'd fall flat on my ass," I confessed.

"That's not a story that you've told me," he said.

"Um, the Cliff's Notes version of it is, I graduated, they kicked me out that night, but they didn't know I'd been pretty much expecting it, so I had money saved up, enough to get me into a place. I was at a fleabag hotel for a week, and then I rented a basement room at this flop-house. It was a shared bathroom, no kitchen, and there were some, um, seriously questionable individuals living in the other rooms. I was stuck there for about a year, kept surfing Craigslist on my phone, Linny helped me where she could, and I eventually landed in Mrs. Sedgwick's mother-in-law apartment, and I've been here ever since."

"Wow," he uttered.

"And on that thoroughly depressing note!"

"Alright, alright," he groaned.

"I love you," I uttered with a slightly seductive edge. I lived to drive him just a little bit crazy, loving the stories of how when he got off of some of these calls he had to pleasure himself before he could sleep.

"Hey now, knock that off," he said, and I could hear the grin in his voice. "I love you, too. Goodnight."

"Goodnight."

He ended the call, and I sighed at the tones in my ear indicating the call was done. I turned my head and looked down at the empty rocker on Mrs. Sedgwick's night-dark porch. The hardest part about all of this would be the one thing I hadn't talked about. It always was. I was sincerely hoping she wouldn't be horribly disappointed. Or that I wouldn't be putting her in a tough spot by leaving.

I went to bed, and was surprised that I actually fell asleep pretty quickly. I had honestly expected to lay awake tortured by my decision, like I usually was by anything big like this.

I guess the fact that I wasn't, in the slightest, meant that I was doing the right thing.

28

*S*erenity…

"Hey, beautiful," he said and I startled and turned around, surprise coating my insides like splattered and dripping paint.

"What are you doing here?" I blurted. "I wasn't expecting to see you until tomorrow!"

"I know, but the guys in the band aren't getting along and rather than sit around with Gideon PMSing or whatever the fuck he's doing, I bagged on band practice, told him to get his shit together, and let 'em know I had better shit to do with my time."

"Oh, and I suppose that shit would be me?" I asked with a wink.

"No, that shit would be me helping my woman pack up her shit."

I laughed slightly, and he leaned his hands on the cash wrap of the department I was working today.

"Anything?" he asked, and I shook my head.

"She's afraid for her job, I think."

That conversation had been unexpected and completely empowering. I'd gone into Lydia's office at the end of the day on Tuesday and had put in my two weeks.

She'd told me, "You can't quit. They'll think it was because of me."

Instead of my usual route of not making waves or of being any kind of apologetic I'd made my first stand in, God, what felt like forever. I'd pretty much told her in no uncertain terms I didn't give a shit, that I was putting in my two weeks, and she could either live with that or I could walk right then and there.

I was sort of bluffing on that last part. I mean, I really could use the last couple of paychecks to help facilitate the move.

I still hadn't looked into the rental cost of a moving truck or any of that. Stoker had told me not to get ahead of myself, to not worry about that just yet, and so I hadn't. I set that bit aside for the time being and let Linny commandeer some boxes from her place of work.

I'd already started packing, but honestly I couldn't wait to unpack Stoker, with him standing there looking absolutely delicious in his jacket and cut, his faded jeans hugging his thighs.

"She should be. Maybe it'll teach her a lesson in respect," he said, and I smiled.

"A lot of those lessons could stand to be passed out," I said, frowning at a woman who took something off the hanger to inspect it, but rather than hang it back up, just slung the top over the rack itself.

"I'll meet you downstairs," he said, and I smiled.

"Love you," I said softly, and went around to ask the lady if she needed any help. Not that I actually wanted to help her, I just wanted to keep her from wrecking the department I'd spent all morning putting back to rights.

People, they were savages, I tell ya.

I finished up what I needed to do and waited for the clock to wind down so I could get out of here. I found Linny talking to Stoker out at the little lounge area outside my department store.

"Hey, you off?" I asked her.

"Nah, not yet, just on my last ten. Saw your man, here and decided it was time for 'the talk,'" she said.

I rolled my eyes. "A little late for that, pretty sure he knows all about the birds and the bees," I said, without missing a beat.

"Ew, God, no!" she cried. "The one about if he hurts my girl, I'm gonna have to get creative with body disposal."

He laughed. "Pretty sure I could teach you a thing or two about that. Gators love ham," he said with a cryptic little smile.

I shook my head and grinned ruefully at the both of them.

"Score any boxes?" I asked her, changing the subject.

"Why, yes. Yes, I did. Why don't you guys come grab them?"

"Sounds like a plan," Stoker said, and we followed her back to her store, through the back corridor, lest we upset the fine sensibilities of any shoppers. Stoker, unfortunately not being an employee of the mall, had to wait for us to come back out. He stood around on his phone while we ran and got the flattened cardboard, and took both mine and Linny's load when we got back out to him.

"Lead the way, baby," he told me, and with a quick hug and a bye-for-now to my best friend, we went out to my car to stow the empty boxes in my back seat for the drive home.

"I rode here," Stoker said, giving me a quick kiss before I got into my car. "Bike's over there, I'll see you at your place."

"Okay," I got into my car and he shut the door for me.

I pulled on my seatbelt and headed for home, taking Sunrise to the I-95 on-ramp to get home. I pulled up onto the freeway, and a short time later, Stoker zipped past my driver's side and pulled two car-lengths in front of me. I laughed a little, thinking at first that he was just fooling around, but a big, black, jacked-up pickup blared its horn at me and barreled past me on the passenger side of my car, using the shoulder of the highway to do it. I watched Stoker pour on the speed and my heart dropped into the pit of my stomach. I reached forward and tapped my phone screen, and thankfully, caught it before it completely went to sleep.

I dialed 9-1-1, but I knew they would never in a million years get here in time.

"9-1-1 What is your emergency?" a woman's voice poured from the speaker on my phone set near my dash, and I hit the power button to shut off my radio.

"Yes, hi, I'm on the I-95 headed north, and my boyfriend is on his motorcycle ahead of me and I don't know what's —" I sucked in a sharp breath as the pickup swerved, trying to knock into Stoker, trying to knock him off his bike.

"Hello, ma'am?"

"Oh, my God, please hurry, he's going to kill him!" I cried. But I knew, they would never make it in time.

"Ma'am, I need to know where you are. Can you give me a description of the vehicles involved?"

I stammered and rattled off random information, the signs stating what exit was coming up, babbling out the truck's make and model as I laid my foot into my own accelerator to try and catch up to them.

Stoker was keeping ahead of the guy who was leaning out his window, screaming at him, and my heart climbed into my throat.

"Oh, my God, this guy is crazy!" I cried, as he swerved at my beloved once again.

"Help is on the way. Can you give me the truck's license plate number?"

"Yes, hang on, I'm trying to get closer."

"Only do that if it is safe to do so, don't speed."

I fought not to roll my eyes and thought to myself, *Fuck that. That's my whole life up there.*

I grimaced as the truck accelerated and Stoker dodged around a car, barely. I checked my speed and my mouth went dry. We were going too fast, way too fast, and traffic was growing thicker. I swallowed hard at another near-miss and said, "You know, what? Fuck it. Just get here already!"

I poured on the speed, and went around two cars, pulling up on the passenger side of the truck, which had switched lanes. My heart beat a frantic tattoo against the inside of my ribs as I gained ground and got ahead of them both. Stoker zipped past me in the lane on the other side of the truck and I took a deep breath, tensed, and made a stand.

I jerked the wheel, cut off the truck and stood on my brakes with both feet, gripping the steering wheel in a death grip with both hands, at ten and two, the tires of my little car screaming against the sunbaked interstate's surface. I braced back against my seat and screamed as the grill of that truck rushed into view, filling up my rearview mirror, and then came the devastating crash as he collided with my little car's back end.

I kept screaming as I was shoved forward even further along the freeway, Stoker still ahead of me and growing smaller as he kept going, and my car finally slowed, the truck growing smaller with the sound of tearing metal as it stopped under its own braking power.

"Ma'am! Ma'am, was that a collision? Ma'am, talk to me!"

"Yes!" I cried brokenly. "He hit me! The man in the pickup truck hit my back end!"

"Right, okay. Just hang on for me, I'm dispatching emergency services right now. What's your name?"

"Serenity…"

I hurt almost immediately, from my neck, down between my shoulder blades into my lower back. My hands gone numb on the steering wheel, though from injury or from how hard I gripped it during the impact, I don't know.

The dispatcher kept talking to me, but my vision was locked on Stoker, far ahead, pulling a U-turn across two lanes of freeway to ride back in my direction. He looped around once more, holding out his hand to cars trying to go around me and the pickup and pulled up in front of my broken car going the right direction.

I could hear sirens in the distance, coming in for the rescue, except I think I'd already provided that. Me. Of all people.

What did I do?

Stoker wrenched on the door handle and I turned my head carefully, wincing, staring up at him. He pointed at the door lock and I got my hands working and got it unlocked for him. He pulled my door open and dropped down into a crouch beside me.

"Serenity, Orchid, baby, where does it hurt?" he demanded, reaching up for me, wiping off my face with the palm of his hand and dragging it across the thigh of his jeans to get rid of the tears he'd collected.

"My head, my neck, and my back. My hands are numb," I said.

"Okay, okay, just hang on for me. Help is on the way."

"Serenity, it sounds like someone is with you," came over my phone.

"Yes, there is!" I called back. "It's my boyfriend, he's here. He came back for me."

Stoker pulled my phone out of the windshield-mounted clip and said, "Stay right here, baby. I'm going to check and see how far away they are."

"Okay," I said, moaning. I daren't try to nod my head again. Oh, my God. It had to be bad if it hurt this swiftly, didn't it?

"Yeah, hi, this crazy son of a bitch –"He'd turned my phone off speaker and was talking to the dispatcher, walking out a little ways from my car to check the emergency team's progress. A big red fire engine lumbered into view, pulling past my car. The whine and hiss of the braking system was startling, but I didn't want to move.

"Hey there, you alright?" One of the firemen came to my open door as Stoker ended the call with the dispatcher on my phone and pocketed it.

A state trooper strode up to him and Stoker kept his hands out to his sides and nodded politely to him.

"No," I whimpered.

"What hurts?" he asked, and I told him what I'd told Stoker.

"Okay, okay, what's your name?"

"Serenity."

"That's a pretty name, Serenity. My name's Jake and I'm gonna be taking care of you. Here's what we're gonna do. First off, I don't want you to move your head, okay? I'm gonna help you get this collar on, and you just don't do anything, okay?"

"Okay."

They put a C-collar on me and extracted me from my car on a backboard. I was terrified. I couldn't turn my head at all, and when they set me on the stretcher, I called out for Stoker. Like a magician, he just suddenly appeared at my side, his warm calloused hand wrapping around mine.

"Hey, baby. They're gonna take you to go get checked out. X-rays, imaging, that sort of thing, okay? I'm going to be right behind you, Orchid. I'm not going anywhere, okay?"

"Can you ride with me?" I asked, afraid, feeling like a child but I couldn't help it.

"No, baby. I gotta ride. I'll be right behind you, I promise. I swear it. Okay?"

"Okay," I whimpered, even though I didn't like it. I didn't like it one bit.

"Okay, you just hang tight. You guys look after her for me, okay?"

"You got it, boss," Jake told him, and they loaded me into the back of the waiting ambulance.

"Any preference on where we take you?" one of the medics asked.

"No," I said. "Wherever's closest?"

"You've got it." The back doors closed, but all I had a view of was the ceiling, my head and neck completely immobilized, the top of the collar digging uncomfortably into the back of my head.

"Woo buddy, that guy did a number on the back of your car. You're lucky he didn't go up and over you, monster-truck style," the ambulance tech said, making notations on his clipboard.

"You good?" his partner called from the front.

"Yeah, we're all good back here. Take us away!"

"He was going to kill him," I said, dully.

"Who? Your boyfriend on the bike?"

"Yeah."

"What'd you do? Brake-check him?"

"I didn't know what else to do," I said. "The police weren't going to make it in time and Stoker was on the bike… I knew I had better chances in my car than he did on the motorcycle. I couldn't watch him get hit. I didn't know what else to do…"

"Wow. Sounds pretty brave to me," the guy said, but he looked like by 'brave' he meant 'stupid.'

I said as much, and he laughed.

"Brave, stupid, the only deciding factor is the outcome. If the guy really was trying to hit your boyfriend like you say, then yeah. Definitely chalk this one up on the winning side for brave. You probably saved his life. A Harley wouldn't have stood a chance against that big ol' pickup."

I closed my eyes and felt hot tears leak down my temples, sucking in a slow breath, trying to breathe through the irritating searing pain of my overworked, whip-lashed muscles.

I could feel my hands again, so I had to take that as a good sign.

At the hospital, I was poked, prodded, and imaged to within an inch of my life and then left to rot, still stuck in the stupid collar, in one of their curtained bays. Stoker found me there. A lot of my clothing had been cut off, my knee had started to throb and ache, and other myriad little hurts had started to surface, though the shot of morphine they'd given me had taken the worst of the edge off of it all.

We were waiting for a doctor to review all of the imagery and to see if they needed to order more before they took the collar off. So, for now, I got to lay here, my hand in Stoker's while we waited and he told me what happened.

"I was trying to catch up to you," he said. "I don't know that fucking guy's deal but I split lanes and zipped past him and it just, I don't know, it must have set him off. Next thing I know he's trying to fucking kill me."

I swallowed hard.

"I saw him try to run you off of the road," I said, and before I could say anything else, a voice outside the curtain called out, "Serenity Bowman?"

"Yes?" I called.

A Florida Highway Patrolman batted the curtain aside and stepped into the little space. Stoker leaned back and the patrolman said, "Here's your purse, recovered from your vehicle, and your citation for reckless driving." He dropped my purse at my hip and set a sheaf of papers on my chest, covered by my hospital gown.

"You're fucking kidding me, right?" Stoker grated out coldly.

"Just doing my job, sir. Several witnesses said your girlfriend sped past the gentleman in the pickup and brake-checked him."

"They also say how he was trying to fucking kill me?" Stoker demanded.

"Not to my recollection, no." The patrolman gave Stoker one of the dirtiest looks I had ever seen and actually smirked. They absolutely had too told him that, but I was betting that it would be omitted from his report.

I swallowed hard and groped for Stoker's hand. He stopped and looked down at me and I pled with my eyes for him to just let it go for now.

"This is bullshit," Stoker growled.

"It's also my only driving offense. We'll go to court and sort it out there."

"Good luck with that," the patrolman snarked, and he went out through the curtain, and from what I could see, left it gaping as his boots thudded against the linoleum and he left the way he'd come.

"Fuck, I'm so sorry. It's because of my patch," he said.

"Don't be sorry," I said. "I'm going to be okay – you're okay, that's the only thing that matters right now."

"You hang tight," he said with a sigh. "I'ma go make a phone call. Call the club, give them the heads-up."

"Call Linny, too. Her number is in my phone. Access code is 4193."

"Got it." He stepped out the curtain and whisked it back into place, hiding me from view, returning to me the semblance of privacy the patrolman had stripped away.

I lay there, and despite my calm words, I was on fire inside with all of the panic. Just what was I going to do?

29

S toker…

"No, I'm not fucking joking, does it sound like I'm joking, motherfucker?" I growled at Radar.

"Slow your fuckin' roll there, Turbo. I get it, your lady's hurt and you got the pigs adding insult to injury. The question was rhetorical. I'ma put out the message and contact the club lawyer. What hospital did you say you were at?"

I rattled it off.

"Okay, now hang up the fucking phone and go be with your ol' lady. We got you," he said.

"Thanks. Oh, and I got this asshole's plate. Doesn't sound like he's going to suffer through the criminal justice system so it's on us for some good ol' fashioned street justice."

"Noted, gimme that too, while you're on the line."

I rattled that off, too.

"Got it. I'll be in touch."

"Thanks, Radar."

"Don't mention it. We're crew and it's just what crew do," he said, with all of his savvy. I could already hear his fingers doing the walking across his laptop's keyboard over the line.

"Later," I said.

"Oh, you have no idea," he said with a malicious sort of glee. He already had the dude's whole life in front of him on his screen. I could see it in my mind's eye.

"Thanks, man." I disconnected the call.

No sooner did I have Linny dialed up on Serenity's phone, than my phone started blowing up with texts and ringing off the hook. I grimaced and rejected the call coming in from the captain, so I could fill in my girl's best friend.

"I thought you went off with lover boy," was how Linny answered the phone.

"She did," I said. "You best be sitting down for this…"

Jesus fucking Christ, Serenity knew how to pick her friends.

Linny was on it like sonic, asking if my girl would need clothes or this, or that, asking about prescriptions, rides, you name it. She was a one-woman organizational army, holding her shit together and getting shit done. She kicked me off the phone so that she could go to work, getting my girl everything she would need, and telling her manager to shove it when she said she was leaving early and I heard him balk over the line.

I smiled to myself and called my captain back on my phone before Serenity's phone's screen had a chance to go blank.

"What happened?" he demanded, and I could hear the general chaos and discord of my crew getting ready to group ride on the other end of the line.

I told him and he muttered, "Fucking son of a bitch."

"Nothing to do but hurry up and fuckin' wait here at the hospital," I told him.

"Radar's already on it, doing his thing. I think he recruited Data up north to get to wiping out some of the financial shit."

"Wow," I said, suitably impressed.

"You look after your woman. We'll be there in a couple of hours," he said.

"Aye, aye, Captain… and thanks."

"Psht! Don't thank me, boy. Be there as soon as we can."

"Copy that."

"Hey," he said, and his voice took on a different quality, one I rarely ever heard from him.

"Yeah?"

"Are you doin' alright?" he asked.

I sighed. "No, Cap. I'm really not. She could have died. She could be in there paralyzed for all I know. I don't know what the hell she was fucking thinking," I said. An anger born of fear coursed through me. and he was silent on the other end of the line for what felt like a full minute.

"She was thinkin' she loves you and she'd rather die than see you die."

I knew he was right. It was still a fucking bitter-ass pill to swallow, though.

"Yeah, well, I'm, um, not okay," I said lamely, not one hundred percent sure what else I should say. I mean, granted the captain was being Captain Obvious but, damn.

"Point of all of this is, she will be okay, alright?"

I nodded and said, "Yeah," clearing my throat, which suddenly had a Gordian knot of emotion in it.

"You keep us posted on the prognosis, yeah?"

"As soon as I know y'all'll know."

"See you soon," he said, and that was it.

I bucked the fuck up and went back to my woman, the picture of positivity and a good outlook, even though I was fuckin' terrified with what was taking so fucking long to read her fucking scans.

We hadn't gotten any answers by the time Linny got there an hour later and we still didn't have anything by the time the captain and the rest of my crew got there, more than an hour after that.

Nine fucking hours, we waited in that goddamned hospital. Serenity was uncomfortable and miserable the whole time. Nine fucking hours of waiting, only to be told time after time, hour after hour, any time we inquired, to wait, to be patient, and that 'No news was good news.'

Finally, the doc breezed in like we ain't shit and told us everything was fine, here was a script for some painkillers for the next few days, and to take some fucking Tylenol after that.

I would have been livid if I wasn't so fuckin' drained, mentally and emotionally.

I let Linny help Serenity get dressed in the clothes she'd brought from her place, and made a mental note to get Linny a key to my place once we had my little orchid all moved in. I wanted to add to my girl's life; I wasn't about disrupting it. Little things like that went a long way.

The captain and crew and I had held church, leaving a couple of the ol' ladies with Serenity while we used the hospital's small chapel to do it. They'd all left hours ago to stake out homeboy in the truck's place, and to do some homework.

First order of business would be to find out what the fuck his deal had been.

Dude's airbags had gone off in his face and he'd been knocked the fuck out at the scene, so there was no telling what was up. It'd been a blessing. If he'd gone after Serenity for having my six, I would have had to kill him right out there on the highway, in front of all those witnesses.

I wasn't about that. I liked my freedom.

Now, it was just me, Linny, and my woman, and she was hurting. She'd stiffened up something awful and was moving around slower and worse than Mrs. Sedgwick, stooped and carefully shuffling her way out the Emergency Department on my arm, while Linny pulled up at the ER's main entrance. She would drive her back to Orchid's and I would follow, hopefully without incident this time.

I'd already called in to work around eleven o'clock at night – much to my foreman's irritation, waking him up like I did. He'd pretty much lost all his irritation when I told him what happened and told me to take Monday too, if I needed it. I told him I'd keep him in the loop. I had to see what happened.

She looked so frail going up the steps to her apartment, and I rushed to catch up. Linny had to go and felt awful about it, and to be honest, even though I'd deny it, and would never in a million years would I say it out loud, I wanted her gone. I know it was selfish as hell, but I needed to be a little selfish right now. I didn't know how much longer I could hold my shit together.

Fuck. I felt like I'd nearly lost her. Way too close, far too close for comfort. It'd be a millennia before my butthole unpuckered from this one.

When I shut the door behind Linny and turned around, Serenity was sitting on the edge of her bed, her hands folded in her lap. She looked exhausted, in pain, and she looked up at me with a mixture of fear and anguish in her eyes that clashed like oil and water. I sank down onto the bed beside her and searched her face.

"You scared the shit out of me," I said.

"I know, I'm sorry." Her voice warbled and her eyes crested with tears, and all I could do was shake my head.

"It's alright. You saved my ass back there, dude was tenacious."

"I couldn't let him hurt you. Not when I could stop him. I didn't know what else to do. He was going to hurt you and the police never would have gotten there in time. I knew I had better chances in a cage than you did on a bike."

I smiled at her natural use of MC terminology, and her face filled with a gentle confused wonder that was likely a byproduct of the good drugs she was on.

"What's so funny?" she asked.

"You, talking like one of us. It's nice. You're assimilating nicely."

She went to nod and stopped. I brushed some of the stray wetness off her cheek.

"Come on, into a hot shower, let's relax those muscles, get you into bed and you can sleep."

"Okay," she murmured.

I stood up and held my hands down to her.

"Wish you had a bathtub," I said, as she took them and I helped her to stand. She toed off her simple black ballet flats and I led her into the bathroom, letting her go ahead of me so I could stand in the doorway. It was far too small for the both of us to be in there at the same time.

I couldn't wait to get her home, to my – to our place – and into a bathroom with some size to it. I wanted to back her into the corner, like

I had our first time. I wanted to taste her, hold her up against my shower wall and make her come against my mouth over and over again. I helped her undress and went back out into the main room to put her clothes away while she showered.

There was never a time I didn't want her. Even now, with as hurt as she was, she was painfully beautiful to me. I wanted to kiss away her tears, love her until there was no more pain and only the good remained. Logically, I knew the sentiment was trash, that it didn't work that way; but it was still what I wanted to do – the urge so strong it drew me back to my feet from the edge of her bed, like I was a damn puppet on a string, when the shower's water cut off.

I reached out to take her hands in mine and help her step over the low lip of her shower. I wrapped her carefully in one of her big towels and ran my hands gently and carefully over the rough material to soak up the water beading on her skin. I leaned down and kissed her gently, carefully. I didn't want to aggravate anything.

She swooned into me slightly, and I backed off with an overabundance of caution and sighed with light frustration.

"What is it?" she asked, and I guided her hand to the front of my jeans. She laughed, blushing slightly and said, "Oh."

"Come on, baby. Let's get you into bed," I whispered, guiding her gently to her bed, lifting the blankets. She ditched her towel, unclipped her long hair from where she had it messily piled atop her head. The artless tumble it made against her smooth skin, the sweeping gentle line of her back was so beautiful, so sexy, and I wanted so badly to do something about it, but there was just no way right now.

She got beneath the covers and I tucked her in gently. Straightening, she looked up at me with wide, startled dark eyes.

"You're not coming to bed?"

I smiled tenderly and murmured, "Not yet, I got a couple calls to make."

"At this hour?"

"Won't take me but a couple of seconds. I'll be right out on the porch." She pouted beautifully and I admonished her playfully, "Stop that. Get some sleep. I'll be in in a minute."

"Okay," she sighed, disappointed, and it tore at me a little. Still, I needed to check in and see what was what with Radar.

I went out onto the porch and wished for a cigarette. I'd quit a long-ass time ago, but right then, a cancer stick would have been real nice. I dialed up Radar and he answered on the first ring.

"Was wondering when I would hear from you," he said.

I grunted. "Just got Serenity laid down to sleep."

"How's she doing?"

"Sore, but I'm pretty sure that's just the beginning. Tomorrow's guaranteed to be worse."

"Maybe not," he said. "Sometimes the day after is the worst, sometimes the day after that is. Just whatever you do, don't baby her too much. Make sure she gets up and does some moving around."

"Sounds like you're talking from experience."

"I am," he said with a sigh. "Marisol got into a bad wreck back when we were together."

"Ouch, sorry, dude. Didn't mean to bring up bad memories."

"It's nothing to get bent out of shape about. My time with Marisol was shit, but I got the best thing I could have asked for out of it with my kids."

"Yeah," I agreed. Radar's kids were his fucking everything. He lived for them first, before anything, even the club.

"So, back to the main event and the real reason you were calling."

"Yeah." I perked up a bit. "You got something already?"

"The fuck you think I've been doing?" he asked. "Jerkin' off over here?"

I laughed a little. "Never know. Lay it on me."

"Okay, sugar – here it is. Dude's name is Gordon Humphries, he lives outside Sunrise, and is one of those early retiree types. He might be a problem in that he's former military, but I don't think so. We're talking like Desert Storm and he wasn't brand new for it, either. He'd been in a while."

"Oh, yeah?"

"Yeah. He was at the same hospital as your girl, but got released before her. The airbag knocked him out, his face is burnt a little from the chemicals and he had a fractured nose, but no other injuries that they know of."

"He's gonna, by the time I get through with him," I said.

"True that. I think the captain wants to send a wrecking crew with you. Definitely no handling this one solo."

"I hadn't planned on it, and as much as I want to head down there now? Nah, I want to make sure she's taken care of first. Get her moved, slow-walk this revenge story a little bit. I don't want anything going sideways for my little orchid."

"Good, glad you're not trying to take it all hot and heavy right from the get-go."

"That's how you get caught. This type of revenge? Best served ice cold."

Radar chuckled. "You're learning. Enough about that asshole, though. You best go in and take care of your ol' lady. We can worry about him after she's moved and the citations and charges, or whatever she's got, are all handled."

"Right," I agreed, clenching my teeth. I was pissed about the citation but that was law enforcement for you. They didn't care about right or wrong, and it was a goddamned lie anytime one of those pigs said they dealt out justice. They didn't know the meaning of the fuckin' word. Shit, they were just all about the fuckin' revenue for the local government. Fuck us little guys.

"Hey, Radar?" I asked.

"Yeah?"

"They cite him?" I asked.

He sighed. "Motherfuckin' cherry on top of this shit sundae… no, they did not."

"Of course not," I snorted in disgust. "If anything, they were probably disappointed he didn't turn my ass into a greasy smear on the highway."

"Probably, but hey, your ol' lady didn't let that happen. A fact that the rest of us are real grateful for. She's somethin' else, man. You better hang onto a woman like that."

"That's the plan," I told him. "Forever and fuckin' always."

"Good deal. Now go snuggle her, since you can."

"Too close for comfort," I agreed. "Scared the fucking shit right out of me."

"I bet, dude. G'night."

"Night, bro."

Yeah, I thought as I pocketed my phone, *a cigarette would be real good about now.*

30

*S*erenity…

I couldn't go to work for a while, I was moving so slowly. Instead I turned my focus on packing. Stoker stayed with me and helped with all the heavy lifting. I was mostly relegated to wrapping fragile items, and telling him what went where, and pouting that I couldn't have him without hurting myself further. He was incredibly beautiful, graceful, and I missed his hands on my skin.

When he did touch me, the touch was light and careful, as if I had somehow become like the thinnest glass, incredibly fragile. It made me simultaneously crazy and love him more, to the depths of my soul, the bottom of my heart. The fear was a real and palpable thing, especially with how uncharacteristically quiet he was about the accident, about the man who had been after him specifically.

I worried, my Spidey senses tingling, that something wasn't right – his silence was speaking louder than words. In retrospect, Kyle had been much the same in the weeks and days leading up to his revenge plot at Rachel Alice Morgan. It all finally came to a head during the rainstorm that kept us indoors in my too-cramped little apartment, what with all the boxes taking up every available surface.

"What are you planning to do to him?" I demanded suddenly, looking up from the books in my hands to meet Stoker's cool and appraising look from across the room where he was building more boxes.

He didn't try to bullshit me, which I was grateful for, but I still didn't like what he said, "That's not for you to know, Orchid."

I scoffed, "Are you serious?"

"As a heart attack," he said, setting down the tape gun on my bed and coming around to sit on its edge closer to me.

"Why? It happened to me," I hazarded, even though that wasn't quite fair. It'd happened to the both of us.

He sighed and swore softly before he looked back up at me. I waited, and he said, "I was hoping it'd be longer than this before you ran into the cone of silence around 'club business.'"

"How is it club business?" I asked, a trickle of fear working its way in a cold shiver down my back.

"You're mine, baby. He almost took that away."

I swallowed hard and stared unflinchingly, wide-eyed at him and asked, a waver in my voice, "You aren't going to hurt his family, are you?"

"No. We don't hurt innocent people. At least, we try not to. Things can…" He cleared his throat. "Things can sometimes happen, but they haven't. Not for a long, long time."

"How long?"

"Mostly long before my time," he said. "Can't really talk about the rest."

"Club business," I said.

"Club business," he agreed.

I fell silent and he watched me as I quietly packed, turning things over and over in my mind.

He sighed finally, and came over to me, getting down on the floor behind me and easing up to me, his chest to my back, his arms going around me and holding me against his chest, his denim-clad legs to either side of mine.

"I don't want you to fret," he murmured.

"Kind of hard," I whispered. "I don't want anyone else to get hurt because of me."

He tightened his hold around my body and I was weak, I admit. I cuddled back into him and took the comfort and shelter he provided.

"Nobody got hurt because of you, baby. You can't take that on…" he murmured.

"Kyle never would ha –"

"Hush, now. Kyle never would have what? Shot up those kids if it hadn't been for the way those kids treated both you and him. You aren't to blame for any of that, that was on him. All on him. And yeah, 'kids will be kids' or whatever, but a lot of it is on the ones who were being little assholes to begin with. Karma has a funny way of workin', and this is no different. The Kraken's been an instrument of Karma's hand a few times now, and we been on the receiving end plenty, too."

"I don't want you guys to do anything," I said, my voice cracking. A bottomless well of emotion had opened up beneath me and was trying to swallow me whole.

"It's out of your hands, baby. Out of mine, too. That dude trespassed against us."

"Aren't we meant to forgive those who trespass against us, though?"

"Our world doesn't work that way, babe. Our world is much more stripped-down. Much simpler than that. In our world, it's blood for blood, an eye for an eye. He hurt you, I won't let that slide."

"But –"

"No buts," he said, and I pulled away from him.

"I don't want this," I said desperately.

He sighed and we faced each other; he searched my face and I searched his.

"A bargain," he said, "and you can never let the rest of the club even know we talked about this."

"I'm listening," I said, hopeful.

"No harm comes his way – at least not physically. Property damage is another story."

"His truck is already destroyed. Isn't that enough?"

"No." His tone brooked no argument.

We stared each other down and I shook my head finally. "I don't know if I can go through with this... moving in... how am I not making a horrible mistake?" I asked.

He sighed out and stared at the ceiling for several seconds, finally saying without looking at me, "I love you. Try looking at this from my side of things for just a second." He dropped his eyes to mine, meeting my gaze unflinching. "That dude, whatever his malfunction is, hurt you. Could have easily killed you, and if that hasn't earned some sort of retribution, I don't know what has."

"Only because I got in his way," I murmured.

He nodded. "To protect me, I know... now it's my turn to protect you back. People need to stop fucking with you. People need to know that you're off fucking limits and you need to get out of your own way and stand up for yourself." He came to me, his voice harsh and passionate, but not yelling. He cupped my face between his hands and, his eyes inches from mine, said, "You need to let me do this. Not just for you, but for me, and if you'd like, for anyone else he might think he could get away with doing something similar, or worse, to, because if you don't let me do anything, that's how this is gonna go. He's going to get the impression he's untouchable and if that happens? What happens to the next guy?"

"That's what the police are for..." I breathed but I was losing this disagreement. He was right.

"What did the authorities do for you?" he asked. "What did your teachers, the principal, the school resource officer – what did any of them do for you?" he asked.

Fuck. He had me there... Because he knew, they hadn't done anything, which is what had prompted Kyle to do what he did. The frustration, the anger, all of it misplaced into a driving need for retribution, and here I was all over again.

I felt my eyes well up, the sight of him, beautiful and earnest, blurring with the tears.

"I feel like such a curse right now," I told him, my voice breaking.

"You're no curse, baby. You're the greatest blessing ever bestowed on the likes of me. Now will you let me take care of you?"

I sniffed, unhappy, but deciding that I loved him, and this too would pass, and it would pass in a way that I honestly would never know.

"I mean, I want to be mad at him, too, but I don't know why he did what he did. How do we know he wasn't just having a bad day, or that he wasn't hurting too for a different reason?"

He sighed pulling me against his chest and holding me firmly against him saying, "You're pure goodness, woman."

"I'm not. I mean, I'm angry too and part of me wants you to do it, but I know in my heart and in my head that man is just not worth it. That he should just be left to his own misery, to rot in it."

"You have a point there, too," he said. "At any rate, ain't nothing going to be done right now, right this minute. What does need to be done is this place needs packed up and you need to come home… that is if you still want that?"

I looked up at him.

"I do want that. I want that more than anything."

He brought his lips to mine and kissed me, and while it was gentle, it wasn't as careful as he'd been.

I admit it freely, I practically fell into his arms. Willingly, enthusiastically, forgetting our near-quarrel of just a moment before in favor of turning my attentions towards getting us both out of our clothes.

I was desperate for his touch, for his lips on my skin, so desperate for us to be close, a sort of way to heal this rift I feared was going to be very real between us. I mean, could I accept it all? Things seemed so wonderful on the surface, things were wonderful for me, but could I deal with it being so at the expense of others?

"Stop, slow down," he growled as I put my hands against his ribs to pull him near, his skin warm, heated with love and lust beneath my hands.

"What is it?" I gasped.

He tipped my chin with his fingers and captured my gaze with his own.

"It's as simple as this, Little Orchid, if nobody hurts you there's no reason to hurt them." I blinked and felt myself lean back and he said, "You aren't a kid anymore. It really is as simple as that."

My mind was caught in a maelstrom of imagined consequences and I realized, much to my own startlement that there wasn't anything they could do to me. I was safe. There wasn't any shunning, or consequence I didn't already know the pain of and I knew so much pain. Pain and I were old friends. Pain, darkness, the familiarity of sadness and fear… were they holding me back?

"Your mind is going a mile a minute," he murmured. "I see it just behind your eyes."

"Make it stop," I whispered. "I don't want to think about it anymore. I don't want to feel this anxiety, this fear…"

"Hey," he murmured in a whispered hush, tracing some of my long hair out of my face, the touch of his middle fingertip against my skin a soothing thing, sending a rush of tingling effervescence across my skin, along the side of my neck, over my shoulder. "There's no bad here, baby. There's just you and me. The road ahead. Better days. It's time to work on leaving all that bad behind."

"I want that," I said breathless.

"Good, because I'm here for it. I'm here for you. I love you."

"I love you, too."

Our mouths came together again but my misgivings had fallen away. I really couldn't believe it was so simple, so easy, but then again I should have believed it to be so. Stoker, the rest of the men of the Kraken, they just didn't care. Didn't care about the false polite constructs of society. Their worldview was something much simpler. Much more black and white.

They hurt you, you hurt them. An eye for an eye, a tooth for a tooth.

I cried out when he stripped my shirt over my head and let it fall to the side, his mouth traveling over my skin, across my chest, between my naked breasts. I hadn't bothered with a bra or panties, just throwing on a tee and a skirt since it was to be just him and me today.

He skimmed his hands up my legs, my back screaming as I planted my shoulders and head against the floor and arched my hips wantonly, momentarily forgetting my hurt.

"You okay?" he asked between kisses, his hands smoothing back up the outsides of my thighs, pushing my skirt out of the way.

"Yeah," I gasped, breathy, as he swept his tongue across my sex, teasing my clit, suckling at me gently and driving me wild.

He gripped my ass, cradling me against his mouth, pulling me against his tongue as he darted it in and out of my body, teasing me unmercifully. I encouraged him, fists wrapped in the material of my skirt, holding it up, out of his way, as he made love to me with his mouth.

I gave myself over to his touch, his mouth, his wicked ways completely. I let the fire of his passion consume me and not for the first time I felt strangely blessed that he was the devil I knew.

31

*S*toker…

It didn't take us any time at all to get her moved out of her place and into mine. She really didn't have that much and I had plenty of room to spare. Of course, she wouldn't hear of moving anything until we weeded out my place to make room for her stuff, swearing that she couldn't abide by any clutter. It was okay. I would have pitched every fucking thing I owned if she'd asked it.

In the end, all I had to ditch was most of the worthless mismatched shit in my kitchen and a worn-out fucked-up chair in the corner of my living room that had been collecting junk mail. Her refurbished reading chair and ottoman fit in well with the rest of the black leather.

She was moving slowly, but determinedly, her body still healing from the accident, and it was really taking a toll on her spirits. The fragile and brittle happiness she had with me seemed thinner, more fragile than usual, even. I knew part of it was the fact we'd had to leave her greenhouse behind and she just didn't feel right without her plants, her own space to hide in.

I loved my lovely creature but she was a creature of habit and I was afraid she was way overwhelmed by all of this newness. So, I enlisted some of the guys – both club and bandmates – to help me the very first

249

chance I got. Now, we were headed in a pair of pickups back to old lady Sedgwick's to break down her greenhouse and bring it home.

Meanwhile, back at base, she was clueless, as she was being inundated by the rest of the club's ol' ladies and Hossler, who were trying to blitz the house and get it up to her exacting standards. Truth be told, I needed those standards. I'd let the place go in my bachelordom.

"What are we going to do with the plants?" Rory asked.

"That's what Galahad's station wagon is for. Put them in the cargo bay and he's gonna rush them to Serenity and we're gonna hope we don't fuck anything up."

"You kill it, you know she's gonna kill you," Marlin grated, cig dangling from his lips. Cutter laughed.

"Don't remind me," I said with an intrepid sigh.

We worked hard, sweating our balls off and lucky us, between moving the plants and disassembling shit, it only took us a couple of hours to get everything locked and loaded.

Galahad had taken off way ahead of us once the plants were safe in his Subaru, and I would be lying if I said I wasn't worried about them. I didn't know if they could go into shock or whatever. I just knew the faster they got to Serenity, the better chances they would have, so I'd told him to get gone, if he wouldn't mind.

"Lemme ask you something," the captain said after we loaded the last board of the greenhouse's frame into the back of my truck.

"Shoot."

"What's the rush on this?" he asked.

I sighed and stared at the pile of boards and some of the windows in the bed, before lifting the tailgate into place and latching it.

"Serenity is upset that I have every intention of dealing with the assclown that hit her."

"And…?"

"And I'm hoping to bury her misgivings in a mountain of the good shit we do."

"She'll never know, y'know… That we deal with him, or how."

"I know, and I don't ever want her to think about him again."

He nodded slowly.

"Let's roll, then. Give her the distraction."

"Let's roll," I agreed, relieved he was picking up exactly what I was putting down.

I went and said goodbye to Mrs. Sedgwick and we got in our trucks and on our bikes and headed back to Ft. Royal. Serenity was waiting at the curb for me to pull in the driveway. Galahad had the side gate open leading into my backyard and she was calling something back to him.

"There you are!" she called, and she looked like she was at war with herself on whether she wanted to nut-punch me or kiss me.

"Uh-oh," I called out as she strode my direction. "I did this wrong, didn't I?"

"Yes and no," she said. "Are you really going to put the whole thing back together tonight?" she asked.

"Well, yeah. Gotta have some place for your plants to go, they can't live in the back of his cage forever."

"You're certifiable!" she cried, but she was smiling again.

"Guilty," I quipped, but I'd already dropped the tailgate and was passing off boards to the next guy and we sort of just fell in, old-school bucket-brigade style, passing things on down the line efficiently so it was all out back and ready for us to rock out my big master plan.

Some of the boys were standing around looking at the decrepit, half-rusting, old corrugated metal garden shed that my gramps had up in the back corner of the yard, which also happened to be one of the sunniest corners that this yard happened to get.

"Well, what're you waitin' for?" Cutter demanded from behind me.

"Pyro's the demolition's expert, figured he should have the honor," Atlas grated.

"Ha, ha, fuck you, man. Hammer's a lot different than blowing some shit up. Way less fun."

I laughed. "I want to keep the bones, so no hammer really required unless it's a claw hammer to pull nails."

"Eh, might need a drill, too. Looks like whoever built it used some Philips and some flat head screws." Galahad scratched the stubble on one cheek with his middle fingernail and looked a touch irritated.

"I got you," I said, and looked down at Serenity. "Can you keep the iced tea coming?"

"You bet," she murmured and drifted to the back slider to go into the house.

"I'll hit the garage and start bringing out useful tools," Hope said, with a faint but proud smile.

"I'll go with ya," Hossler agreed.

We got to work.

If there's one thing I learned working construction, nothing ever goes one hundred percent according to plan or smoothly, but, on occasion, it actually did, and this ended up being one such occasion. My plan had been to strip the old garden shed of its shell and to use the bones to put up her existing windows, utilizing the bones of her greenhouse as an expansion to give her more room – once I could pour another cement pad to join up with the existing one where my granddad's shed used to be.

I expected there to be a hiccup if the windows from the old greenhouse would be too few or too many to encompass my gramp's old garden shed's skeleton but the gods, or whatever, smiled upon us, it was almost a perfect fit. We got the fan up and centered first, because Serenity said that was one of the most important parts of a working greenhouse, and then it went together almost like magic from there.

It was dark by the time we slid her roughed-out workbenches of old timber and warped plywood in there, but it was enough to get her existing plants moved in by flashlight and the light of the fire from my old rusting hulk of a backyard firepit, while most of the brothers and old ladies enjoyed a cold one to cap off their job well done.

"You've really outdone yourself," my little orchid murmured, her arms going around my waist as she leaned into my side. I put my arm around her and caressed her arm. She was beautiful in her favorite faded black hippy dress that she loved to wear around the house. I kissed the top of her head as we looked at her relocated little greenhouse.

"Excited to fill it again?" I asked.

"Yeah. The plants should be okay overnight in the back of the station wagon and Galahad said he could leave it parked here for a couple of days which will give me plenty of time to get everything sorted. I thought we were going to wait, though."

"We were, but I couldn't. I knew how much it was chewing you up not having your own space around here," I said, and she glanced up sharply. She visibly flinched, just the look in her eyes and the expression on her face, and I chuckled.

"Don't read more into it than what I just said," I told her.

"I can't believe everyone —"

"I told you," I said gently, cutting her off, "this is what it is, being club, and belonging. I know you haven't had much of this, that you've had a rough go of it, but those days are over, baby. Those days are gone. You belong now, and we take care of what's ours, protect our own, and are here for each other no matter what. This is how it's supposed to be, this is how it is."

She let her eyes wander across the fire-lit backyard and over the faces of my crew gathered around the flames. She took a deep breath and let it out slowly, gazing at the little reclaimed window greenhouse with its solitary hanging lightbulb, dimly lighting the interior. That's why I'd chosen to retrofit my granddad's shed. It had power to it, no ugly orange extension cord running up a support pillar to an outlet on the porch like she'd had set up at her old place. I was planning on fitting her with something essentially state-of-the-art while keeping her rustic eclectic vibe alive and well.

It was the least I could do. Her feeling calm, feeling safe, having a place of her own to go was important. So said Marlin, and he was the expert when it came to anxiety-riddled abused women – at least among us. Charity and Galahad had had a lot to add, but it all amounted to the same.

Trauma was trauma, and Serenity had it in spades, even before the shooting at her school. All the years of bullying and mental abuse, all the emotional abuse, the systematic and intentional psychological chipping away at her self-worth and her psyche… it left her with a serious case of C-PTSD, PTSD's insidious and harder-to-diagnose big ugly cousin. Often mishandled as depression with generalized anxiety disorder, it didn't react the same to the general medication and treatment for the two.

I'd done some heavy talking, heavy thinking, and some solid research, and knew that this change of scenery, this new life with me, was just the beginning. Serenity didn't know it yet, but I'd talked to my boss, we'd fudged some paperwork and we were getting her onto my insurance, and as soon as she was ready? We'd make her an appointment with the same shrink lady that'd been helping Faith. The one that specialized in trauma.

It was time for my little orchid to stop just living. It was high time for her to be transplanted to a place where she could thrive and I knew that she was ready for it. She'd said as much, told me how she wished that the doctor's visits and physical therapy to deal with the aftermath of the car crash she'd been in could lead into more, for the other stuff.

Well, here we were, and I was going to make it happen, come hell or high water. I wanted her to do better, to be better, and I wanted to grow and be better, for her and with her.

"I love you," she said finally, on a soft exhalation of breath, her eyes slightly unfocused as she stared over the new arrangement back here.

"I love you too," I murmured, giving her a gentle squeeze. "Let me take you back in the house and show you just how much."

She shook herself as if waking from a dream and looked up at me a bit stricken. "But we have guests!" she protested and I chuckled darkly.

"We have crew and my bandmates over; they're family, and they know their way around the place and don't need us. Come on." I led her by the hand toward the back door.

"Have fun, you two!" Hossler called out, raising her bottle of beer in salute in our direction.

Laughter broke out around the fire, and bottles and glasses were raised. Serenity shrank into my side, her nose and cheeks flaming to match the glow of the fire as I ushered her through the back door.

I stopped outside the bathroom when she went to head into our bedroom, and I liked the thought of that so much – our bedroom. Still, as much as I liked the thought, I shook my head and drew her into the bathroom with me, shutting the door firmly behind us and throwing the lock.

"Suppose somebody has to use it!" she exclaimed and I grinned.

"We're a bunch of party animals. The guys'll just go against the other side of the house."

"Oh my God!" She stuffed her hand against her mouth to stifle her laugh and it was the cutest thing.

I smiled, and went over and started up the shower. She gave me a long slow blink, like she was surprised I was serious, and that I wasn't backing down. I gave her one of my slow, sexy smiles and arched an eyebrow.

"Get naked," I ordered, and she just stood there like a rabbit in the headlights so I started first, propping one of my work boots against the closed lid of the john and working the laces out of their secure knot.

She watched me, mesmerized, as I stripped my dirty sweat-stained work tee over my head and tossed it in the open hamper, her gaze thirsty as she drank in the sight of me and I gotta say, when she looked at me like that, I felt ten feet tall.

She watched me undress, shirt, boots, socks, and when I went for my belt, I cocked my head and said, "Serenity…" a reminder that she should get undressed, too.

Her name galvanized her into action, her fingertips flying to the dark wooden buttons on the front of her dress, plucking them through the button holes, the material parting, giving me glimpses of her black lace bra and panty set and short circuiting my brain for a hot minute.

"Stoker?" she asked, amused, and I shuddered like a dog coming out of a pond and got back to work freeing my erection. I dropped my cargo shorts and boxers in one smooth clean movement as she slipped her bra off her body, her breasts free, nipples tightening in the cooler air of the bathroom, the steam from the shower reaching out to caress her.

I've never been so jealous of water vapor in my life.

I couldn't wait to have her in my arms but I seriously needed to rinse off first. I was sweaty and grimy, and while I was down for defiling her hot little body it certainly wasn't intended that *way*.

My cock throbbed as she gave a little shimmy of her hips, her panties skimming over her thighs and dropping to the bathroom rug and I held out my hand to her after I stepped into the tub. She stepped behind the glass doors with me and I groaned with pleasure as the hot water beat a little soreness out of my back and she stepped into me, pressing her body against mine, turning her face up for my kiss.

I pulled her against me and she melted into me. Tongues twining, the pleasure from our joined mouths... there really wasn't any describing it. There honestly wasn't any woman who came before who gave me the same feeling. Serenity filled every one of my senses and it was completely indescribable the amount of love, lust, and other things I felt for her.

Her hands smoothed over my water-slick skin and she tore her mouth from mine, breathing heavily, snatching the bath poof I kept in here from its on-demand hook stuck to the back shower wall.

She lathered it up while I stood and watched her in a sort of half-dreamy state from her kiss, shuddering when she ran it over my chest.

That was the other thing. I had never had a woman treat me as well as Serenity treated me. I closed my eyes and let her take care of me for a few minutes, relaxing under her gentle touch as she lightly scrubbed the grime of sweat and hard labor from my skin.

I sucked in a sharp breath and held it when her fingers wrapped lightly around my cock and she began to stroke me. Root to tip and back down, adding a bit of a twist at the wrist, her soap-slick fingers expertly played me, and I didn't have any complaints.

I was so turned on that I warned her, "Not gonna last long, baby but I'm gonna make it up to you."

"You don't have to make anything up to me," she said, so quietly I almost didn't hear her over the working showerhead. "I just want you to feel good."

I grunted and drew in a deep breath, the air passing through my nose and deep into my lungs as if filling an endless well. I gasped, my breath cut off as the pleasure surged, my balls giving a deep and satis-fying – I don't know. The sensation was like an ache, but different somehow, as if an ache could be less pain and more pleasure.

I reached out a hand and braced it against the shower wall, the other gripping her shoulder, my thumb smoothing against her skin as, with every stroke, she brought me closer and closer to going off like a shot.

Fuck, when I came, it was so damn hard I saw white stars flitting at the edges of my vision and her lovely face swam in a fog created by a haze of pure euphoria as my come spilled hot and heavy over the back of her hand and ran down her wrist.

"I fucking love you so hard," I growled, reaching for her, murmuring, "Your turn," just before I let my mouth devour her lips as if it was the last kiss I would ever get.

32

Serenity…

He backed me into the corner and I laughed, delighted. His mouth dropped kisses against my skin, warming me through in the cooler atmosphere of his house – our house. 'I needed to turn down the air conditioning' was the last rational thought I had before he pressed me back into the corner and lifted my legs over his shoulders.

I swear, his mouth against my pussy was his favorite place to be during sex and I was so not even complaining. I did, however, feel a little guilty that all I'd managed to give him by way of foreplay this time was – in my estimate anyway – a sad hand job.

He lavished his tongue over me and I gasped, throwing my head back and bracing it against the wall, secure that he held me fast and I wouldn't fall. I trusted him to hold me up, to not drop me, and he had never and probably would never disappoint on that front – no matter what iteration or form it took. My fingers wound through the long, wet strands of his hair, pulling his mouth tighter against my body as he darted his tongue in and out of me, teasing me, pleasing me, in every way that stoked the fires of my desire without outright pouring gasoline on it.

Problem was, at least I thought so, I wanted the accelerant. I whimpered as he kept me just on that edge without letting me take that shining fall, the pleasure building and building until I seriously began to panic in wonder if I could take anymore.

"Stoker!" I gasped, and he grunted as his only answer, but I knew that grunt. He might as well have said aloud, 'Wait for it...' and I didn't know if I could.

"Stoker!" Again I gasped my lover's name, a half-warning that I was so very close and a half-plea for him to please, please let me have it, to please finish me! To catch me as I fell among the stars that he'd catapulted me expertly into.

He might as well have hung the moon for me, with how much I loved him, how much my body sang his praises as he teased me with the very tip of his tongue. I writhed as much as our position would let me while keeping me secure, and with a cry that bordered on victorious, I came, nipples tightening, sparks flying along every nerve ending, the dam that'd been holding me back breaking and a flood of warmth and the golden glow of orgasm sweeping through me, pouring out from my middle in wave after wave until I felt all used up. I leaned against the wall panting, still somehow unfulfilled, even after all of that, aching to have him inside of me.

"God, please tell me you're ready to go," I gasped. "I need you inside me."

"Let me grab a condom," he said, helping me shakily off his shoulders and to my feet, not letting go until he was sure my legs could hold me.

"No, now," I gasped, trembling.

"What if you get pregnant?" he asked, arching an eyebrow.

"I don't care," I said, surprised to find that I meant it. "I mean, would it be so bad?"

"You want kids, now? With me?" he asked, and there was a weight behind his words, a hopeful anticipation.

"I mean, if it happens – but yes, I want children at some point, with you..."

"Fucking bend over," he ordered, and turned me around, shoving me forward at the hips, pressing my hands flat against the shower wall and rising like a leviathan behind me. He was as hard as I'd ever seen him, his cock fully engorged, bobbing thickly between his legs. I only caught a glimpse of it, of him, that way but a glimpse was enough. The memory seared into my mind even as my pussy throbbed like it was giving a glad little cry, knowing that it would soon be filled.

He pressed into me and groaned, shoving into my body, the hot, slick folds of my twat welcoming him, gripping him, my body pulling him deeper into me even as I thrust my hips back to meet him. My fingertips mottled white against the faux-marble shower wall in front of me as I braced my trembling arms, so many endorphins rushing through my blood I didn't even think about how sore I might be later from this. Right now, my back and shoulders were fine, as he ran himself in and out of my pussy, adjusting his hips, looking for that perfect angle that would make me yowl like a cat in heat.

He found it, of course, and I definitely wailed, and he took that as an invitation to really fuck me, which I loved. We didn't stop, we didn't even slow down, even when someone knocked on the door, a masculine voice cursing and boot treads retreating as Stoker expertly worked his way in and out of my body.

The sensations were intense, made even more intense, insanely intense, when he gripped my shoulders and plowed forward into me, bottoming out against my cervix in a delicious shock of pleasure wrought into a work of art turned pain, an exquisite feeling that I generally had to be in the mood for and I was right there, in that perfect headspace, ready for him to dish out whatever he wanted and to accept it as holy writ. My body was practically levitating, the sex so good it was almost an out-of-body experience as he fought and won to bring me to orgasm again.

He pulled me into a standing position as I came, still deep inside of me, holding me back against his body, my feet not touching the slick tub floor, holding me steady, holding me tight, and I loved that, giving myself over purely to the bliss flickering through my veins and along my limbs as I trembled like a newborn deer calf.

He slipped out of me, reluctantly, and he was still hard. Setting me down gently, he turned me, and I looked up at him, still a bit dazed, and asked, "Did you come?"

"No," he shook his head with a shy grin. "Held off."

"Can't have that," I murmured and slipped to my knees to finish him with my mouth, rinsing him with my hand and the shower spray, I could still faintly taste myself and that was okay. I didn't care.

All I cared about was pleasuring him as he had pleasured me, until the end of time.

Taking care of each other, from now until we grew old; I wanted that so much, needed it like a plant needed the sun, good soil, and enough water to thrive. That's what I wanted us to do. I wanted us to both be healthy, to both thrive, so that when we did bring children into this world, we could give them a better life than we had growing up.

"Oh, Orchid, don't stop," he breathed, and I looked up at him, as he leaned one shoulder into the shower wall and gazed down the length of his chiseled body at me. God, he was beautiful; it was another sight forever burned into my brain.

God, I loved him. I would love him until the end of time, no matter what, if he would let me.

EPILOGUE

*S*toker...

"You ready for this?" Pyro asked, flicking his cigarette out into the street off the curb.

"Oh, I've been ready," I declared.

"Sweet," Atlas grunted.

"Let's fuckin' do it!" Lightning grinned a little too enthusiastically, like he pretty much did every time he was about to strike.

"Wait until he gets a little further out, into the parking lot. No cameras and it's dark as fuck, should give us plenty of cover."

I nodded, and we waited for him to stumble around that way. As luck would have it, he stopped to relieve himself against the cinderblock wall of the watering hole he'd just stumbled out of.

We crept around the back of his shiny new good 'ol boy pickup and flanked him to either side.

Atlas asked him, "You uh, weren't planning on driving that shiny new rig of yours drunk, now, were ya?"

"What's it t' you, motherfucker?" the guy demanded.

"Might hurt another little girl," Lightning said at my side, and the guy turned and he did crash, right into my fucking fist.

He went down, but only for a half second before he bounded back up like a rubber fuckin' ball. Pyro got him though, his arms looped into a full nelson, fingers laced behind the guy's sweaty neck. Alcohol fumes were coming off of him so bad, I thought my next punch into the dude's gut might spark off his belt buckle or something and catch us all on fire.

I did the most of the wailing on him, whooped his ass but good. He was on his hands and knees, coughing and retching, and I got down near him.

"You ever fuck with anyone else, the next time? We'll kill you, you get me?" I demanded, my breath heaving from the workout I'd put in.

He laughed and wheezed saying, "I know you. I'ma run every last one of you fuckers off the road." He spat, "Fuck you! You fucking fucks."

"Brave man," Atlas said dispassionately.

"Let's beat it out of him," Lightning suggested, and we stomped his ass into the fucking blacktop.

He wasn't laughing anymore.

"I think he needs a fucking reminder every time he looks in the mirror that he needs to watch his fuckin' mouth," I said, and I knew just what kind of reminder to provide. I exchanged looks with Pyro and he gave a curt nod. He knew exactly what I was thinking.

"Get him up," Pyro ordered. Atlas took one side, Lightning the other, and they dragged him over to the bumper of his shiny new rig. Pyro grabbed him by his lolling head and positioned his mouth against the front bumper for me.

"Hit it," he said, and I brought my boot crashing down on the back of the motherfucker's skull, his teeth and jaw giving a satisfying, juicy crunch against the chrome. The boys dropped him and I wiped my sweating palms against my jeans. None of us were wearing colors. Hell, none of us had even ridden. We'd jacked some stripper's car from a joint not far from here and ridden in a cage.

We piled back in it, drove back to the strip club where the bikes were parked, wiped down the interior of the car, and left a wad of cash in the center console for the damages. She'd be alright with a story like that for the pigs. They were used to that shit.

We went back inside with the rest of the crew, cleaned up in the john and I dropped into a seat between the captain and Gator. The captain handed over my colors.

"Smooth?" he asked.

"Slicker 'n owl shit," I confirmed, and that was that.

A lap dance or two, to get enough of a bitch's stink-water and body glitter on my shit and we rode out as one big pack later that night after we had our fill of titties and beer. As far as the ol' ladies knew, we were just out being a bunch of guys, the only one with us was Cutter's woman, Hope, because she was just as much one of us, but we all knew she would keep her pretty mouth shut.

I wasn't really down for that last part. The lap dances. The only woman I wanted in my lap was my little orchid. I just wanted home, a shower, and to slip inside her. I guess you could call that the biker's method of slipping into something more comfortable.

She was curled in her reading chair when I came home, the picture of smart girl, her legs tucked under her like a cat as her eyes skimmed the page of her book open in her lap, an oasis of light in the otherwise-dark room, sitting under a little golden pool of lamplight from her little side table.

She was a sight for sore eyes.

I watched her for several moments until she said, without looking up, a small smile on her lips, "Aren't you going to say anything?"

"No," I told her, my voice husky with desire.

She looked up, her smile faltering as her dark gaze fell upon my face.

"What's wrong?" she demanded.

"I had a good time," I answered.

She frowned.

"I don't understand."

"Got a few lap dances from some pretty girls, got into a decent brawl with another patron," I held up my scraped fist, the story already pre-established with the rest of the crew. "Drank my fill of beer and got rowdy as hell. Good for the soul, right?" I asked.

"But...?" She cocked her head expectantly.

"All I really wanted to be doing was you," I said with a smirk. "I just wanted to be here, with you in our bed, making love to you all night."

"Night's not over yet," she said softly.

"No," I agreed. "It's not."

"So why don't you go take a shower, get cleaned up, and you might just find me in bed."

"Naked," I demanded.

"Naked," she threw in for my benefit, laughing. "Waiting for you."

"Couldn't ask for a better ending to my night," I said softly.

She and I stared across the living room at one another, the desire rising from the floor and shimmering almost palpable between us.

"What are you waiting for?" she asked, softly.

"Could ask you the same thing."

"I'm waiting for you to get in the shower," she said, closing her book.

"I'm waiting for you to get in bed."

She smiled and set her book aside. "One of us has to go first."

"Yes, ma'am," I said, and put one foot in front of the other up the hallway, despite not being able to take my eyes off of her.

She smiled and shook her head, planting her hands firmly on the edge of her seat and levering herself up out of her chair.

I carried the sight of her all through the shower, which I made quick work of. When I stepped out, the house was silent and dark. Towel slung low on my hips, I went to our room, the door cracked, and Serenity nude in our bed, the moonlight spilling through the bedroom window caressing her naked back, and the sight was so beautiful. I could swear she was a siren from the sea, not a woman when she looked like that.

I let the towel drop and she opened her eyes.

"Don't move, I want to look at you, like this a minute," I said, stroking myself. She watched my hand move over my flesh, a hungry heat in her gaze and I smiled and went to her, nudging her legs apart with my knee between them as I got up onto the bed, sliding myself along the crack of her ass, teasing her, listening to her soft little pants of want, her hips rising off the bed in offering.

I found her opening with the head of my cock and paused, murmuring against her ear, covered by the silk of her hair, "I love you, babe. It's good to be home," before sliding into her.

She sucked in a sharp breath in response and I chuckled, working my way carefully in and out of her, intent on delivering on my promise.

I'd be making love to her until sunrise. I'd be making love to her, and only her, for the rest of our lives.

The End

ALSO BY A.J. DOWNEY

The Sacred Hearts MC

1. Shattered & Scarred

2. Broken & Burned

3. Cracked & Crushed

3.5 Masked & Miserable (a novella)

4. Tattered & Torn

5. Fractured & Formidable

6. Damaged & Dangerous

The Virtues

1. Cutter's Hope

2. Marlin's Faith

3. Charity for Nothing

The Sacred Brotherhood

1. Brother to Brother

2. Her Brother's Keeper

3. Brother In Arms

4. Between Brothers

5. A Brother's Secret

6. A Brother At My Back

7. A Brother's Salvation

Indigo Knights

1. Her Thin Blue Lifeline

2. His Cold Blue Command

3. A Low Blue Flame

4. His Wild Blue Rose

5. Her Pained Blue Silence

6. A Cold Blue Call

7. Her Reluctant Blue Cavalier

Paranormal Romance (with Ryan Kells)

1. I Am The Alpha

2. Omega's Run

3. Hunter's End

ABOUT THE AUTHOR

A.J. Downey specializes in writing real and relatable contemporary romance stories. She's from Seattle, WA and loves the Pacific Northwest. She finds inspiration from her surroundings, through the people she meets, and likely as a byproduct of way too much caffeine. An avid reader all of her life, it's now her turn to try and give back a little, entertaining as she has been entertained.

Stalker Information:

Website
www.ajdowney.com

Sign up for her newsletter at
http://eepurl.com/dkQiIH

Facebook Group - AJ's Sacred Circle
https://www.facebook.com/groups/authorajdowney/

facebook.com/authorajdowney

twitter.com/authorajdowney

instagram.com/ajdowney

bookbub.com/authors/a-j-downey